A Long Way From Yesterday

by
Lynda J. Cox

Dedication

To my husband, Ken Cox,
who never stopped believing,
and Champion Wych's Rolling Thunder
—a.k.a. "Colt"—
the original "Devil's Own Desperado."

Chapter One

ear Red Deer, Wyoming Territory

N Colt Evans learned at an early age never to sit with his back to a door. Any door. At a poker table in the corner of the room, he sat with a log wall, darkened by age and smoke, protecting his back.

A lanky kid no more than fifteen pushed open the saloon doors and paused for a moment. A gusting breeze swept through the saloon, stirring the lamp flames and swirling the hazy smoke hanging near the rafters. Shadows skittered across the floor and danced up the walls. Colt nudged his hat back a little on his head and spared the kid silhouetted in the doorway little more than a glance before he turned his attention to the cards in his hands.

Aces and eights and the nine of diamonds—a dead man's hand. A superstitious chill crept up Colt's spine, despite the heat of day lingering in the dark night. Same hand Hickok had been holding when he'd been shot in the back—when Hickok had forgone his rule of never sitting with his back to a door. Colt pulled out the nine and was dealt a third ace.

Colt looked away from the cards. He was getting too damn old for this. Just that morning, he'd found several gray strands shot through the black of his hair, and he'd been forced to squint to see his reflection that closely in the mirror. Somehow, that blasted dream he'd held onto all these years—the one of a small house sheltered in some mountain valley, with a couple of kids, a few head of cattle—seemed to be getting further out of reach.

He grimaced. He wasn't simply getting old. Hell, he was getting maudlin. He knew better than to grab at a dream. A shootist didn't settle down with a woman to raise kids and cattle, and he certainly never stopped being a shootist, no matter how many years passed after hanging up the hardware. It was a bitter realization, but one he'd learned to come to terms with.

He spared his cards another glance. They weren't changing. Colt peered through the haze of cigar and cigarette smoke for the kid. What was a boy with peach fuzz on his face doing in a saloon?

The kid approached the bar, walking as if the gun strapped to his thigh was too heavy for him. After a moment of being ignored by the barkeep, the boy knocked on the wood bar top and demanded a whiskey. Colt lifted a brow when the barkeep placed a tumbler full of tarantula juice in front of him. Ordering a whiskey in Dale Carrie's saloon was always a questionable proposition. Everyone knew the liquor was cut with something, but no one knew what Dale added to the whiskey barrels to make it last longer. Colt had once bet that Dale used turpentine. He wasn't going to buy a shot of red-eye to find out if he won that bet though.

A smile tugged at one corner of Colt's mouth when the boy slammed the rotgut down and fought to hide the fact he was choking on it. Probably the kid's first taste of whiskey. And, more than likely, his first time to wear a gun too. The kid's walk bellowed that to the heavens. He was uncomfortable with its weight and over-strode to try to adjust for the heaviness.

"You in or out, Colt?" Bear Mulligan's rumbling voice dragged Colt's attention back to the game.

Colt spared his cards one last look. Ghostly fingers traced a chill up his spine and lifted the hair at his nape. He nudged his hat back a little on his head and dropped the cards face down onto the table. "Out."

"Then I'm calling. Beat 'em if you can," Hank cheerfully announced, and dropped a straight to the queen on the table. Still grinning, he bent to the side and spat a glob of dark tobacco juice into a spittoon before raking his winnings in.

Bear and Joe snorted something unintelligible, and Joe pushed away from the table.

"I'm done," Joe said. He picked up his hat and plunked it on his head. "If anyone else wants any more of my hard-earned money, tell 'em to come looking for me upstairs. I'm going to spend the last of it on one of the girls."

Bear picked up Colt's cards and raised his brows. Colt shrugged. "Not a hand I wanted to play," he said. "It ain't against the law to fold a decent hand, is it, Sheriff?"

Bear laughed, sounding like a huffing grizzly bear. "Boy, keep on riding me about this here badge, and I might just have to throw you in a cell for a day or two."

"Save me from paying for a night sleeping on a lumpy mattress over at Bullfinch's if you did that."

"Now, that could be considered being on the wrong side of the law, getting arrested so you don't have to pay for a good night's sleep."

"Who said it was a good night's sleep?" Colt snorted. "It's like trying to sleep on a sack of potatoes."

The boy at the bar straightened and ambled to the poker table. He stood within a circle of flickering yellow light cast by the lanterns overhead, his gaze skipping over the three men, lingering for a moment on the badge pinned to Bear's shirt. "Can anyone sit in?" Colt glanced at Bear and Hank, and then shrugged.

"So long as we see the color of your money before you sit down."

The kid met Colt's eyes and reached into his pocket. Another chill brushed up Colt's spine as the boy glared at him. His instincts warned this boy was some Johnny Quick Draw, looking to make a name for himself.

The kid dropped two gold double eagles onto the table. "That enough to cut me in?"

"Your momma know you're here? Or that you been robbing banks to play poker?" Hank asked with a grin. His amusement died when the boy aimed a frigid stare in his direction.

Bear whistled low between tobacco-stained teeth. "That's a good start, kid. What do they call you?"

"I didn't rob no bank for it, Sheriff. You always go without a gun?" Without waiting for Bear's response, the kid glanced again at Colt. "Most folks call me Mitch."

"Well, Mitch, usually I'm big enough to intimidate people, so I've never felt the need to pack iron. Have a seat." Bear flexed his fingers, cracking his knuckles. "We'll see if we can't lighten your load just a little."

Mitch swung his leg over the chair back, sitting directly across the table from Colt.

Colt's nerves strummed with the aggression and cagey tautness radiating from the kid. For the third time in as many minutes, an indistinct warning whispered in the back of his head.

Bear shuffled and began to deal, in an obvious attempt to break the tension. "This hand, we're playing five-card draw, nothing wild."

Hank groaned. "Again?"

"Don't know what you're belly-aching about. You've won the last three hands," Bear said, tossing cards onto the table. "And I know you wouldn't try cheating with me sitting at this table."

Mitch never removed his dark glower from Colt. Finally, Colt rocked his chair onto its two back legs. "Son, most men get real nervous when they're being stared at."

"Just trying to place where I know you." Mitch didn't break his steady stare. "You're Colt Evans, ain't you?"

"That's the name my mother gave me. I'm at a disadvantage, because I know I have never seen you before." Tension thrummed in the air. Bear eased his chair back slightly from the table, and on Colt's other side, so did Hank. "I don't recall ever knowing anyone with the name of Mitch." Colt casually reached for his cards, fanned them, and spared them a quick glance.

"How about Frank Matthews?" Mitch's sharp voice pulled Colt's gaze away from the cards. Fury had filled the emptiness in the kid's eyes.

Colt's stomach twisted. Damn. This kid wasn't just some Johnny Quick Draw. Frank Matthews—some fool who'd called him out a year ago and paid for it with his life. Who was this blasted kid? One of Matthews's brothers? Or his son? He'd bet brother. The kid had the same dark hair, same dark eyes, same hooked nose. He should have seen the resemblance earlier. And if this brother was here, where were the rest of the Matthews boys?

Just as casually as he'd picked up the cards, Colt lowered them, face down, to the felt-covered table. "Can't say I recall that name either." Colt reached above his head to flick a speck of daubing from the wood wall behind him. The moment Mitch's attention strayed to his raised hand, Colt slipped his gun hand under the table. His palm curled around the cool wood of the revolver's handle, and he slid his finger against the trigger. A strange, numbing calm settled over him with the comfortable feel of the revolver in his hand.

"He was my brother," Mitch snarled. "You telling me you don't recall the name of a man you gunned down in cold blood?"

"To hear some people talk, I've gunned down a lot more people than I really have, but no one's ever said it was in cold blood." Colt's finger tightened on the trigger. The grooving on the hammer brushed against his thumb as easily as a lover's caress. The familiar sensation of ice water in his veins knotted deep in his stomach. "If Frank Matthews was killed in cold blood, it sure as hell wasn't at the end of my gun."

Mitch bared his teeth and leaned closer. "You're a liar, Colt Evans."

"That's not something most people would take kindly to being called, Mitch." Colt held the kid's narrowed gaze until the boy eased back in his seat. Damn, he was getting too old for this. "Far as I know, I don't have a single lawman on my trail for shooting any man in cold blood. Hell, I'm sitting here playing cards with the sheriff." Colt used the table to hide his slow easing of the revolver and holster along his thigh.

God have mercy, he didn't want to do this. The fact the kid had let him get his gun hand under cover was proof enough the boy was still wet behind the ears. Colt was acutely aware the chatter and drunken laughter in the saloon had stilled as the patrons became aware of the tableau playing out at the table.

"I'll forget the accusation I shot a man in cold blood, but I don't think I can let your accusation of being a liar pass," Colt said, keeping his voice level. "I think the best thing for you to do would be to apologize and then leave."

"I'm not leaving, Evans, until you're dead." Mitch's voice rang harshly in the silent saloon, as fierce as barking gunfire.

"Son, you might want to rethink this," Bear said.

"Stay out of this, old man. This isn't your concern."

Colt raised a brow but maintained his gaze on Mitch's face. This kid had to be crazy. "How old are you?"

"What the hell does that have to do with anything?"

The ever-present wind moaned softly through the chinking of the walls and over the shake-shingled roof, mournful as a funeral dirge. "Everything. How old are you, boy?" Colt had his revolver, still in the holster, twisted on his thigh and pointed into the kid's gut. Not the shot he wanted to take because it wouldn't stop a return shot if Mitch pulled iron, but at the moment, it was the best he had. He sure as hell didn't want to shoot a damn kid.

"I ain't no boy," Mitch said. "I'll be nineteen in a month."

"If you live that long," Colt said. The kid might be older than he appeared, but he didn't have a lot of smarts. "That's too damn young to die. Threatening to kill anyone in these parts is a surefire way to get yourself shot." He deliberately softened his tone, hoping for some sense of reason from the boy. "I'm willing to let the whole thing go to hot-headedness on your part. Apologize for calling me a liar, live to see your next birthday, and your momma won't be burying another son."

"I'll see them put you in a hole six feet deep, Evans." Mitch shoved his chair back from the table. He dropped his hand to the revolver on his thigh in a blurring motion. The instant Mitch came out of the chair, Colt rolled from his. In the same motion he slipped his revolver from the holster, thumbed back the hammer and aimed for the kid's chest. Even as he squeezed the trigger, Colt knew he was a second too late.

Mitch's bullet tore into Colt's chest. A few feet from the table, Mitch stood statue-still, disbelief and shock widening his eyes. A bright red flower blossomed over his heart. He fell to his knees and slowly collapsed onto the rough wood flooring. Colt slumped against the wall behind him, struggling to hold onto consciousness.

Shouts echoed in the shadow-and-smoke-shrouded saloon, mingling with the rasping of chairs across the rough-hewn flooring and the screams of the saloon girls.

Colt managed to pull himself to his feet. Bear grabbed his swaying form and jerked Colt's vest away from his shoulder to reveal a growing bloodstain. The older man blanched under his sun-weathered complexion. "Damn it, Colt, how many times do I gotta tell you that dying ain't much of a living? You gotta get to the doctor."

Colt shoved Bear away. "I have to get out of town, not go see any damn sawbones." He ripped the bandana off his neck and pressed it into the bullet hole in his shoulder. "That kid isn't Frank Matthews' only brother. He's got a couple more and several cousins."

"Ain't no one gonna say anything, Colt," Bear said, grabbing Colt's arm as he staggered through the saloon. "He drew on you."

"You think that's going to matter to the Matthews?" Colt stumbled to the door and down the boardwalk. "The law ain't what I'm worried about, Bear."

"Nah, I guess that ain't your biggest worry." Bear kept a firm grip on Colt's arm, and strode at his side as far as the livery. "Stay on this side of legal, son. You don't need to go crossing that line."

Colt managed a grin. "I've stayed on this side of it so far, haven't I?"

He pulled his white gelding from the stall. The livery owner had thought he was crazy when he said he wanted the horse left saddled and bridled. Thank heavens the man had done as he'd been instructed.

The gelding snorted and rolled his eyes with the scent of fresh blood but didn't sidle away.

Colt's head swam and the pain throbbed throughout his chest, setting his stomach roiling. Blood seeped through his fingers, hot and sticky, soaking the bandana pressed to his shoulder. Huge black holes danced in his vision. Thankfully, though, the bullet seemed to have missed bone and vital organs.

Colt grabbed the horn and with Bear's help dragged himself onto the gelding's back. Bear grabbed the bridle. "You take care of yourself, son."

"I'm trying, old man." Colt pulled the reins, breaking Bear's hold on the bridle, kicked the horse into a gallop, and headed west in the darkness.

Chapter Two

B *etween the towns of Federal and Yesterday, Wyoming Territory*
Amelia McCollister shielded her eyes against the afternoon sun, searching the distant horizon for thunderheads. The sun hung halfway between zenith and the horizon, a white-hot disc in a metallic blue sky. Not a single cloud dared to mar the cobalt expanse. Even the birds were silent in the heat of the afternoon, and the breeze could have been straight from the mouth of a foundry.

Amelia pulled at the bodice of her calico dress and winced with the sweat dripping down her spine and between her breasts. Another August day of searing, blistering sun and brutal, dry heat. Hot enough to make the devil sigh, she remembered her father saying more than once.

"Saul, we've got to get the garden watered again," she called to her younger brother.

Saul emerged from the small cabin, his shirttail hanging, his face smudged with dirt. "Again? We just watered yesterday."

"I'm well aware of when we last watered. If we don't water again today, everything in that garden is going to shrivel to nothing. I'll remind you that you didn't want to water when we're reduced to chewing shoe leather this winter." Amelia grabbed his shoulder and marched him to the well. "I'd like to know where you've been all afternoon other than out wasting time, when you should have been here helping me and your sister with the chores. And you need to tuck your shirttail in."

"Who cares if my shirttail is hanging out? No one comes out here, anyway." Saul pulled up the bucket. "Next year, when I'm all grown up, I am never going to haul up another bucket of water."

Amelia let her brother's comments pass, noting he hadn't told her where he'd been. She also carried a pail of water to the garden and doled out the precious liquid to the wilting plants. "Jenny," she paused to call, "the chickens need watered and fed."

Silent as a wraith, keeping as close to the cabin as possible, Jenny drifted across the yard to the chicken coop. She collected the water dish and scooped water from Saul's bucket. The chickens crowded around Jenny as the seven-year-old scattered cracked corn for them.

At the unmistakable sound of her herb garden being trampled, Amelia lifted her head to scold Saul for his carelessness. Her gaze was drawn to Jenny who stood frozen, corn falling from her slack fingers. Amelia followed her sister's stare.

A white horse shuffled through the herb garden into the yard, his head down at his knees. The chickens scattered, squawking angrily. A man slumped over the horse's neck, not moving. Amelia dropped her bucket and ran to him.

Blood, both dried and fresh, painted a lurid path down the horse's shoulder. Amelia caught the animal's reins and brought the lathered horse to a halt.

"Amy, he's been shot," Saul said in a breathless whisper.

"I can see that." Amelia dragged the weary horse closer to the house. "Help me get him down."

He didn't seem to be breathing. Amelia grabbed the man's arm, and together she and Saul managed to pull him off the horse. Amelia staggered a step back and a low groan broke from the man when his weight settled into Amelia's arms. His hat tumbled to the ground. She and Saul half-carried, half-dragged him into the cabin, leaving tracks in the dust from the heels of his boots. Fresh blood pattered into the dirt.

"Where are we going to put him, Amy?"

She hesitated for a moment, and then said, "In my room."

Amelia panted with the exertion of carrying the unconscious man. They stretched him out on the bed and Amelia stared at him. He wore a gun. She should turn him away.

The moment she thought that, her conscience railed at her. So much blood stained his white linen shirt and blue trousers. His build was slight, but substantial. How could he be alive after losing all that blood? Did a man have that much blood in his body?

"Saul, go put his horse in the barn and then you saddle up and ride into town. Tell Dr. Archer we need him here."

Suddenly the man grabbed her wrist. Amelia yelped and tried to pull free. He glared up at her with eyes like a snowy winter's sky, set under a deeply furrowed brow. Her heart leaped into her throat.

"No doctor," he grated out. His gaze darted around the room, making Amelia think of a cornered wild animal. "No sawbones."

"You've got to have a doctor. I don't know what to do for you." Amelia struggled to pull her wrist free.

"No doctor." He eased his hold on her wrist. "If it's as bad as it feels, he's going to take my arm. Please, lady, no doctor. I can't lose my arm."

Amelia loosened his fingers and lowered his hand to the bed.

He clenched his fists, tensing. "God Almighty, it hurts."

"Let me see how bad it is."

He nodded and closed his eyes. His fingers uncurled as he slipped into unconsciousness again.

Amelia spun, looking for Saul. The boy stood in the doorway, his eyes as wide as cake plates, his face whiter than January snow. "Saul, look at me."

She waited until he broke his gaze from the lean man on her bed. "I want you to bring me a bucket of water and then go put his horse up. Make sure the horse has water."

Amelia unbuttoned the man's shirt and tried to pull it from him. Dried blood had stuck the fabric to him as surely as if it had been applied with wallpaper paste. Amelia wrinkled her nose at the smell of infection, took a deep breath, and pulled on the fabric as hard as she could.

The shirtfront peeled from his chest. Amelia staggered a step backward. Fresh blood and a thick, yellowish fluid oozed sluggishly from the bullet wound. Her stomach roiled with the smell and the sight. Gagging, she spun away and fled the room.

Just outside the doorway, she met Saul and had to grab his shoulder to steady herself. The water in the bucket he carried sloshed over the floor.

"Saul, saddle up, quickly. Ride into Federal and get Dr. Archer." She took the bucket. "Tell him to hurry. If he's not in town, ride out to the Running Diamond. Rebecca can tell you where he is."

Amelia returned to her bedroom. She soaked several clean rags in the bucket and washed the man's shoulder and chest as best she could without removing his shirt. He shivered, despite the heat blazing from his skin. A ghostly pallor colored his face under his sun-darkened complexion. His chest rose and fell in short, shallow breaths. She applied cool rags to his forehead. He felt so hot. He had to be burning up with a fever.

A short time later, a horse galloped up to the house. Amelia straightened, went to the window, and pulled the gingham curtains aside. A huge spotted horse stood near the barn, and a tall, muscular man walked across the yard. Thank God, Dr. Archer was here. With his practice covering the towns of Forgotten, Federal, Eagle Springs, and Yesterday, Amelia had feared he wouldn't be in his office.

With lowered brows, Dr. Archer crossed to the bed and bent over the bloodied man. He was silent for a few moments. "Not a pretty sight, is it, Amy?"

She shook her head. It was an ugly sight, brutal and filled with violence.

He opened his black bag, retrieved a pair of scissors, and cut what was left of the shirt from the man. "Good thing you got that wound open, though. It's draining and I don't see any signs of gangrene." Archer wrung out another rag and scrubbed at the wound. "Amy, go start some water boiling. We're going to draw the rest of that infection out with some hot compresses."

Amelia fled the room, burning bile rising in her throat. She gulped air and willed her stomach to remain where it belonged. When she was certain she was not going to retch, she pumped water into a large pot and set it on the stove.

Who was the man in her room? Who had shot him and why? Thank the Almighty, Saul had been too shocked with the blood to notice the gun on the man's hip. Lately Saul had been fascinated with gunfighters like Wyatt Earp, Doc Holliday, and Bat Masterson.

When Amelia carried the pot of steaming water into the bedroom, Archer glanced at her over his shoulder. "Any idea who this gentleman is?"

Amelia shook her head while she set the pot on the nightstand. "I've never seen him before. He rode in almost unconscious." She backed to the doorway. Surely Dr. Archer wouldn't need her to stay, would he?

Archer's brows shot up and he dropped several lengths of white cloth into the steaming water. "From the looks of that bullet wound, he was shot at pretty close range and it happened several days ago."

The man on the bed slid his hand to his gun, struggling to free it from the holster. Amelia gasped as he pulled the gun clear and pointed it at the doctor's back. Those gray eyes were even harder than before, and colder than a glacier.

"I told you no doctor."

Dr. Archer did little more than spare the man on the bed a glance over his shoulder. If the gun or its owner intimidated him, he never revealed it.

"Nice piece of hardware, mister." The lightness in the doctor's voice belied the unwavering gun barrel mere inches from his heart. "Put the gun down."

Amelia marveled at Dr. Archer's calm demeanor as he rummaged through his black bag. He dropped more bandaging material, metal instruments, and what appeared to be a spool of thread onto the nightstand.

"You're not taking my arm, Sawbones." Panic and desperation lent a hard edge to his voice. His gaze skipped from Amelia to Archer and then to the medical supplies on the bedside table. Sweat beaded on his forehead and ran in rivulets down the side of his face and the length of his throat. The gun wavered and dipped. He gritted his teeth and a muscle ticked against the plane of his jaw. Tendons in his wrist stood out and his knuckles grew white as he struggled to hold the weapon steady.

"I have no intention of taking your arm. You were shot in the shoulder, not the arm." Archer dropped the bloody rag that had once been the man's shirt to the floor, and then pulled more white bandaging materials from the black bag. "When Amy pulled your shirt from you, it started that bullet wound to draining. There's no sign of gangrene, so the way I see it, sawing your arm off would be a waste of time."

The man's gaze darted from Amelia to Archer. Pain and terror darkened his eyes and left him panting like a cornered creature. "More like I'm so far gone, ain't no sense wasting your time to cut my arm off because I'll be dead in a day or so, anyway?"

Dr. Archer pushed the gun into the mattress with one hand and lowered the back of his other onto the gunman's forehead. "You could still die, but until that arm has gangrene, I am not about to saw it off. You can keep it for now. The fact the wound is draining will probably keep you alive. You're a lucky man."

Amelia moved toward the doorway. It appeared the doctor had things under control. She had done her Christian duty. There was no need for her to stay in this room any longer.

Archer pried the gun from the stranger's hand. "Amy, come and put this gun somewhere."

Archer's words halted her retreat. Amelia crept closer but stopped when the man tried to push himself up.

"Give me my gun. I need it."

He fell back when Dr. Archer gently held him by the other shoulder. "Lie still, you damned stubborn fool. You're so weak you can't even hold that gun steady enough to risk a shot. God knows what you would hit if you fired it." Archer's voice hardened. "But if you ever point another gun at me, I don't care how nicely Amy asks, I won't come out here to take care of you."

Archer held the revolver out to Amelia, and then shook it when she didn't move any closer. "Take this, Amy. I'm going out to my horse. I've got a few things in Chief's saddlebags that I need."

Amelia took the gun, though her stomach twisted, and her hands shook, as if Dr. Archer had handed her a coiled rattlesnake.

The wounded man turned his gaze to her, his eyes hard and un-yielding. "Give me my gun, lady.

"You don't need a gun in this home," Amelia said. The weight of the revolver in her hand sickened her. She hated guns and didn't think highly of those who felt they needed to wear them. "No one here is going to harm you."

"Like I'm going to believe you after you said you wouldn't send for the doctor and you did anyway." He shut his eyes. Goose flesh pebbled his skin. "God, I'm so cold."

"I never said I wouldn't send for Dr. Archer." Amelia set the revolver on the nightstand and tugged a blanket up over his shivering form.

Those wintry gray eyes snapped open again. "Lady, you had better hope I die if he takes my arm, because I'll kill you otherwise. I told you not to get a doctor."

He didn't seem to be in any condition to do anything, but she wasn't about to find out if he was more bark than bite. Amelia shook her head. "You can't kill me if I have your gun."

His gaze darted to the nightstand and the revolver lying among the doctor's things. He reached for it but fell back into the mattress with a deep groan. Sweat dripped from his face into the silvered-black hair at his temples and his chest rose and fell in rapid succession. "Lady, please, give me my gun. You don't understand."

"You don't need it. No one is going to shoot you here." Amelia picked up the revolver again and dropped it into the pocket of her apron. No, it didn't need to be put somewhere, as Dr. Archer had suggested. It needed to be well hidden. Somewhere Saul's inquisitiveness wouldn't find it.

She paused in the doorway. "And my name is Amelia, not lady."

Chapter Three

He was delirious, that had to be it. He drifted in and out of consciousness, trying desperately to hold onto a single thought...any thought other than the memory of that kid's face the moment the bullet entered his chest and ended his life.

He knew if he slipped under again, everything of that night would flow across his memory again. He wanted to forget it, forget all of it, because then it might not have happened. And he also knew that was a vain hope. It had happened.

An angel hovered over him and pressed a cool cloth to his burning skin. He shivered, despite the heat roiling through him. He knew beyond a shadow of a doubt he wasn't dead, because there weren't angels where he would be spending eternity, and definitely not angels who ministered cool water and bathed his fevered flesh. He'd been told too many times where he would end up to think that place had a single angel with cool water.

He couldn't figure out where he was. His brain was too muddled to reason it through. His shoulder throbbed like a son of a bitch. There was a vicious demon in his head, beating his skull with a hammer. He shuddered with the fever racking him. His throat was dry, and when he ran his tongue over his lips, they were peeling, and rougher than a corncob. He tried to ask for a drink of that heavenly cool water but couldn't form a word. As if she'd read his mind, the angel gently lifted his head with her oh-so-cool-and-soft hand pressed into the nape of his neck. She held his head up and lifted a glass of water to his parched lips. He gulped the sweet-tasting liquid, only to have her pull it away.

His stomach lurched as the water hit it. He gagged on something vile lurking in the liquid.

This was hell, after all.

"...said the medicine he left for your pain has a very bad taste."

His eyes slid shut. He was too exhausted and too weak to hold them open anymore. He was too sick to care about any medicine. He'd figure out who said that later, when his brain wasn't fuzzy and his whole body didn't ache. Later he would figure out what that vile brew was, as well. At the moment, it just didn't seem important.

What seemed to be most important was surrendering to the darkness once more, where a soft voice whispered that he was safe, that no one was going to come gunning for him, that he was protected and would be cared for.

"...Mathews that live around here."

Who were the Mathews? He knew he should know and that it should matter.

The angel smoothed another cool rag over his burning face and neck, pressed a wet cloth to his cracked, dry lips, and murmured that he was safe. The water, this time, was sweet as it trickled down his throat and he swallowed instinctively. It tasted just like heaven would taste to a man burning.

For the moment, he was willing to believe that the words were true and that the Mathews, whoever they were, were not a threat to him.

AMELIA DOZED IN A CHAIR at the wounded man's bedside. He had been in and out of consciousness for three days. At times, his fever raged so high the heat radiating from him was like the warmth rolling off a red-hot stove. Other times, he was nearly cool to the touch. The wound in his shoulder had stopped draining.

Dr. Archer had been out daily to check on him and seemed pleased with the way the wound was healing. He was lucky, Dr. Archer had said. He was young, despite the gray in his hair, and in good physical condition. The past day he had been sleeping deeply, an exhausted, but healthy sleep without delirious ravings and fevered thrashings.

Amelia could attest to his physical condition. In his delirium, she had struggled more than once to keep him quiet. There was more strength in his lean body than she would have thought. More than once, the muscles across his chest and in his arms had knotted as he struggled against some assailant known only to him. Amelia had a bruise on her arm where his iron fist had connected in one of those struggles.

A quiet groan broke from him and he stirred. His eyelids fluttered and he opened his eyes. His gaze darted around the room before he scrutinized her with cool, lucid eyes.

"You're awake." She looked away from that level expression. Those gray eyes hinted at things no person should ever see, or that no respectable lady should even try to imagine. His delirious ravings had convinced her he'd lived a life she never wanted to contemplate. His language had been enough to peel the hide from the toughest mule. Her mother would have been mortified to know that Amelia had heard such words.

"Yeah," he grunted, his voice rough from lack of use. "I guess I am."

Amelia stood and set her book on the seat of the rocker. "That's good. Would you like something to drink?"

He shook his head and winced. His eyes closed for a moment. "That was a mistake," he ground out. "Shouldn't have moved my head. It feels like it's splitting into lots of little pieces."

Amelia pressed the back of her hand to his forehead. "I think your fever has broken."

"I still have my arm too, I see." A thin ghost of a smile crossed his mouth. No warmth reached his wintry gray eyes. "Not sure if I should thank you for that or not."

"Thank Dr. Archer. He didn't see it necessary to amputate." Amelia crossed the room to the doorway. She chose not to mention his delirious ravings, and his plea for the "sawbones" not to take off his arm. "I've got some broth on. I'll go get you some of it."

"Lady, I'm hungry enough right now to eat a whole yearling steer."

"My name is Amelia, not lady. And Dr. Archer said I wasn't to give you any solid food for at least two days after you woke up."

He shot a bitter-cold glare at her. Amelia smoothed the front of her dress and suppressed the shiver threatening to rush over her. "You haven't had solids in several days and with the fever you ran, the doctor is worried that you will vomit. No solid food, only broth and water to drink."

"I don't want broth, lady." His brows lowered. The tone of his voice sounded younger than he appeared. "I want real food. Steak, fried potatoes, green beans, and carrots, with coffee to wash it all down. I don't want broth."

A smile tugged at Amelia's mouth and she bit the inside of her mouth to stifle a laugh. Perhaps he was not quite so rough around the edges as he tried to act. "You sound exactly like Saul when he's pouting and wants something he can't have."

"Who the hell is Saul?" He tried to push himself up but gave up the effort. Sweat dripped off him, and his face drained of color again.

"My twelve-year-old brother. I'm sorry, but Dr. Archer was very plain about what you could and couldn't have when you finally woke up. No solid food for two days." Amelia walked to the bedroom door. "I'll bring some broth for you."

"Don't bother," he flung at her back.

A few minutes later, Amelia returned, carrying a tray. She set the tray on the nightstand, taking a moment to steady the wobbling table. "I'll help you sit up."

He shot a glance at the bowl of broth on the tray and shoved it to the floor. Amelia jumped back in time to avoid being splattered with the warm chicken broth. Anger with the waste, with the loss of one of her mother's china pieces, and anger for his seeming ungratefulness flared up.

"That was rude and uncalled for."

"I said I didn't want that."

Amelia forced herself to draw a calming breath before she turned her gaze to the man lying in her bed. He was in pain, he was in a strange place, and from the things she had heard him say in his delirium, he was on the run from someone, but none of those reasons was an excuse for his behavior. "You're acting like a spoiled child, Mr. Evans."

Something very dangerous glittered in the icy depths of his eyes. "How do you know my name?" The quiet, even quality of his voice was more chilling than an angry shout would have been.

"Saul went through your saddlebags and found a Bible with your name inscribed on the cover. At least, we assumed it was your name." She neglected to mention Saul's constant chatter about the man's supposed reputation with a gun. "I've been reading your Bible while I watched over you." Amelia knelt, and placed the shards of the bowl onto the righted tray. She slowly rose to her feet. "I'll be back with a rag to clean the rest of this. Then I have chores to do. I'm afraid you'll be by yourself for a while."

"Suits me just fine, lady." He looked out the windows, though Amelia knew he couldn't see much with the gingham curtains drawn to keep the harsh light and heat of afternoon out of the room.

Amelia paused in the doorway, studying him. Her anger sparked to life, and this time, she didn't quell it. "If you are always this rude and this uncivilized, it is no small wonder someone tried to kill you."

He turned his head to her in a deliberate motion and his gray gaze raked up and down her frame before settling on her face.

Amelia had the uncomfortable sensation of being evaluated by a large predatory animal. She wanted to do nothing more than turn and flee the room. She forced herself to meet his gaze.

He was silent for a long moment as his brow slowly arched upward. "You've got an awful lot of grit for such a little bit of calico. I bet you've got enough grit in you to take a shot at me right now and kill me."

Amelia forced a shiver away. That gaze could freeze a mountain lake in minutes. "Actually, Mr. Evans, I wouldn't want to kill you. I have spent too much time over the last four days keeping you alive." She backed out of the room and quietly pulled the door shut behind her.

Chapter Four

Four days? She'd been taking care of him for four days? His often dormant conscience railed at him for his behavior. Colt made a mental note to apologize to her, but other concerns soon crowded out his guilt.

How far was he from Red Deer? Had he put enough distance between himself and the Matthews brothers, or at least enough to give him a few days to regain his strength? He recalled at least three, maybe four sunrises on the painful, hard ride from Red Deer. He hoped a four days' ride was enough, because at the moment, he doubted he could stand, much less ride. But once he could ride, he would really put space between himself and the Matthews.

Colt shut his eyes for a moment, cursing whatever Fates were toying with his life. He was so damn tired of never staying long in one place, of forever looking over his shoulder, waiting for the inevitable to happen—a bullet in the back, or being a fraction of a second too slow. Like he'd been in Red Deer. That fraction of a second had almost cost him his life.

His eyes flew open. Where had she hidden his gun? If the Matthews clan showed up while he was flat on his back in a bed and without his gun it would be bad. The Matthews weren't known for their genteel treatment of women. He sure as hell didn't want to see the woman or anyone else caught in the crossfire between himself and the Matthews. He could handle himself in a straight-out gunfight, but if there were people who would be caught in the middle—he shivered.

Even if the damned woman was stubborn and refused to listen to him when he said he wanted food, not broth, he didn't want to see her get hurt. She'd spent four days taking care of him, keeping him alive, nursing him. He hadn't known there were people like her left in the world, people who cared about other folk, and even took in total strangers because it was the decent thing to do. Heaven knew he'd met very few people like her in his life.

Colt sat up. He ignored the way the room spun around him and grabbed the rounded newel of the headboard, willing his stomach to stop roiling. He had to find his clothes, his boots, and his gun—not necessarily in that order.

A breeze stirred the gingham curtains, and he caught a glimpse of a small barn and a narrow set of wagon tracks leading away from the house. At least he could keep an eye on the road. No one could ride up unannounced to the place. It had that much going for it, if nothing else.

Sparrows chattered in a small bush outside the window. Chickens clucked and squawked, and a rooster crowed loudly. Horses whickered from the barn and a cow lowed somewhere. The woman's family was probably small-time farmers. Squatters, a lot of the larger ranchers called them. And that was one of the kinder things ranch owners had to say about small-time farmers. He'd been approached by more than one cattle baron who'd wanted to hire his gun to rid the land of squatters. At least he still had some semblance of decency. He'd never hired out his gun for that, or for any other reason. He was able to sleep with his conscience on most nights.

His stomach rumbled at the mouth-watering aroma of baking bread. He added another item he needed. Food—and not her damned chicken broth.

The door crept open and Colt fell back into the pillows. Maybe if he pretended to be asleep, that blasted woman would stop trying to feed him broth. She didn't seem to understand a body needed real food, not something a toothless old man would slurp down.

"Mr. Evans? You asleep?"

Colt pried one eye open. A tow-headed kid with a remarkable resemblance to the woman stood in the doorway. This had to be her brother. "Not asleep anymore," Colt said.

The kid was between hay and grass, perched on the threshold of awkward, not yet all knees and elbows, but darn close to it. His trousers were a good inch too short for his legs, his wrists peeked out at the ends of his shirt sleeves, and his hair stood out at all angles to his head, as if he hadn't dragged a comb through it in days.

"I'm sorry. I didn't mean to wake you up." The boy slipped into the room, and quietly closed the door. "Amy said I wasn't to disturb you if you was sleeping."

"Well, I'm not sleeping, now." Colt managed to push himself to a semi-sitting position before the room began to spin in lazy loops again and his stomach threatened dry heaves.

He pulled in several long, slow deep breaths and the nausea faded. He shot another appraising glance at the boy. Actually, being confined in the room with only his thoughts had been a lonely proposition. Maybe the kid could help him pass the time of day. And maybe the kid also knew where the woman had hidden his gun. He just had to remember what she'd said the boy's name was. Forgoing the effort, he demanded, "What's your name, kid?"

"I'm Saul McCollister." The boy's eyes were wide as pie pans as he approached the bed. "Are you really Colt Evans, the gunfighter?"

"Yeah, my name is Colt Evans." Colt surveyed the room again. The gingham curtains billowed into the room like brightly colored sails with the warm breeze, and sunlight dappled the wood-planked floor. "Speaking of guns, where did she hide mine?"

Saul shook his head and shrugged. "I don't know. Amy won't tell me. She's afraid I'll try to shoot it. I'm almost thirteen. I can handle a gun. I've shot a gun too, and Amy ain't caught me," he said with a note of defiance. He took another step closer to the bed. "I'll bet you've killed a lot of men with that gun, haven't you?"

A chill rippled up Colt's spine. Dear God, the kid thought he was some kind of a hero. He sure as hell had never felt like a hero, and especially not lately. No matter what he said now, it wasn't going to be right. He could put wrong ideas into the boy's head. Picking up a gun was not a way of life, and certainly not anything a boy should want to do as a lifetime pursuit.

Bear's voice echoed in his memory. *Dying ain't much of a living.*

When Colt didn't answer, Saul went on, "Amy hates guns, but I want to be a gunfighter, just like you and Doc Holliday and Wyatt Earp and Bat Masterson."

"Hold on, there, kid. You rattled off a hell of a list. Those men walk a knife-blade between enforcing the law and stepping over that line." Colt's chest tightened. Holliday was notorious for his short temper and quick trigger. Earp had probably crossed that line more times than anyone knew, and Masterson wasn't any better. "Most shootists have really short careers. Holliday, Earp, and Masterson were just damn lucky, and they had someone to cover their backs most of the time."

"You're lucky too." Saul's head bobbed as he spoke. "I read one of those dime novels about you, and it said—"

"Stop right there. I don't care what those damned books said." Colt shook his head, wincing when his shoulder jarred with the movement. What the hell was his sister letting him read? "I ain't that Colt Evans."

The glow in Saul's eyes faded and his grin slipped away. Colt's stomach twisted again. Where did this boy get the idea being a shootist was a life of adventure and excitement? If he'd had a choice, he wouldn't have been a fast gun. It hadn't been how he had seen himself living when he'd been younger and a lot more naive. Ranching had been his dream, not living his life constantly on guard for the next young gun wanting to make a name at his expense.

"Kid, most gunfighters die young." Colt's memory flashed with the look of stunned shock and fleeting horror on Mitch Matthews's face as the boy realized he had been fatally shot, the denial on his face even as he crumbled to the floor, dead before he hit the planking. "They die real young, and those that don't, spend the rest of their lives looking over their shoulder, wondering what hothead is going to try to make his own name by shooting them."

Saul stepped back from the bed. "You're not Colt Evans?"

"Not *that* Colt Evans."

Saul frowned and pinned his gaze on the heavy white bandaging covering Colt's left shoulder and encircling his chest. "That how you got shot?" He lifted his gaze to Colt's face. Replacing the crushing disappointment was something Colt could only define as concern. "Someone thought you were the other Colt Evans?"

"Yep." Even though the lie stuck in his craw, Colt suddenly saw a way out of being Colt Evans, fast gun and target for every Johnny Quick Draw out there. He was getting too old to continue living on his reputation with a gun. Twenty-eight, and I'm too old.

The bedroom door banged open and Amelia strode into the bedroom. Saul whirled around, and then cast a pleading look at Colt.

"Saul David McCollister, I thought I told you not to disturb Mr. Evans."

Colt grinned at the boy. "If she's like most women, you're in big trouble now. She used your full name."

She was like some kind of avenging angel garbed in calico and a pristine white apron. Her eyes blazed and her mouth settled into a grim line as she swept into the room. "Out now, Saul."

"You said I wasn't to disturb him if he was sleeping," Saul said. "Mr. Evans wasn't asleep when I came in here."

"Out." She pointed at the door. "Now."

Saul sighed. His shoulders slumped and he slunk to the door.

"Do not slam that door on your way out either, young man. And tuck your shirttail in. You have not been raised to be a hooligan."

"Yes, ma'am," Saul mumbled, shoving the tail of his shirt into his trousers. He stomped through the doorway and shut the door more firmly than Colt guessed she liked if the further tightening of her mouth and the stiffening of her spine was any indication. She appeared to have a ramrod sewn into the back of her dress.

"I'm sorry, lady, for my temper tantrum a little while ago."

His apology momentarily took her aback. Amelia turned on Colt. "I certainly hope you weren't filling his head with silly, foolish notions of being a gunfighter."

His gray eyes darkened to nearly black, like a threatening thunderstorm. The grin on his lean features vanished, replaced with a mocking upturn of one corner of his mouth. "How can I do that, lady, if I'm not a shootist—or gunfighter, as you put it—myself?"

"Mr. Evans, he's an impressionable young boy. I don't know what lies you told him, but I know better. When I took that holster off you, it was tied down low over your thigh, and the sight on your revolver was filed away. Saul might believe you if you told him you aren't the Colt Evans, but I am not that naive." She wasn't about to tell him she'd harbored suspicions when she first removed his weapon, but it had been Dr. Archer who had confirmed her fears that the modification made it likely Colt was a gunfighter.

His jaw clenched for a moment and a muscle ticked along the stubble-covered plane of his cheek. Amelia was afraid she might have pushed him too far.

"Lady, I never did take kindly to being called a liar. I'm a lot of things, but a liar usually isn't one of them. And if I am that Colt Evans, you've got a hell of a lot of trouble laying here in your bed. Wouldn't it be better for everyone involved if I'm not that man?"

Amelia ground her teeth, her hands on her hips. He had a valid point, but it didn't mean she liked being spoken to in such a manner. "My name is Amelia. I am not a..." She trailed off, realizing what she'd almost said.

He arched a jet brow upward. "Not a lady? Lady, I'm not that naïve. If you ain't a lady, I'm President of these here United States."

Amelia flushed. Attempting to hide her discomfort, she asked, "Would you like some broth, now? And your apology for your ill manners a little while ago is accepted."

"No, I don't, thank you. I want my clothes and I want my gun."

"What could you possibly need your gun for if you're not *that* Colt Evans?" Amelia smiled in her sweetest manner.

That muscle ticked faster in his cheek and his eyes darkened. "Either you bring me my clothes, or I'll go find them myself." He clutched the blankets, bunching them up, and levered himself off the pillows.

Amelia couldn't suppress a gasp. "Mr. Evans, Dr. Archer said—"

"I don't give a damn what that sawbones said. I want my clothes, I want my gun, and I want something to eat." He flung the blankets off and stood.

"Mr. Evans!"

A moment later, he toppled to the floor. Amelia rushed to his side and slipped an arm around his bare back. Grunting, she managed to get him to his feet. She scrunched her eyes shut and assisted him into the bed. Heat seared her face. With her eyes still shut, she rummaged for the blankets and pulled them over him, covering his nude body.

His low groan forced her eyes open.

"Are you all right?"

"No, damn it, I'm not." Pain thickened his voice. "I landed on my shoulder and it hurts like hell." Sweat dotted him and all the color had fled his complexion.

"Well, you shouldn't have tried to get out of bed. I tried to tell you Dr. Archer said you shouldn't be out of bed until you've eaten solid food for a day or so." She lifted a washrag from the basin at his bedside and wrung it out. Wiping away the sweat from his face, neck and chest, she added, "You've been without solid food for who knows how long. You also lost a lot of blood. Of course, you're going to be too weak to stand, much less go looking for your clothes, your gun, and food."

He caught her wrist in a gentle grasp. "How in the hell did you take care of me for the last couple of days if the sight of a naked man makes you so embarrassed you turn as red as a hot branding iron?"

Amelia's heart raced. Her throat seemed swollen shut, making breathing nearly impossible. She swallowed. "Actually, it wasn't all that difficult when you were unconscious. It was rather like looking after a very large baby."

He released her wrist and chuckled low. "Well, that puts a man in his place." Colt slipped his hand behind his head and grinned at her. "How about we make a deal, lad—Amelia? I'll promise to drink every drop of broth you bring me, provided you bring me some solid food with it."

Why did her heart thump even harder with his smile and her skin tingle where his fingers had held her wrist? She dropped the washrag into the basin, her gaze on the fabric sinking into the porcelain bowl. "I don't know. Dr. Archer said—"

"Well, you don't have to tell him, do you? I could smell that bread you're baking all the way in here, and it's torture telling me I can't have any of it."

Amelia glanced down at him again, her resolve fading before his deep, entreating voice.

"I can just about taste it, dripping with hot, melted butter and drowning in some jam." His grin widened, and his brow lifted in another slow arch. "Or are you going to tell me you like making a man suffer?"

Amelia opened her mouth, cocked her head, and just as quickly snapped her mouth closed. "No, I don't like seeing any creature suffer. I'll bring some broth in here, and I'll bring you a piece of hot, buttered bread with jam. I only have blackberry. Will that be all right?"

"I haven't had blackberry jam since I was a kid." His expression softened, taking the edge from his features. Amelia was taken aback by the youthfulness and vulnerability of his face in that moment. Something deep inside of her lurched and tightened in an odd, new sensation.

She walked to the doorway, needing to put distance between herself and this man who stirred her emotions and fired strange, new sensations in her. "I'll be back with something for you to eat, Mr. Evans."

"You think the sawbones would mind if you brought me a cup of coffee too?"

Amelia paused in the doorway. "I'm sorry. I don't have any coffee here. I never learned to like the taste of it, or the knack of brewing it right. I never could make a horseshoe float in it."

"No coffee?" A decidedly wicked gleam danced in the depth of his eyes and a rogue's smile curled the corners of his mouth. "How about some whiskey, then?"

Amelia's heart hammered. She shook her head. "I should say not."

His dark chuckle escorted her through the doorway. Amelia fled to the kitchen of the small cabin. She gripped the edge of the table so tightly her knuckles whitened.

He was impossible. This was impossible. Dr. Archer was wrong. She couldn't do this. Colt Evans was going to have to go to the doctor's house. Let Rebecca deal with this. Rebecca was married to the doctor and that man was the doctor's patient.

Amelia straightened her shoulders. No, she would manage to get through. Rebecca didn't deserve to have this placed on her doorstep. After all, she and Dr. Archer were newlyweds.

Just a few days more and then she could send him on his way. Send him away from Saul, who saw him as some kind of hero and away from Jenny who was terrified of guns and thunder and any loud noise. Send him away from her too, so her body would stop reacting to his smile, to his deep, velvety voice and his agate eyes. She didn't need his kind in her home, and she certainly didn't need his temperament. Did all gunmen have such mercurial moods?

"Whiskey," she muttered under her breath. She poured simmering chicken broth into a bowl, and then sliced a thick chunk from the cooling loaf of bread. She slathered butter onto it and slapped a large spoonful of thick jam over the butter. Lastly, she poured him a glass of freshly made lemonade. "Whiskey. I should say not. Not in this house."

Returning to her bedroom, she set the tray on the nightstand. "I'll help you sit up, so you can eat."

He pulled his gaze from the meal. "La—Amelia, that looks better than it smelled. I think I can sit up on my own."

"I'll help. You couldn't stand a moment ago." Not allowing him a chance to argue, she slid one arm around his waist and slipped the other under his uninjured shoulder. He grunted when she raised him into a sitting position.

Amelia felt that strange sensation again when his arm tightened around her. Butterflies swirled in her stomach and an unfamiliar ache invaded her. He inhaled deeply, murmuring when she straightened, "You smell good...like rainwater and vanilla."

She had no idea how to respond. Instead, she reached for the tray. In her discomfort, she knocked the tray to the floor, shattering both the glass and the bowl. Another of her mother's dishes shattered, and she could hear her father scolding her for her clumsiness even as she mumbled, "Oh, no. Momma's china..."

Without another word, she fled the room, mortified. When she returned a few moments later, she was carrying another bowl of broth and a new glass of lemonade. She couldn't look at him, afraid of the mockery she would see there—or worse yet, pity for her clumsiness. She carefully set the glass on the nightstand and handed him the bowl. "I'll be right back with another piece of bread."

Before Colt could answer her, she disappeared again. A moment later, she brought in a piece of bread on a small plate. She handed the plate to him and set about cleaning up the shattered glass. Keeping her back to him, she stood, the ruined meal on the tray.

"Amelia, how old are you?"

His voice caressed her like sun-warmed velvet. She turned to him, puzzled by this question. He set the empty glass on the nightstand.

"I'll be nineteen in a week."

His brows lowered. "Where is your husband?" "I'm not married." Amelia laughed, her cheeks flooding with bright color. Daddy had been so careful of the boys he allowed to court her. His rules had been so intimidating most of the young men had never gotten past him to even talk to her.

"Where are your parents?"

The question forced a bright lance of pain through her and she wondered for a moment if that pain would ever stop being so sharp. "They're both dead."

He reared back, and his brow shot up. "You're raising your brother all by yourself?"

"My brother and my sister. You've met Saul, but you haven't met Jenny yet." She gripped the tray tightly. "They are all the family I have left, Mr. Evans. I was not about to relinquish them to an orphanage, as a few of the finer citizens of Federal suggested I do. I'm managing."

"Soothe your ruffled feathers." His mouth twisted in a parody of a smile. "I wish someone had cared as much about me. An orphanage would have been preferable to living with my stepfather. It was a blessing when he finally threw me out."

Amelia's throat tightened. "How old were you when he did that?"

"Thirteen." His gaze moved to the small window in the room. "I'm kind of tired right now. I guess I'll go back to sleep."

Understanding she had been told he wanted to be left alone, Amelia nodded and pulled the door shut behind her.

Thirteen? Saul was only twelve. Thirteen and thrown into the world to fend for himself? No wonder Colt Evans had such hard mannerisms. No wonder he had picked up a gun. It had been for survival.

Amelia wrapped the still-warm bread in a towel to keep it fresh and placed it in the breadbox. Her heart had finally stopped its frantic pounding and the strange ache in her body was easing. She glanced over her shoulder at the closed door to her bedroom.

When he had been unconscious, she hadn't felt any of these things. Now that he was conscious, she had the oddest sensation she was harboring some kind of feral, dangerous thing. Perhaps it was the way he arched his brow, or the black hair combined with those gray eyes. That gray could change from warm to brutally cold in a blink. Or maybe it was the week's worth of stubble covering his hard jaw and lean cheeks that made her think of him as dangerous.

She supposed he wasn't terribly hard on the eyes. Other than the bullet hole in his shoulder, there had been nothing else to disfigure his lean, muscular form.

She had been fascinated by the ridges and hollows his muscles created on his frame. He had the most interesting eyes, and his face was made all the more remarkable by the slant of his cheekbones and the strength in his sculpted, nearly square jaw. Heat flushed her face and Amelia pressed her hands to her cheeks, trying to cool them. That odd, not-quite-unpleasant ache began to gnaw at her insides again. No, he certainly wasn't hard on the eyes.

Why did he have the power to make her heart hammer and her throat tighten? No boy she knew ever made her feel those things. But Colt Evans was far from a boy. Even she with her limited experience knew that.

COLT STARED OUT THE window. God, had it been fifteen years since the cold, rainy night his stepfather had thrown him out the door?

You'll never amount to anything.

The words still held their crippling intensity.

You know what most people do with a colt in their barnyard, don't you, boy? They either geld him or get rid of him. I can't geld you, but I sure as hell can get rid of you. Get out of this house and out of my life. I'm getting rid of the colt in my barnyard.

"Burn in hell, old man. Burn in hell." Colt recognized the warning signs he was going to have a screaming headache if he didn't force his thoughts away from Jackson Hayward. He eased his clenched fists and drew several deep breaths. Hayward was dead, and he was still alive.

He veered his thoughts from his stepfather to Amelia. Saul had called her Amy.

Pretty name for a beautiful lady. He would have doubted she had enough strength in her reed-slender body to pick him up from the floor, but she'd surprised him. She was a lot stronger than her appearance would allow. And come to think of it, she wasn't reed slender. She had all the right, soft curves a woman needed. He'd felt some of them twice in less than half an hour. She smelled good, clean, of rainwater and vanilla. Things that made him think of a safe place.

He grinned. Despite the soft curves, there was an iron will hiding in her. He knew he wouldn't have argued with her if she had ordered him from the room as she'd ordered Saul earlier.

They were similar, Saul and Amy. Both had the same pert nose and the same blue eyes, like Texas bluebonnets in May. But that was where the similarities ended. Amy's brows were delicately arched, adding openness to her heart-shaped face.

So what did Jenny look like? Another version of her sister? Did Jenny have Amy's hair color, a color that reminded him of strawberry wine? Would Jenny be just a younger version of her older sister?

With a sudden insight, he realized who the angel was he had dreamed in his fevered state. It was Amelia. She had been the figure bending over him, pressing cooling rags to his burning body, holding his head up to give him drinks of water, and murmuring promises of safety, her face wreathed with a halo of red-gold hair.

Amelia wasn't married. Good Lord, were the men in these parts blind? And no wonder he rattled her. He wasn't the damn best-looking thing, but he knew he could throw off a woman's balance. He'd learned at a very young age how to melt the hardest heart with a winsome smile and a slow arching of his right brow.

He'd practiced it on every dance-hall girl and saloon whore from the Rio Grande to the mighty Missouri.

Colt shook his head.

She was neither dance-hall girl nor saloon whore. She was probably a virgin, and an unkissed one at that. And she was a lady, through and through. He'd bet a small fortune on that one. Lady to the core and it showed in the way she walked, the way she held her head, even the way she kept her voice moderated.

He clenched his jaw, staring a hole through the door. Even when she broke that second bowl she hadn't lost her ladylike demeanor. He could read the thoughts on her face as if he were reading a book, and he knew she was calling herself clumsy. Hell, clumsy wasn't the word that came to mind when he saw her. She flowed like a gentle spring breeze over the prairie, graceful and ethereal. He wondered if someone had told her she was clumsy.

Colt shook his head again, disgusted. He knew how deeply words could wound and how tightly they clung on like cockleburs in a hound's coat. He still carried Jackson Hayward's words around with him. They were deep in his hide, no matter how he tried to dig them out. Hayward had been right. He hadn't amounted to much. A gunman wasn't much of anything, except a dead man walking.

And he sure as hell didn't have time to be filling his dance card with sweet, young virgins, no matter how tempting she might seem, or how big the challenge involved.

Chapter Five

Amelia paused in front of the closed door to the room where Colt Evans slept. Even though she had moved into it shortly after her parents died, she still had difficulty thinking of it as her room. She lowered the wick on the lamp she carried and plunged the small home into a gray-shrouded gloom. Quietly, she worked the latch and pushed the door open.

Colt lay on his back, snoring softly, sprawled across the width of the bed. In sleep, all the hard edges he seemed determined to keep around himself were gone, and the pale gray light of dawn removed much of the coldness and menace from him. She paused, startled. He didn't look much older than she was.

His muscled chest rose and fell in a level rhythm, one arm stretched out to the side. She crept closer to the bed. His lashes were a dark smudge over his cheeks. She knew girls who would kill to have eyelashes that long and that thick. His silver-shot, jet-black wavy hair was tousled, and Amelia curled her fingers into her palms to quell the sudden desire to smooth a shock of it from his brow.

As if sensing her presence, his eyes snapped open and a hard, predatory expression slid across his face. Amelia leaped back from the bed. Faster than a rattler striking, he rolled onto his side and reached for the nightstand.

"It's only Amelia, Mr. Evans." She forced her heart from her throat. "Go back to sleep. I just need to empty the chamber pot."

He rolled onto his back, clutched his injured shoulder and groaned. The wildness faded from the depths of his eyes. He dragged his hand down his face and drew a yawning breath. He rubbed his nose with the back of his hand and then stretched, raising his un-injured arm above his head. "What time is it?" he asked, his voice roughened with sleep.

"It's not even dawn. Go back to sleep for a while." She picked up the pot. She detested this part of housekeeping, but it had to be done. "No one else is up."

"Amelia, if no one else is awake, why are you up before the dawn?"

"I get up this early every morning. The chickens need fed, eggs collected, and the cows need milked before I can do anything else. And I need to have breakfast ready for Saul and Jenny before they wake up."

He pushed himself into a sitting position. The sheet dropped lower over his hips, barely covering him. Dark curls wisped lightly over his chest and wedged down his trim, flat stomach. The white bandage contrasted starkly against his ebony hair and sun-darkened skin.

Amelia averted her eyes. Unable to breathe for the sudden con-striction of her throat, feeling her heart hammering madly and heat creeping up her face again, she fled the room and the house, dumping the pot in the outhouse.

Dropping the chamber pot to the floor Amelia shoved the door shut and leaned back against the rough wood of the outhouse. What were these things he did to her? She had never struggled to breathe, felt her heart race so, or felt that ache deep inside around any other man. What was the matter with her?

She surveyed the familiar landscape and took a moment to re-store her equilibrium. The sun broke over the horizon, flooding the vista with a brilliant, golden glow. Dew glittered on the tall, sun-burnt grasses and the birds sang their melody of welcome for the new day. The Medicine Bow range rose into the rapidly brightening sky.

Glaciers cradled by the quartzite peaks caught the early sunlight, glittering and sparkling. Tableau Mesa dominated the nearest horizon. She had been awed by those mountains when she had first seen them, but now they were as familiar as her own reflection. At times she hated them. If Daddy hadn't come here, hadn't needed to see mountains like his native Scotland, he and Momma would still be alive.

Her heart stirred again with the memory of her father singing a lullaby to Jenny that was a call to return to the mountains. The recollection of his gentle, hushed voice lulling Jenny to sleep, the words carrying through the house with their soothing melody, brought a smile to her face.

The chickens scurried around her feet and Captain crowed lustily from a fence rail. Amelia smiled at the cock. "You are such a silly bird. Do you know that, Captain?"

The rooster hopped off the fence and strutted over to her. Amelia bent and scooped the black-and-white-speckled bird in her arms. "Such a silly bird," she crooned. He preened in her arms, cackling deep in his throat. Amelia took a small handful of cracked corn from the pocket of her apron and offered it to him. Captain daintily ate from her hand. His comb bobbed with the motion of his head as he dipped repeatedly into her palm. When he had finished his treat, Amelia set him on the ground. "I'm going to collect the eggs now. I promise, if any have your babies in them, I'll give them back."

The rooster strutted at her side to the small henhouse. Amelia collected the eggs and carried them in the basket made of her gathered apron. Captain paused at the doorway of the cabin, and then strolled with supreme arrogance back to the henhouse. Amelia chuckled. Daddy had been right. Captain was definitely the cock of the walk. Of course, it didn't hurt he was the only cock of the walk.

Amelia sat at the table, lit a candle, and peered at each egg in the egg candler. Two she set aside to be returned to the henhouse.

The rest she placed in a towel-lined basket. They would have eggs for breakfast, and there was still a side of bacon in the smokehouse.

Amelia returned the fertilized eggs to a nesting box in the coop and went to the small barn. Colt's horse whickered at her as his head emerged over the stall. He shook his head, ears flicking back and forth.

"You are the hungriest horse I have ever met," she said while pouring a mixture of corn and oats into his trough. The horse shoved his nose into the wooden box and crunched contentedly. "You are also the most beautiful animal I think I have ever seen. You weren't very happy when Saul and I scrubbed all that dried blood off you, were you?"

He blinked large, black, white-lashed eyes. Amelia patted his neck once more, and then picked up a bucket and a stool and approached the first cow. "Good morning, Buttercup."

The cow chewed her cud, shuffling a little when Amelia placed the stool next to her. A moment later, the rhythmic swish-swish of milk squirting into the bucket disturbed the quiet of the barn. Finished with Buttercup, Amelia approached the other cow. "Good morning, Dolly."

Dolly bobbed her head, a trick Amelia had taught her a long time ago. "Are you going to give me a little more milk than you did yesterday?"

Dolly bobbed her head again. A few moments later, Amelia pushed away from the cow. She sighed and peered down into the half-full bucket. "You didn't tell me the truth. This is less than yesterday. I think you need to have a baby again, Dolly. You're drying up on me."

Amelia put the bucket-and-a-half to the side, untied the two cows, and shooed them out the doors. Back in the cabin, she placed the half-bucket from Dolly on the table and covered it with a clean piece of cloth. Even though Dolly wasn't giving as much milk as usual, the cow's milk had more butterfat in it than Buttercup's ever did. She needed to churn out more butter.

Amelia measured out oatmeal and set a small pot onto the stovetop to boil. Oatmeal, eggs, bacon, and toast sounded good to her that morning.

Saul wandered into the kitchen, rubbing the sleep from his eyes, and parked his bottom in a chair. He propped his elbows on the table and dropped his chin into his cupped palms. "What's for breakfast, Amy? I'm hungry."

"Are you awake enough to eat it?" She smiled at him. "And Saul, lately you're always hungry."

"I'm always awake enough to eat too." He yawned, belatedly covering his mouth when Amelia glared at him. "Sorry, I forgot."

Amelia tousled his hair. "Why don't you go wash your face, comb your hair, and put your clothes on? By that time, I should have most of breakfast ready and you can wake Jenny then."

"Okay." Saul padded from the kitchen. The tail of his nightshirt dragged the floor, gathering dirt along the hem. She should scold him for wearing another of their father's nightshirts, but she didn't have the heart to do it. Too soon, she knew, he would grow into the garment.

Amelia sighed. The floors needed to be mopped again. How had her mother ever managed to do everything that needed done? There was always laundry to do, floors to sweep and mop, dishes to wash, animals to care for. Amelia squared her shoulders. And complaining about it wasn't going to get any of it done either.

She went out to the smokehouse. The empty hooks were a vivid reminder that they had to find the funds to purchase another hog for butchering and curing in the fall. She returned to the kitchen but halted just inside the door. Colt Evans sat at the table, a bed sheet wrapped around his waist.

"You shouldn't be out of bed."

"I know," he admitted with a quick smile, "but the chamber pot was missing, so I need directions to the little house."

"I'm so sorry." Heat flashed up her neck and face. "I forgot to bring the chamber pot back into the house. Go on back to bed. I'll go get it and bring it in to you, Mr. Evans."

He shook his head, and a shock of that blue-black hair fell over his brow. He shoved it away in a gesture that reminded her of Saul. "I'm up and walking and I'd like to stay that way. Just point me in the right direction."

Amelia nodded out the door. "To your left."

"Thank you." He paused in the doorway. "Where did you hide my clothes? I can't wander around wrapped in a bed sheet, and I doubt you want me strolling around buck naked."

"I'll find you something to wear. My father was a little larger than you, but I think we can manage with his clothes." Amelia waited until he went out the door, and then went to her bedroom to gather up some clothing for him. Pulling open a drawer of the old bureau, she gave in to the crippling sense of loss for a moment.

All her father's clothing lay neatly folded in the drawer, as if he would be back at any moment. She pulled out a pair of trousers, a shirt, and a pair of socks. It was probably too warm for a union suit. She lifted her father's shirt to her face and breathed deeply of the faint, lingering scents of pipe tobacco, talcum powder, and saddle soap.

She turned and found Colt blocking the passageway between the bed and chest of drawers. He held the bed sheet wrapped around his waist, clutching it closed with his wounded arm. "I'd like my own clothes, if you don't mind."

He was standing so close to her, she had to look up to see his face. He stood a full head taller, and she had never been accused of being short. "I'm sorry, Mr. Evans, but your shirt was ruined when Dr. Archer cut it from you, and I can't get the blood stains from your trousers. I tried. I scrubbed them twice with strong lye soap, but the stains are set. They're ruined."

His brow lifted with his slight smile and he tipped his head to the clothes in her hand. "Then I guess those will have to do. Where are my boots?"

"They're drying still. I had to wash your left one out, because so much blood ran into it." She held the trousers, socks, and shirt out to him. "Do you need some help?"

A predatory grin split his face. The depths of his eyes took on a new, disconcerting heat. "This is a new one on me. Most times, women are asking if I want help getting out of my clothes." He shook his head and a shock of silver-shot ebony fell over his brow again. With a grimace, he shoved it back. "No, I think I can manage on my own."

Amelia ducked her head to hide the heated color searing her cheeks. He took the clothes from her and she fled.

She went back to the kitchen and began to fry the bacon. The water boiled for the oatmeal and she started that cooking as well.

"It smells really good, Amelia."

She whirled. Dressed in her father's black shirt and trousers, Colt seemed to fill the tiny kitchen. Any vulnerability she might have seen on his face when relaxed in sleep was gone. Even without a gun strapped to his thigh, this man was danger embodied. Uncertain what to say, she smoothed her suddenly damp palms down the front of her apron.

"I'm not going to bite you." Amusement danced with bright glitters in his eyes and tugged at the corners of his mouth.

Amelia's mouth went dry and her heart hammered.

"Breakfast isn't ready yet," she finally stammered.

"Is it all right with you if I sit?" He gestured at a chair behind him. "You seem very uncomfortable with me being in the same room with you."

"Please, sit down," she managed, forcing away the desire to run from him.

"I know there isn't any coffee so I won't ask for any." He pulled a chair from the table, wincing when he moved his bandaged shoulder. He lowered himself into the chair and cradled his left arm to his stomach. His breath hissed in through clenched teeth and his tanned face blanched.

When he sat, he didn't look quite so imposing and his obvious pain stilled her fear. "I think if we put your arm in a sling, it would keep your shoulder from moving quite so much and you'd be more comfortable." "That's probably a good idea." He scratched his cheeks and chin, his fingernails rasping on the stubble. "I'm trying to figure out how I'm going to shave with only one arm."

Without thinking, Amelia said, "I can give you a shave after breakfast." She clamped her hand over her mouth for a second. "You probably don't want me to shave you. You might be cut."

His smile revealed white, even teeth that contrasted starkly with the dark stubble. "I'll take my chances, la—Amelia." He scratched his chin again. "Worst that can happen is I'll get my throat slit. But if you don't give me a shave, I'm not going to get rid of this face hair, and it's itching like the devil."

"Mr. Evans!" Saul plunked himself across the table from Colt.

Amelia winced. If Saul had brushed his hair that morning, it had been with a rake. His idea of being dressed seemed to mean the tail of his shirt hung out from the waist of his trousers. He looked more like an urchin without any supervision or guidance than the young man her parents would have wanted him to be. She wondered if he had even wet a washcloth to try to fool her into thinking he had washed his face.

"You're walking," Saul said in a bright voice. "Maybe Amy will give you your gun and you can show me how to shoot it."

"No." Amelia was startled to hear her denial echoed by Colt Evans.

"Come on, Amy." Saul's mouth twisted down into a pout. "I can't even go hunting if I don't know how to shoot."

"Absolutely not," Amelia said through clenched teeth. "I forbid it."

Colt glanced down at the table and then up at Saul. "Kid, you don't hunt anything edible with a revolver. You use a rifle for that. You want me to show you how to shoot a rifle, I'll be glad to do that. But my gun ain't ever going to find its way into your hand."

A motion at the doorway caught Amelia's attention. She smiled and held her hand out to her sister. "It's okay, Jenny. You can come in here."

Colt twisted on the chair, a grimace of pain flashing over his chiseled features. Without turning from Jenny's thin frame and downcast eyes, he locked his intense gaze onto Amelia. Aware of his scrutiny, and that most people considered Jenny simple-minded because of her perpetual silence, Amelia crossed the kitchen and took Jenny's hand into hers. She waited until Jenny lifted her gaze before she led the child to Colt. "Jenny, this is Mr. Evans. He is our guest."

Jenny studied his face, and then with solemn dignity rounded the table and sat down. Amelia quelled her shock. Colt Evans was the first stranger Jenny hadn't backed away from.

Saul asked, "When do you think you'll feel up to showing me how to shoot, Mr. Evans?"

Amelia whirled. "Saul, that is enough! You do not pester a guest like that."

Colt dragged his hand through his hair. "Let's see if I feel up to it tomorrow. Okay, Saul?"

Saul nodded. He lifted his angry, glum face to Amelia. "You're not my mother, you know. I'm getting old enough to decide what I want to do. You're only my sister."

A new stab of pain lanced into Amelia. She was only his sister, and she would give anything in the world not to be in the role of his parent.

Before she could respond, Colt leaned across the table and grabbed the boy's arm. "You want me to teach you how to shoot a rifle, son, you apologize right now to your sister."

Saul's eyes widened. Amelia took a step back from the icy gaze Colt leveled on Saul. Jenny blanched white, her eyes wider than wagon wheels.

Colt added in a low growl, "I mean it. Apologize now, or all deals are off. You don't talk like that to any lady, but especially not to your own sister."

Saul dropped his head. "I'm sorry, Amy," he mumbled.

Colt released Saul's arm and smiled, his expression softening. "Saul, part of growing up means knowing when to bide your time and when to bite your tongue. It means a well-raised young man does not talk in a disrespectful manner to a lady. Respecting a lady means coming to the table with your hair combed and the tail of your shirt tucked into your trousers."

"She's just my sister." Despite his protests, Saul stood and shoved his shirttail into the waist of his trousers and dragged his fingers through his hair.

Amelia bit back a laugh at Saul's instant obedience.

Colt ignored Saul's last comment. Instead, he smiled across the table at Jenny. "Does he talk like that to you too, Miss Jenny?"

Jenny nodded, her long walnut curls bobbing, a shy smile curling her bow-shaped lips. Amelia's heart lurched. She hadn't seen a smile on Jenny's face in months.

Colt leaned back in his chair and winced again with the movement. Amelia hunted through a small cabinet next to the stove. She pulled out a large square of white cloth and folded it into a triangular shape. "Let's see if putting your arm into a sling helps, Mr. Evans."

He nodded. Amelia bent over his shoulder and slid the cloth under his arm. She drew the ends up and tied them behind his neck. His thick hair curled around the knotted white fabric. A deep wave marked where his hat normally rested on his head. Again she felt an inexplicable need to smooth those waves.

He released a slow breath of relief. "Thank you. That feels better."

"You're welcome, Mr. Evans." She straightened and shoved her hands into the pockets of the apron.

"Colt," he said, tilting his head up to her face. "My name is Colt."

Amelia scurried over to the stove, willing her hands to stop trembling and hoping her knees weren't knocking together so loudly they could be heard. "How do you want your eggs, Mr. Evans?"

"It's Colt, and I like them scrambled."

Amelia scooped oatmeal into bowls and set them on the table. She poured the milk into a large pitcher and set it out as well. If she went about her normal, everyday routine, perhaps her heart would stop its maddened cadence and the butterflies would leave her stomach. "Saul, will you get the sugar bowl and put it out? Jenny, everyone will need a spoon, fork, and a knife."

Silent as a drifting fog bank, Jenny set eating utensils out for everyone. Amelia's skin tingled when Colt's voice rumbled, "Thank you, Miss Jenny."

Amelia cracked several eggs into a bowl and whisked them into a yellow froth. She poured the liquid into the hot frying pan, listening to the banter at the table. Saul prattled on and on about the injustice of the chores he was expected to do, when all Jenny had to do was feed and water the chickens. Amelia bit her tongue. She could tell Saul a thing or two about the injustices of the workload around the house.

Colt said, "Tell me again how old you are, Saul."

"Twelve. I'll be thirteen in three months."

"And how old is your sister?" There was a deceptive gentleness to his voice, one that raised the hair on the back of Amelia's neck.

"Jenny or Amy?"

Colt's laughter filled the warm room. "Saul, never, ever ask the age of a grown lady. It isn't polite. How old is Jenny?"

Amelia bit her tongue again. She wanted to point out Colt Evans had asked her how old she was...but maybe, asking in private was another thing entirely.

"Jenny's seven."

Amelia scooped the eggs out and glanced over to the table in time to see Colt lean his elbow onto the edge of the pine planks. Incredulity rang in his voice. "You can't do more than your seven -year-old sister can?" Colt smiled and winked at Jenny, taking the sting from his voice. "I have never heard tell of a twelve, almost thirteen-year-old boy, who can't do more work than his little sister."

Jenny's smile beamed across the room, her dark eyes twinkling with mirth. Amelia brought her attention to the sizzling bacon and blinked away tears. In less than ten minutes, Colt Evans had coaxed two smiles from Jenny.

After breakfast, Amelia sent Jenny and Saul from the house with orders for Saul to hoe the vegetable garden and Jenny to weed the small herb garden. She cleared the plates from the table. "I'll start some water heating for your shave, Mr.—"

"Colt. My name is Colt," he interrupted.

She froze for a moment near the stove. "I would feel very forward to address you by your given name, Mr. Evans."

His laughter boomed through the room. Amelia whirled. His head was tilted back, and the strong cording of his throat stood out in relief. "Amelia, you didn't have a problem taking care of me while I was unconscious and naked as the day I was born, but you think it would be forward to use my given name. There is something that doesn't add up there."

She twisted her apron between her hands, staring at the floor. A moment later, Colt caught her chin in his palm and tilted her head to him. She hadn't heard him cross the floor. Her breath caught in a mingling of fear and some nameless anticipation.

"My name is Colt. Try it, Amelia. Colt."

Amelia's skin burned with the light touch of his fingers and her heart hammered against her breastbone. She wet her parched lips.

"It's a simple name, really. Four little letters. Colt."

Her throat was frozen. She was falling into the depths of his gray eyes. The pad of his thumb brushed along her lower lip. The butterflies returned to her stomach and that curious ache renewed. She shook her head, freeing herself of his gentle hold. She staggered a step away and broke the spell.

"I still have my father's shaving things. Will that be all right, or do you have your own?"

Amelia risked a glance at him. He was studying her. She couldn't look away from that intense scrutiny. At long last, he said, "If the razor's sharp, your father's things will do."

Amelia set a pot of water on the stove to heat. She went into her bedroom and in the trunk at the foot of the bed, found her father's straight- edge razor, razor strop, shaving mug, and brush. She carried them into the kitchen. Without looking at Colt, she handed the razor and strop to him. "Perhaps it should be sharpened."

A second or so later, the rhythmic zip of the razor along the strop broke the silence. How many mornings had she woken to that sound, and the sounds of her mother's soft, hushed voice as her parents shared a peaceful moment alone before anyone else joined them in the kitchen?

She dipped her finger into the water. It was warm enough. She carried the pan to the table, draped a towel around his neck, and swished the brush into the water. Swirling the brush in the mug, she lathered the long, soft bristles.

Amelia applied the lather to his cheeks, chin, and throat, until he appeared to have a heavy, thick, white beard. She picked up the razor and hesitated. "Are you sure you want me to do this?"

He caught her wrist. His thumb moved in a light caress over her palm. A delicious chill shivered up her spine, and her breath caught in the back of her throat. His smile lanced into her. "Don't slit my throat and anything else will be fine."

Amelia pulled her wrist away. She bit her lower lip, tilted his head to a side, and dragged the blade down his hollowed cheek. The rasp of the razor over his beard stubble was a familiar sound. How often had she sat at this table, watching and listening to her father shave? She wiped the build-up of lather on the towel and made another stroke down his cheek.

There was something intimate about standing this close to him and performing this routine ablution. Her heart raced, that ache deep in her was almost a pain, and her chest was tight. She concentrated to keep her hand from trembling. The warmth of his skin seared her palm and fingers, as surely as if she'd grabbed a hot pan from the oven.

Carefully, she shaved his chin, tilted his head to the other side, and shaved that cheek. She was so close to him she could see flecks of black and even white in the depths of those gray eyes. With one finger, she tilted his head back and slid the razor down the column of his throat. His pulse tapped a slow and steady cadence.

Finally, she was through. Amelia stepped back. Colt dipped a corner of the towel in the still-warm water and wiped the last of the shaving lather from his face and neck. Then he pulled a hand along his jaw. "No blood, Amelia. Didn't miss a single spot either. You did a right fine job." He stood and dropped the towel onto the tabletop. "You'd almost think you've had practice shaving a man's face."

Did he think she had been this close to any other man? "No, I haven't." Amelia shook her head. "I've never done this before. I was just very careful."

She needed to flee the suddenly too-small confines of the house. Colt caught her elbow as she turned and pulled her into his chest. He winced but didn't release her. "I didn't mean it as if I thought something wrong, Amelia. I just wanted you to know you did a good job."

She dropped her gaze to the long, elegant fingers wrapped around her elbow. The irrelevant thought struck her that he had pianist's fingers, just as Daddy had said Momma did. "Please, Mr. Evans, let me go. I have chores to do. I have to clean the stalls—they haven't been done in a week—and the garden needs to be watered or it's going to shrivel up to nothing." She was babbling and she couldn't stop the tumble of words from her mouth. "If I don't supervise Saul, he'll weed out the vegetables along with the weeds. He isn't too careful about what he gets with the hoe."

"Colt." His fingers shifted on her wrist, sending a jolt of raw energy through her suddenly quivering insides. "Say my name, and I'll let you go."

His deep velvety voice snaked into her and grew into a scalding heat. Her chest tightened, her heart quickened, and her mouth went dry again. His thumb traced a light circle on the inside of her wrist. The sensation was nearly overwhelming, and it shimmered through her, coiling around her limbs with a dizzying lethargy.

"Please...Colt, let me go."

Chapter Six

A melia fled the kitchen as if the hem of her skirts were ablaze. If Colt was any judge of women, he'd say she had never been that close to any man other than her father. Dear heavens, a nineteen-year-old woman who had never been close to a man. Hell, he was damn sure now she'd never been kissed.

The room dimmed in his vision and he grabbed the table to steady himself against the lightheaded exhaustion hammering at him. He took a moment to gather his waning strength and then staggered into the bedroom. He collapsed on the bed and stared up at the low, flat roof of the cabin. Maybe if he fixed his gaze on one point on the ceiling, the room would stop spinning around him. This was worse than being drunk. At least with a roaring drunk tied on, he would have an excuse for the room whirling around him. He let his thoughts drift and the room slowly stopped dancing, easing his nausea.

Letting Amelia shave him had been torture. It had taken everything in him to keep from grabbing her around the waist and pulling her onto his lap so he could kiss her. She had smelled so good, the scent of rainwater and vanilla in her hair and on her skin. He wondered for a moment if she put vanilla in her bath water. If he'd bent his head forward, he could have pillowed himself on those soft mounds swelling under the bodice of her blouse.

And gotten his throat slit for his impertinence.

The rapid, dramatic pounding of her heartbeat at the base of that long, creamy neck had driven him to distraction. Would she have tasted like vanilla if he had pressed his mouth to her throat? His loins tightened with the thought of pressing his mouth against her racing pulse and tasting her warm skin. If she put vanilla in her bath water, she'd taste like a sweet sugar cookie just meant to be savored.

He groaned. Was he out of his mind? He didn't have time to cool his heels here, seducing a virgin. He had to find his gun before the Matthews brothers picked up his trail and found him. Colt draped his arm over his eyes. Find the gun and get the hell out of this two-bit town, while leaving a trail plain enough a blind man could follow—at least for a day or two. He slid his arm to his side. He had to find that gun for more reasons than that he felt naked without it.

If he were a stubborn, headstrong woman, where would he hide a gun? There weren't a lot of places in the room to hide a revolver. He glanced around the low-ceilinged room, over a short chest of drawers, a wobbly nightstand, and a battered trunk at the foot of the bed. He smiled.

He sat up, ignoring the way the room spun around him, and forced himself to take long, slow breaths until the motion ceased. He stood. The room didn't loop around him this time. He pulled the lid up on the travel-scarred trunk at the foot of the bed. A heavy down comforter rested on top, and Colt tossed it onto the bed.

His hand brushed against silk and he lifted an ivory wedding dress, tucking it under his injured arm. Under the dress he found a fading tintype. Colt picked up the picture and dropped the dress into the depths of the trunk. A woman, clad in the ivory dress, stood stiffly next to a man in a high-collared shirt. If this was a picture of Amelia's parents, she didn't look like either one of them, but there was a marked resemblance between the woman and Jenny. The woman had been beautiful. The man wore a preacher's suit, had his hair slicked back, and sported a narrow mustache. The white collar around his throat made Colt think of a noose.

Colt raised a brow. Her father had been a preacher-man? No wonder Amelia was so sheltered and naive. It would also explain why she wasn't married. Most men that he knew—and those who believed themselves to be men—weren't keen on courting a preacher's daughter.

A wry smile lifted a corner of Colt's mouth. A preacher's daughter had taken him in and nursed him. He returned his scrutiny to the picture. The father was evident in the son, as well. Saul was just a younger version of the older man. And as he studied the picture of the couple, a different memory clicked.

He imagined the man in the picture with a thick mustache, a spade beard, and a slouch hat perched on his head. Colt's jaw dropped. Thirteen years before, or thereabouts, one of the most notorious shootists in Missouri had just up and vanished. A few had taken credit for gunning down Brimstone Phillips—so named for his habit of quoting the Good Book in a thick, Scottish burr—but when no one could come up with a body, no reward was ever paid.

"What are you doing?" The words sounded in the room with the startling quality of gunfire.

Colt straightened. Amelia stood in the doorway, her eyes glittering and her lips compressed into a thin line.

"Looking for my revolver," he said.

"It's not in there." She stalked over to him and snatched the tintype from his hand. Her expression softened for a moment as she gazed down at it. She brushed her fingertips over the glass front before her other hand tightened on the gilt wooden frame.

"Your parents?"

She nodded, her expression hardening again. She carefully set the tintype in the trunk and tossed the comforter back in before slamming the lid with the finality of a coffin. Colt knew he had just been told in very certain terms not to look through the trunk again.

She marched to the window and flung the curtains open, her motions sharp and short. Sunlight flooded the dark, low-ceilinged room. Her shoulders were squared, and she held herself as if a ramrod had been sewn into the back of her starched calico dress.

"What were their names?" he asked.

"Mary and Phillip McCollister."

Maybe it wasn't old Brimstone Phillips. Colt slid his hand into his trouser pocket. "I'd like my gun back, Amelia."

"When you leave, I will give it back to you. I will not have a weapon like that in this house."

She seemed as unwavering as the mountains visible through the windows. Yet pain radiated from her, a pain he knew had nothing to do with physical hurts. Finding that tintype had opened wounds he was willing to bet hadn't healed.

"What happened to your parents?"

"They died." She fussed with the curtain over the window.

She could be as close-mouthed as a padlock, Colt decided. "I gathered as much. How?"

"Does it matter how?" Her voice cracked and her hand closed around the hem of the curtain. "It won't bring them back to Saul and Jenny."

Colt caught hold of her shoulder. He gently pulled her away from the window and caught her chin in the palm of his hand, forcing her to meet his gaze. "Or bring them back to you, Amelia? How did they die?"

Damn it, he shouldn't care. All that mattered was getting his gun back and leaving here...leaving her. He couldn't afford to care about anyone other than himself, and yet, he cared how her parents had died. He cared that she was raising her brother and sister by herself, that she was carrying that weight on her slender shoulders. He cared that the longer he was with her, the greater the odds became that the

Matthews brothers would find him here, and that she or those kids could be hurt.

She shook her head, the loose tendrils of her hair brushing her face. "It doesn't matter how, it just matters that they are dead, and I have to raise Saul and Jenny."

"Did a gunman kill them? Is that why you're so opposed to a gun in your house?"

Amelia didn't answer. Colt brushed several long, wispy tendrils of strawberry-blonde hair from her slender cheeks. "It's not an easy job you have. Raising kids, especially a boy, can't be easy."

She stilled under his light touch, and her eyes widened. Colt trailed his fingertips down the length of her neck, resting them for a moment in the hollow of her throat. Her pulse leaped under his fingers. She scarcely took a breath.

Dear God, she was innocent as a newborn. Colt's chest tightened and a heavy weight settled in his groin. He caught her chin between his thumb and forefinger and tilted her face up to him. He bent his head to her. He doubted it would have been possible, but she stilled even more.

Colt hesitated. "You've never been kissed, have you?"

Her tongue darted out, skimming along her lips. Colt ground his teeth with the effort to keep from claiming her mouth at that instant.

"Yes, I have." Bright color splashed on her cheeks, matching the defensive tone of her voice.

"Really kissed, or just a peck on the cheek by some sweaty-palmed boy behind the church?" He bent closer, his mouth nearly on hers. "Did some boy press his lips to yours for a second and tell you that you'd been kissed?"

The bedroom door flew open and Saul raced in. "Amy, the cows got out again."

Amelia leaped back as if scalded. Colt smothered a groan when she slipped from his fingers and brushed past him. "I'll help you catch them," she said to Saul.

Colt dropped his head to his chest, ruthlessly quelling the desire firing through him. The tormenting, faint scent of vanilla lingered in her wake.

AMELIA RACED FROM THE bedroom as if a pack of hell's demons was dogging her heels. Her body tingled and her skin burned along the path his fingers had traced down her neck. Thank heavens Saul had intruded when he did.

As she looped a rope around Buttercup's horns and dragged her back to the small pasture next to the barn, Amelia wondered what the difference was between being kissed and really being kissed. A kiss was a kiss, wasn't it? After securing the cow in the enclosure, Amelia leaned her elbows onto the fence and attempted to sort out her cascading emotions. She dropped her head to her hands, admitting in that instant Colt Evans had fully intended to kiss her.

Somehow she knew kissing Colt Evans would not be like the quick, cool kiss Donnie Morris had stolen from her behind the Methodist Church a year ago. Being near Donnie Morris didn't make her stomach fill with butterflies or make her ache deep in her core. Donnie Morris certainly didn't make her insides tremble when he touched her and holding hands with him had been like holding a cold, dead trout.

It wasn't that she didn't like Donnie. She'd known him ever since her parents had moved to the Wyoming Territory. He had been the only one brave—or foolish—enough to try to fulfill all the Reverend Phillip McCollister's requirements to court his oldest daughter. Even then, it wasn't until after her parents' deaths that Donnie had actually announced he wanted to court her. Donnie was sweet on her, she knew that. And he was good-looking, in a boyish manner. But when she compared him to Colt Evans...that was unfair, and she knew it. Donnie Morris was a boy and Colt Evans wasn't.

Amelia laughed, embarrassed with the direction her thoughts were taking. Colt had asked if she considered a peck on the cheek by some sweaty-palmed boy a kiss. That was Donnie Morris, and Donnie's kiss, and that honestly was the extent of her knowledge of kissing. Oh heavens, Colt had to leave. She didn't need this added difficulty in her life.

A horse trotting into the yard caused her to turn. She was startled to see Marshal Taylor rein in his huge, black gelding and silently regard her. That level gaze reminded her of the day her parents had been killed. He had been so kind and understanding, but there had also been a cool, distant shading to his eyes that day, as if he knew something he would not tell her.

The ever-present Wyoming wind gusted, tugging on Amelia's skirts and blowing the long strands of the black gelding's tail to the side. "Marshal, what brings you out here?"

Taylor sat still as a statue. "Everything all right, Amy?"

His question startled her more than his unexpected visit. "Why would you ask that?"

He swung down from the horse and dropped a rein. Tipping the brim of his hat to her, he said, "Doc Archer tells me you've been taking care of a man who wandered in here with a bullet hole in his chest. Doc says his name is Colt Evans. So I'm just checking up to make sure you, Saul, and Jenny are all right."

"We're fine, thank you." She wiped her palms down her skirt and brushed a long strand of hair from her face, the whole while meeting Taylor's level gaze.

"In my experience, when a woman stands with her head buried in her hands, she's upset about something. Are you sure everything is all right? You're all right?"

Amelia glanced at the house and her stomach knotted. Taylor followed her glance.

Colt stood on the top step of the small porch, his face shrouded by the shadow of the overhang, the white sling a stark contrast to his all-black attire. The slash of white accentuated the width of his shoulders and drew attention to the narrowness of his hips.

"Introduce me," Taylor said, leaving no doubt this wasn't a request. Under his soft, Kentucky drawl was the strength of railroad-track iron.

Amelia led the way to the cabin. Every line of Colt's expression was chiseled from the same granite that formed the peaks of the Medicine Bow Range. One corner of his mouth curled in a brief, mocking smile. No January day ever held the bitter cold his eyes did at that moment.

Amelia stopped a few feet from Colt. She tipped her head to the man behind her. "Marshal Taylor, Colt Evans. Mr. Evans, this is our marshal, Harrison Taylor."

Only Colt's level, icy gaze shifted, moving from Amelia, to the silver badge on Taylor's chest, and then up to the man's face. "Marshal."

"The Colt Evans?"

Amelia had the sensation of standing between two snarling mountain lions sizing each other up. What might have been a smile skated for a second across Colt's face. He still hadn't moved, but Amelia sensed there was a coiled, dangerous energy in him just waiting for the slightest misstep to be unleashed.

"If I said no would you believe me?"

"Nope," Taylor said.

Amelia stepped between the two men. "Marshal, Mr. Evans has assured me it is a simple coincidence—"

"Amy," Taylor cut her off. "Don't bother. I've seen enough shootists pass through Federal that I could probably pick them out of a crowd." Taylor's brutal glare returned to Colt. "Far as I know, you've managed to keep your killing legal. But let me find out differently..."

"I've never shot any man who didn't draw on me first." Colt leaned against a post. "I rather like my neck the length it is. I'd prefer not to have it stretched." Colt's brow arched up. "Anything else, Marshal?"

"Yeah, there is, Evans. Some of the folks in Federal feel downright protective toward Amy, Saul, and Jenny. I'm one of those folks. Don't overstay your welcome."

In the moment of silence between the two men, a meadowlark near the house trilled liquid notes from the tall grasses bending in the face of the breeze. Captain crowed from his post on the fence. Taylor's horse shook his head, the bit jangling.

Colt's frigid gaze slid over to Amelia and thawed. "That's rather up to the lady, Marshal, not you or anyone else."

Taylor took a step closer, forcing Amelia out of the way. "You do anything to hurt her or those kids or do anything that puts them in harm's way, and you will answer to me."

An insolent smile curled Colt's mouth. He lifted his brow again and crossed one ankle over the other. With a jolt Amelia realized that even though he was shorter than the marshal, he had forced Taylor to look up at him by not stepping off the porch. "Answer to you, or answer to the badge?"

"Whichever you want, Evans." The marshal's voice sharpened. "You do anything that threatens any one of the people I care about, and I'll take it very personally. The last man who pushed me on that point ended up dead."

Amelia cringed with the arctic quality of Colt's laugh. "And you despise me for never killing a man unless he's already drawn on me? Were you wearing that badge when you killed him, just to keep it all legal?"

Taylor's frame grew rigid. "Yes, I was. He's dead because he abducted my wife."

Amelia had no idea exactly what it was in Taylor's words, but some of the chill melted from Colt's expression. He dipped his head. "Good to know where I stand, then." Colt turned on a heel and walked into the house.

Taylor hesitated a moment, and then touched the brim of his hat. "You have any trouble, any at all, Amy, and you send Saul or Jenny into town or out to the ranch for me. I'll be here as fast as I can."

Amelia forced a smile. "We'll be fine, Marshal. Mr. Evans is not a danger to me, or to Saul and Jenny."

Taylor's brow arched into his hairline. "He's more dangerous than you can possibly imagine. Take my advice, Amy. Move him along as quickly as you can. He's trouble for you and the kids, the likes of which you've never seen."

Colt was sitting at the table when Amelia came into the cabin. The white lines at the corners of his mouth matched the white of the sling around his neck. Cold, controlled fury shimmered in his eyes.

Before she could say anything, Colt said, "Let me guess, he told you if you have any trouble with me, he'll take care of it."

Amelia recoiled at the bitterness in his voice. "He said something to that effect, yes."

His laugh was harsh. "I can probably make a better guess than that, Amelia. According to him I'm nothing but trouble to you and he said he'd be here as fast as possible if you needed him, didn't he?" Colt slammed his fist onto the table. "Damn it, does he really think I picked up a gun because it was how I wanted to spend my life?"

"Doesn't what you do ever keep you awake at night?" Amelia asked, needing to understand what the fascination with the power of life and death over another was.

"What the hell do you think whiskey is for?" Amelia recoiled from the vehemence in his voice. "For nights after I've killed a man,

I drink myself into oblivion. I learned damn quick a conscience was a commodity I couldn't afford." Colt shook his head. "No, I sure as hell can't afford a conscience," he added, almost to himself.

"Why did you pick up a gun, Colt?"

His shoulders slumped. "Because I didn't have a choice."

"There's always a choice. Even if your stepfather made you leave, surely your mother—"

"Leave my mother out of this." There was a different pain in his voice at the mention of his mother. "When my stepfather threw me out, I got caught up with the wrong kind. Pretty soon, people were talking about how fast I was on the draw and how accurate. The next thing I knew, I got called out in some little one-horse town down on the Rio Grande." He clenched his fists. "I was so damn scared I about wet my britches. After that, there was no turning back. I was fourteen the first time I got called out."

"Colt..." His posture, the tone of his voice and the ravaged expression lining his face allowed her to imagine that terrified fourteen-year-old boy, trying to face down a grown man and knowing the only thing that would keep him alive would be his ability to draw a gun faster and shoot more accurately. And where was his mother when he had been cast into the world, little more than a child? Why that undercurrent of pain at the mention of her?

"I couldn't stop shaking after I'd killed him. I was shaking so badly I couldn't even put my revolver back into the holster. And then I started puking, right there in the street and couldn't stop. I thought I would turn inside out." Colt lifted his head. His lean features twisted, and his mouth was a bitter gash. "I still get the shakes, but at least I don't puke."

He came to his feet. "Trust me, Amelia, I will not do anything to encourage Saul to ever pick up a gun. It's not living. It's surviving." He bowed his head. "Taylor's right. I'm nothing but trouble for you and those two kids you're raising."

"I don't see it that way."

Colt's head snapped up, his mouth open.

"I don't think you've lost your conscience either. If you had, you would have told Saul the truth about who you really are, because you wouldn't have cared that he's enamored with being a shootist and you know that's a sure way to shorten a young man's life."

Colt staggered back and sagged against the wall, his face drained of color. Amelia leaped across the room and caught him as he slid down the wall. "Colt?"

"I think I've been on my feet too long." A lopsided grin flashed across his pale face, erasing some of the bitterness. "You tried to tell me I'm not strong enough yet to be up and walking around. I admit it, you were right."

"Put your arm around my shoulder." She wasn't entirely sure that was the reason for his slide down the wall, but she was willing to let it go at that. She slipped her arm around his waist. "You need to rest for a while. I'll help you get into bed."

"What an offer," he drawled. "Be thankful I'm not myself, or I might even take you up on that."

"It is not an offer of anything other than assistance," Amelia said, heat filling her face and coiling around her insides.

As Amelia eased him down onto the mattress, Colt caught her wrist. "Look, Amelia, as soon as the sawbones takes this bandage off my shoulder, I'll be gone from your life. In the meantime, I'll try not to be too much trouble to you and those kids."

He rolled onto his uninjured shoulder, presenting his back to her. He curled his arm under the pillow and drew a deep breath. Once more she knew she had been dismissed, that he needed to be left alone with the memories that obviously haunted him.

Uncertain why the prospect of watching him ride away left her feeling so empty, Amelia left the room. She also realized that her questions of why anyone would choose to continue in such a way of life had gone unanswered.

"GOOD MORNING."

Amelia spun around, a shock of hay dribbling off the end of the fork. "Hello, Colt." She tossed the hay to Colt's horse, and then propped the hayfork against a wall. She wiped her hands down the front of her apron. "You were sleeping when I fixed breakfast, so I let you sleep."

He pulled his hand through his hair. "Thanks. Where are the kids?"

"Saul took Jenny into town to go to church." Amelia stroked the gelding's warm neck. He was so soft and sleek. The horse pressed his head against her shoulder. She pushed him away and scratched his poll.

"You don't go to church?" Colt leaned against the doorjamb. "What do folks in this little town think of that, the preacher's daughter not going to church?"

"I haven't been to church since my parents were ki—since they died."

"They were killed?" His brow arched. "Who killed your parents, Amelia?"

The gentleness in his voice belied his glacial expression. Amelia shook her head. "No one knows. They were on their way home from town on a Saturday afternoon. Jenny was with them. When they still weren't home by dawn on Sunday, Saul and I went looking for them. Marshal Taylor was with them by then and tried to keep me and Saul away."

Colt took a step closer. The chill melted and an unexpected gentleness softened his expression. She held her hand up, halting his slow progress. "They were dead, and Jenny was hiding under the seat of the buckboard, under a buffalo rug. They had been robbed and Momma..."

Amelia couldn't force the last words out. She dropped her gaze to the floor. Her stomach twisted again with the memory of her parents' frozen, bloodied bodies, partially drifted over with snow. Since that day, she had been forced to be strong for Saul, stronger for Jenny. What she wanted to do was exactly what Jenny had done. She wanted to retreat into her own shell and go back to a world that included her mother and father. Nightmares still tormented her.

"It's okay, Amelia." He caught her hand and squeezed it once before releasing her. "I don't need to know what they did to your mother. Unfortunately, I can guess."

Amelia lifted her eyes to him, grateful for his understanding. "We almost lost Jenny. She must have seen it all, and she got so sick afterward. She doesn't like to look anywhere but at the ground, sometimes she won't eat for days, and she hasn't made a sound since that day. Dr. Archer thinks someday, she'll be able to talk again, but he's also afraid it may take something just as terrible to break through"—she struggled to recall the exact words the doctor had used—"to break through the walls her mind put up."

"How old was Jenny when this happened?" Colt pushed the white gelding's head away from his injured shoulder.

"It happened in January. She was six, almost seven." Disoriented with the gentle sympathy in Colt's expression and needing to change the subject, Amelia tilted her head to the horse. "He's a beautiful animal. What's his name?"

"He doesn't have one." His cold mask slipped into place faster than an avalanche roaring down a mountainside. "I don't name animals. Not anymore."

Not anymore. What had happened to him after his stepfather had thrown him out at the tender age of thirteen? "May I name him?"

"Suit yourself." Colt poured a scoopful of cracked corn and oats into the horse's trough. "Amelia, I feel undressed without my gun. Where did you hide it?"

"I think I'll call him Angel. He's as white as a Christmas angel." She hoped if she ignored his question, he wouldn't ask again. She wondered for a moment if her parents had ever had a conversation like this one when her father decided to walk away from his previous life and put on the vestments of a clergyman.

"My gun, Amelia." He spoke each word clearly, adding a little more force to each syllable. "Where did you hide it?"

She shot a glance at him. Again, she was struck with the contrast of the pristine white sling against the black shirt. Black gave him an intimidating air, but also lent a new depth to his silver-shot, jet-black hair and added a startling deep cast to his eyes. "Are you leaving?"

"Not yet. I'd just like to know where it is."

She nodded to his saddle on a rack across the barn. "The gun and your holster are in your saddlebags."

He strode across the barn. Amelia turned her back to him and stroked Angel's face. A harsh, metallic click broke the peaceful quiet of the warm barn, followed by the unmistakable sound of the barrel spinning. She winced but continued to stroke the gelding's broad face.

Another sharp click traced a chill up her spine.

A quieter, but no less harsh double click lifted the hairs on the back of her neck.

"Amelia, look at me."

With a sigh, she faced him.

"We both know you can't leave my gun in my saddlebags. If Saul gets really curious, this is going to be the first place he goes looking for it." Colt lowered the hammer against the chamber, slipped the revolver into the holster and wrapped the belt around the gun. "I know he's already been in my saddlebags, because you said he found my

Bible. I suggest you hide this wherever you had it hidden when he found my Bible. Obviously, my gun wasn't in there then."

Amelia recoiled from the gun. "I don't ever want to touch that thing again."

"Then tell me where to put it and I'll go hide it."

"You said you feel undressed without it, Colt."

His grin made her heart skip. "Yeah, I do."

She searched his face. He could have been one of the serene marble angels she had seen towering over the sanctuary of a Roman Catholic Church once. Those beautiful and majestic creatures had left her awestruck, transfixed, her original mission of stealing in to see the stained-glass windows forgotten. She had spent an afternoon in the quiet, incense-scented sanctuary of the church, befriended by a priest with an Irish brogue who had told her who each angel was, and his role in the Roman Catholic view of heaven. Even her father never knew of her infatuation at the age of five with angels, or that the priest had said anytime she wished to view the angels she was more than welcome to come back. She never had though. Shortly after her discovery of those beautiful marble beings, her father had moved them to Missouri.

"But," Colt's voice brought her back to the barn, with its dust motes dancing in the sunlight and the chattering of sparrows and swallows, "you're also jumpier than a long-tailed cat in a room full of rocking chairs because of my revolver. As long as I'm here, I won't wear it. So, we need to agree on someplace to hide it. The only non-negotiable part of this agreement is I have to be able to get to it at a moment's notice."

"Why?" Amelia envisioned him again carved of gleaming white marble. She tingled with the nearness of him, the way his voice caressed her like velvet.

"Because I may need it. When I was shot, I also killed the boy—the man who shot me. He has other brothers who will come looking for me sooner or later."

"You shot a boy?" Amelia's stomach twisted and then sank through the floor. Nausea left her head spinning. If Colt was an angel, he was a fallen, damned one.

"He was nineteen. He just looked a lot younger."

Amelia's heart leaped into her throat. The last person he had killed had been the same age as she was. She couldn't imagine her life ending at nineteen. Most likely, neither could that boy when he pulled a gun on Colt.

"He wasn't a boy any longer. He stopped being a boy when he picked up a gun and tried to kill me." Colt held the revolver out to Amelia. "Anytime anyone picks up a gun with the intent to kill someone else, they stop being a child. That's a simple fact of life out here, and you damn well know it."

Amelia shuddered. Colt was right. Saul would go looking for the revolver again. She cautiously took the gun from his extended hand. Colt had stopped being a boy when he was fourteen, whether or not he had wanted to. And now he stood in her barn asking her to hide his gun, a weapon he had used to take the life of another human, from Saul. Not hide it from this man, this killer, but hide it from Saul. Even as part of her argued that it was wrong to continue to give this man refuge, another part of her knew that this was not the life he wanted for himself and certainly not the life he would want for Saul.

"All right, Colt, I'll hide it. And if you need to get it immediately, that will be possible, as well."

Chapter Seven

Amelia paced the cabin, pausing regularly to peer out the windows. Saul and Jenny should have been back from church almost an hour ago. Where were they? Why were they so late? Had something happened to them on the way home? Even though their homestead was less than a mile from Federal and she didn't want to believe anything could happen to Jenny and Saul, the death of her parents had brought home just how dangerous that short mile could be. Sometimes she regretted giving away her father's revolvers and his shotgun in a thoughtless rage after her parent's death.

A wagon rattled into the yard and she flung open the door. Relief weakened her knees, and she clutched the doorframe to support her trembling legs.

Jenny sat between Saul and Donnie Morris. Donnie's dark bay mare was tied to the back of the wagon. Amelia's relief was short-lived, and she bit back a groan, too conscious by far of Colt's presence. Donnie Morris...of the stolen kiss and the hand like a cold, dead trout. Donnie Morris, who was not much more than a boy himself.

Colt sat in the cane-bottomed rocking chair on the small porch, whittling a large piece of pine into shavings. He tilted his head toward Donnie. "You don't seem to be really pleased to see that gentleman there. Friend of yours?"

"Donnie Morris, the livery owner's son." How had he realized her discomfort with Donnie's presence? Her spine stiffened under Colt's continued scrutiny. "And, yes, he's a friend of mine."

71

Colt shifted his gaze back to the young man assisting Jenny from the wagon. "Real dandified gentleman there, Amelia."

"He's going away to college in a month." Colt's sarcasm forced Amelia to defend Donnie Morris. "He's been accepted at the Indiana State Normal School in Terre Haute. He's going to be a teacher." Amelia waved to Donnie, but instantly regretted the welcoming gesture for the message it sent to both Donnie and Colt.

"Teacher-type, huh?" Colt rocked back and propped his feet on the railing. Amusement added a bright glint to his eyes. "He looks like a bookworm."

"My Daddy always said that education is the only thing that truly separates us from the savages. Being able to read and write and teach others to do the same isn't something to be scoffed at," Amelia said.

"I didn't say it was." A tormenting grin lifted one corner of his mouth. "I said he seems to be a dandified gentleman and a bookworm. You're putting more into what I said. Way you're acting, I'd be inclined to think he's more than just your friend. I'd almost say you're sweet on him."

Donnie trotted toward them in a gait that had earned him the nickname Duck as a child. Amelia bit the inside of her lip. He did run like a waddling duck— a waddling duck dressed in a gray pin-striped suit and high-collared shirt. Amelia would bet his collar was even celluloid. His dark bowler did nothing for him, only emphasized the roundness of his face.

"Amy, I'm sorry Saul and Jenny are late," Donnie said. "It's my fault, so don't yell at them. The church had an ice-cream social as a goodbye for me. I told the children if they wanted to stay, I would bring them home. Everyone said to say hello to you and to ask when you're going to come back to church." He glanced back at the wagon, shouting, "Saul, just tie my horse up by the barn. She'll be fine there until I leave."

Amelia ground her teeth. She wanted to tell Donnie she wasn't ever coming back to church until someone could explain to her why God would allow her parents to be so brutally murdered, especially when they had worked so hard to put their past behind them. Instead, she nodded and ignored the unspoken censure. "I'm grateful for everyone's concern and their greetings."

Jenny smiled shyly at Colt as she walked by. Colt chuckled. "You had chocolate ice cream, didn't you, Miss Jenny?"

Jenny's smile widened and she nodded vigorously.

"I'm Donnie Morris. You must be Colt Evans." Donnie stopped on the first step of the porch and gave Colt a quick once-over. Again, Amelia had the uncomfortable sensation of watching two bristling mountain lions challenge each other. She amended that comparison to a mountain lion and an angry house cat. There was no way she could ever see Donnie Morris as dangerous. Colt certainly did bring out the best in people.

"I'm him." Colt spared Donnie a glance but didn't get up. He continued to shave chips of wood from the piece of pine. "That get-up the newest fashion back East?"

"Yes, it is." Donnie glanced down at his clothing, a frown marring his round face and then he shrugged, as if dismissing Colt's question. "Saul just prattled on and on about the man Amy had staying here who had been shot." He stepped onto the porch. "Seems you're getting along right well. How long are you planning on staying here?"

Colt's eyes narrowed and the shavings flew off a little faster and with more force from the stick.

Donnie retreated a step and Amelia slipped between the two men. "Donnie, Sunday dinner is just about done cooking. Would you like to stay and have a meal with us?"

"I'd like that very much." He smiled. "I was rather hoping you would invite me to Sunday dinner."

Behind her, Colt coughed. Amelia whirled. With deliberate motions, Colt uncoiled from the rocker and drove the whittling knife into the porch railing. "I'm going to the barn so you two can...talk about going back to church. Call me when dinner is ready."

"What do you mean by that?" Amelia fought the urge to shake him.

"Nothing. Just that I'd like to know when dinner is ready." He walked away from the cabin toward Jenny who was scattering feed to the clucking chickens. Colt tossed the stick he had been whittling and held his hand out to the girl. "I'm going out to the barn to brush my horse. Want to help me, Miss Jenny?"

Her walnut curls bobbed with her vigorous nod. Jenny tossed the rest of the feed to the cackling hens and raced to Colt. She slipped her hand into his and skipped alongside him.

Donnie tugged on the collar of his shirt as if his tie was knotted too tightly. "Jenny certainly has taken to him."

Amelia pulled the door open. "Yes, she has. I'm glad too, Donnie. She's been so terrified of strangers."

"With good reason." Donnie followed Amelia into the house. He swept his bowler off and hung it on a peg by the door, and then smoothed his mousy-brown hair, slicked back with Macassar oil. He sat on the edge of a chair at the table and cleared his throat several times. "Amy, folks in town are talking," he finally said.

"Talking about what?" she asked leaning over the large black oven. Amelia didn't know why she asked, as she was certain she and Colt were the subjects of the conversations.

"About you and that man staying here and how it isn't appropriate," Donnie said.

Amelia glanced at him over her shoulder, a pot of boiled potatoes in her hands. "What was I supposed to do? Turn him away? He'd been shot and he was unconscious and bleeding profusely."

"How long are you going to let him stay?"

"Why, Donnie Morris, you sound as if you're jealous." Amelia poured the water off the potatoes. She added milk and a bit of butter and rummaged in a drawer for the masher.

"Truth be told, I am." Donnie's voice took on an unaccustomed hard edge. "Where does he sleep?"

"In my bed." She found the masher and took some of her anger out on the hapless potatoes.

Donnie's *harrumph* grated Amelia's nerves.

She wagged the masher at him. "And I am sleeping in Jenny's bed with her. You should be ashamed of yourself for what you are thinking. We both know that I don't turn any heads. I doubt I hold any attraction for Mr. Evans. You are the only one who has ever tried to court me, and that's only been after Momma and Daddy died."

If Donnie was embarrassed, he didn't act it. He closed the distance between them. "You still haven't told me how long he's staying here."

"Until Dr. Archer says he's fit." Amelia returned to mashing the steaming potatoes. A fierce, bright anger shimmered through her. How dare he? "Donnie, this isn't like you."

Donnie grabbed her arm and spun her around. "And this isn't like you, letting a man like that stay here."

Amelia glared at the chubby white fingers encircling her arm. "Letting a man like what? What kind of a man is he, Donnie?"

He shook her, his face inches from hers. "Do you have any idea the number of men he's killed? Especially after what happened to your parents, I wouldn't think you would want a man like him staying here. People in town are really wagging their tongues too."

His hair oil, his strong cologne, the faint, acrid odor of cigarette smoke and soap made her head swim. His fingers dug into her arm. The jealousy and anger on his face twisted his features into something unpleasant, something she had never seen in Donnie before.

"Let go of my arm, Donnie." Amelia forced herself to meet his angry gaze. "The last sermon Daddy preached was about the injured man on the road to Jericho and the people who passed to the other side. Let the people in town wag their tongues. If my parents were alive, they would have taken him in, and you know that. I will not be one who passes to the other side."

"But Mary and Phillip aren't alive, Amy. Do you know what they're saying about him and about you?" Donnie shook her arm again. "They're saying he's a killer, a gunman, and they're calling you a Jezebel...and worse. If your parents were alive, people wouldn't be talking about you and that man staying here. You're out here, all alone and without a chaperone. Anything could happen to you with him here."

"Let go of my arm." Amelia flung his hand from her. "I will state this again. I was not raised to pass to the other side of the road, and Colt Evans has not acted anything but a gentleman toward me." Even as the words slipped from her lips, she recollected the near-kiss Saul had interrupted the previous day.

"Then send him on his way. He's obviously getting around well enough if he's up and walking." Donnie stepped back, bright color suffusing his rounded cheeks. "Amy, it won't matter to me if you and he...when we're married...if you and he had...if the reason he's still is here is because..."

Amelia's spine stiffened. "I never said I would marry you, Donald Robert Morris. And for another thing, Colt Evans has never done anything that could even be considered inappropriate."

"It's appropriate to have that man here, sleeping in your bed...?"

A red haze filtered her vision, and Amelia slapped Donnie as hard as she could.

Shocked silence reigned for a moment until Amelia broke it. "He sleeps in my bed, yes, but as I have already told you, I am sleeping with Jenny." She pressed her stinging palm into her hip and resisted the urge to hit him in the head with the potato masher. "Maybe you had better leave, Donnie."

"I was going to ask you to marry me today." Donnie backed another step away. "I'm the only one who will marry you, Amy. No one else in this town will, now that you've let him stay here. Too many people already think the worst. I'm beginning to think there is something more going—"

"Get out!"

Donnie grabbed his bowler from the peg. The same moment he reached for the knob, the door opened from the outside. Donnie shoved past Colt, slamming him into the doorjamb.

"Shit," Colt hissed through clenched teeth and slumped against the doorframe. He covered his injured shoulder with his good hand as color drained from his face, leaving him ashen under his sun-darkened complexion.

Amelia dropped the potato masher and raced to his side. She caught him around the waist before he fell to the floor. Ignoring Donnie's wide-eyed stare and the angry tightening of his features before he marched away, Amelia led Colt to the table. "Sit down."

He didn't argue with her. He dropped into the chair and clutched his shoulder, his head falling forward. "Jesus, that hurt."

Amelia pulled the knot on the sling and eased it off his arm. She knelt in front of him and unbuttoned his shirt. "Let me see if it's bleeding again."

His shirt parted and she carefully pulled the thick bandage away from his shoulder. Fresh blood welled against the protective cloth. She slipped the shirt from his shoulders and tugged his right arm free of the sleeve.

"What happened, Amy?" Saul asked from the doorway.

Amelia glanced over her shoulder. Jenny and Saul stood in the doorway, both of them as white as Colt. "Jenny, go get me the bandages Dr. Archer left for Colt. Saul, saddle up your mare and ride in-to town. Go get Dr. Archer."

Colt shook his head. "Saul, ain't no need for him." He sent a watery smile to Jenny. "Go find those bandages, like your sister asked, Miss Jenny."

His smile went a long way to remove the worry from Jenny's slender face and dark eyes. Amelia tilted her head up to him. "She really likes you, Colt," she said.

He nodded. Sweat dripped down his throat and chest. "Actually, Saul could go into town and see if one of the saloons will send a bottle of whiskey home with him."

Amelia reared back, and then nodded. "Saul, take your mare and go to the Thirsty Dog Saloon. Silas knows you. Tell him what happened and that we need a bottle of whiskey."

Jenny returned with a wicker basket filled with rolled white bandages. Amelia shook one of the rolls out and folded it into a thick pad. "Jenny, I am going to need your help. Can you help me?"

The child's eyes widened, and the remaining color leeched from her face. Colt shook his head again. "Don't ask her, Amelia. I'll help as best I can. Jenny, go on out and finish brushing my horse down, will you?"

Jenny raced from the house. Amelia handed the thick pad to Colt. "Some tough killer you are."

Colt's grin was lopsided. "Let her pull a gun on me and see how tough I can be." He sucked a hissing breath in through his teeth when Amelia unwrapped the bandaging on his shoulder. She grabbed the fresh pad and pressed it onto the welling wound.

"Son of a bitch. That hurts like hell," he grated out, swaying in the chair.

"You've got to hold this in place until I get the first wrap around it." She glanced away from his face, adding, "And please watch your language around Jenny and Saul. They're very impressionable."

"Yes, ma'am." He covered her hand with his to hold the padding in place. Amelia started wrapping new bandaging around his shoulder, then encircled his back with the wide, white swathing, and crossed up to his shoulder again.

He was as white as the bandaging when she finished. Sagging in the chair, eyes shut, Colt breathed shallowly.

Amelia rose and wet a washrag from the hand pump at the sink. She returned to him and gently wiped the cold sweat from his neck and chest. Finished with that, she eased his arm into the sleeve and tugged the shirt up onto his shoulders.

She bent over him to close the buttons, but her hands froze when he captured her chin in his palm. With a gentle, insistent pressure, he tilted her head to him. The gray of his eyes had deepened, more like the billowing, deep thunderheads of a spring storm, adding a new depth and dimension to his gaze.

"Why'd you slap him?" His rich, velvety baritone caressed her, warm and vibrant.

"How'd you know I...?"

"He was wearing your handprint on his face. Why'd you slap him?"

Amelia twisted her head from his palm and resumed buttoning his shirt. "He said something inappropriate."

"He one of those sweaty-palmed boys who's stolen a kiss from you behind the church?" The amusement in his voice raked over her already raw emotions and left her aching. First Donnie Morris with his self-righteousness and his assumption that because Colt Evans slept in her bed, she had become a woman of loose morals, and now Colt tormenting her about the only kiss she had ever had.

"That is none of your business, Colt Evans." Amelia rose and stomped over to the cooling, partially mashed potatoes.

His laughter rumbled from deep in his chest but was aborted. "It hurts to laugh, Amy."

"You shouldn't be laughing at me," she shot back as she scooped the masher from the floor. She rinsed it off and continued to beat the potatoes. And why was he calling her Amy now, not Amelia?

"Amy, would you please come here and help me get this sling on?"

How could his voice change in range from cold-enough-to-shatter-steel to molten honey so quickly? And why did the sound of that voice slide over her skin like the caress of warmed velvet? Without a word, she abandoned the potatoes again and carefully lifted his arm. She slipped the sling under and bent to tie it. A second later, he held her captive, his hand cupping the nape of her neck. To keep from falling against him, Amelia braced her hands against the chair back.

He pulled her closer to him. "You need to be really kissed, and not by that dandified boy who just left."

His mouth was inches from hers. Her heart leaped, and butterflies fluttered in her stomach. She had to swallow before she managed to croak, "Donnie Morris is not a boy."

"Did he ever kiss you?"

"Once." She wasn't about to tell him that at the time she wondered what all the fuss was about. Why folks seemed to think kissing was such a wonderful thing.

"Once?" His brow shot up. "Only once? Either he didn't kiss you right, or else this isn't the first time he's worn your handprint on his face."

"Donnie Morris is a gentleman." For a moment, Amelia reflected that this was the second time she had defended one man to the other by claiming each was a gentleman. It was almost amusing that the one man she wished would act as a gentleman hadn't recently, and the one who had been accused of not being a gentleman had so far been just that.

"Donnie Morris is a boy." Colt slid his hand into her hair and cradled the back of her head, pulling her closer to his mouth. "You need kissed by a man who knows what he's doing. You need kissed by a man who will make your knees weak and every inch of you ache for more."

Everything in her stilled with the veiled promise in his deep voice. The depths of his eyes were as fathomless and warm as anything she could imagine. Amelia pushed away from him. "I suppose you think you're that man?"

"Amy, darling," he said in a deeper voice, "I know I'm that man."

More butterflies fluttered in her stomach and her breath caught. She wiped her damp palms down the sides of her skirt.

Jenny shoved the door open at that moment. Colt smiled in the manner Amelia was beginning to realize was for Jenny alone.

"All done with my horse, Jenny?"

The girl nodded. Her pointed gaze fell on Colt's shoulder and she lifted her brows in a silent query. He spared his shoulder a glance. "All bandaged and it's going to be fine. Come here. You've still got chocolate ice cream on your chin." He picked up the discarded washrag from the table and dabbed the dried splotch from Jenny's chin.

Jenny's smile wreathed her face. Amelia turned away. A twinge of jealousy pinched before she quelled that baser emotion. Jenny's easy and light-hearted relationship with Colt was a blessing. The smiles he brought to her little sister's face should be treasured.

AMELIA WALKED FROM the barn to the house, deep in thought, a half- empty milk bucket in her hand. The last bit of daylight had faded, leaving the land bathed in gathering shadows of gray and black, and the sky streaked with myriad hues of blue, purple, red, orange, and yellow. The Medicine Bows rose in the west, the peaks golden in the last of twilight. A vesper sparrow sang lustily from a small bush near the house, whistling the day to sleep. This was a beautiful place, and she did love it here, despite the harshness of the land and the difficulty of forcing a living.

Amelia sighed. Dolly was dry. She was going to have to talk to Marshal Taylor about getting her bred. She stumbled to a halt when Colt emerged from the deepening shadows of the small porch.

"What the hell was your beef with Jenny this evening?" he asked, his face set in harsh lines and his voice tight.

"What are you talking about?" Guilt stabbed Amelia. She had been short-tempered with Jenny all evening.

"You snapped her head off when she said she didn't want to go to bed. If you're still angry about that dandified twit this afternoon, or with anything I've done, take it out on me." He raked a hand through his hair, dragging it from his brow. "I'm an adult and I can snap back. She's just a kid."

"It was past her bedtime and I was not going to have her stand there, shaking her head at me and giving you calf-eyes to plead her case. And she didn't say she didn't want to go to bed. She won't talk."

"Oh, yes, she does talk. You just have to listen to her. She makes herself known in very uncertain terms."

"You're coddling her." Amelia started past him. He caught her arm and spun her around. Milk sloshed from the bucket, splashing Amelia's skirt.

"Oh, no, look at what I just did. Now, I've got to wash this skirt again. If I wasn't so—"

"Don't you dare say you're clumsy, because you didn't do it, Amy. I did when I caught your arm." Colt stepped closer to her. "What is eating at you? This isn't like you."

"That is twice today a man has told me I'm not acting like myself." Amelia jerked her arm free of his hold and sloshed more milk onto the fieldstone porch. "You don't know me well enough to know how I should or shouldn't be acting. I'd like to think that I know how to be myself without other people telling me I'm not."

She stalked past him into the cabin and set the milk bucket on the table. She searched for a clean towel to cover the bucket. It should remain cool enough she could put the milk outside in the small stone vat to allow it to separate.

Colt grabbed her elbow from behind and spun her into his chest. Before she could react, his injured arm snaked around her waist. He caught her chin in his other hand, fingers splayed across her cheek, and bent his head to her.

Amelia's breath caught in her throat. Butterflies darted through her stomach when he ran the pad of his thumb along her lower lip. Without thought, Amelia trailed the tip of her tongue along the path his thumb had traced, and met his gaze, startled to see the cool gray was gone, replaced with molten pewter.

When he pressed his lips to hers, they were light as a downy feather, and Amelia stilled. He tightened his arm around her waist and lifted her closer, while his lips coaxed her mouth open. She shivered as his teeth grazed her lower lip. She parted her lips to the demanding pressure and his opened mouth claimed hers.

It wasn't butterflies in her stomach now. They were huge, soaring hawks.

His hand crept up her back and his palm pressed between her shoulder blades.

Oh, heavens, this wasn't anything like the cool, fast kiss Donnie Morris had claimed from her.

Her breasts were crushed to his hard chest, and she tingled everywhere his body made contact with hers. That new ache jolted through her, warming her and coiling in her innermost region.

His mouth left hers and burned a path down her throat. She arched back against the arm holding her captive. Her skin felt branded where his mouth had been, and a delicious shudder passed over her when his tongue flicked at the pulse throbbing in the hollow of her throat.

Without any warning, Colt released her and stepped back.

Caught off balance, she staggered a step forward. Breathing in short gasps, Amelia stared at him. A satisfied smile twisted up the corners of his mouth.

"I told you that you needed to be kissed and kissed by a man who knows what he's doing. I also told you I was just the man to do it."

Humiliation seared through her, followed with the icy chill of anger. How dare he? Pushed beyond her patience, Amelia snapped her hand back, palm open.

Lightning-quick, he caught her wrist. A mirthless smile crossed his face as he slowly uncurled his fingers and released her wrist. "Never try to outdraw me, Amy. Even with my arm in a sling, I'm still a hell of a lot faster than you."

Shocked, Amelia lowered her hand and stepped back from him. She had barely seen him raise his hand to block hers.

He dipped his head, the smug expression wiped from his features. "I think it's time we both went to bed."

He walked into the bedroom and shut the door with a quiet click behind him.

COLT EASED HIS ARM from the sling. He crossed to the window and let the cool night breeze wash over him. Stars glittered in the velvety expanse. Somewhere in the darkness, a coyote lifted his voice in a yapping song. Colt was trembling and he wasn't sure whether it was a physical reaction to Amelia's charms or a more honed reaction to her upraised hand.

It was both, and he knew it. She was sweeter than hell. Holding her against him, claiming her mouth and feeling her trembling against him had just about driven him mad. He leaned his head against the window jamb and concentrated on the cool glass against his forehead. Jesus...he envied the man who would marry her.

He shook his head. She'd marry some dandified twit like Donnie Morris and the damn fool would never know what he had. And then, like an even bigger fool, he'd taunted her. No wonder she tried to slap him.

Colt straightened and walked to the bed. He struggled to un-button his shirt. With one hand, it was damn near impossible, but thanks to Donnie Morris, his other shoulder hurt too much to risk moving it any more than he had already done—not if he wanted to keep his stomach where it belonged.

At last he had the buttons parted and he shrugged out of the black fabric. He tossed it across the foot of the bed and sat down to work his boots off. He fell back on the bed, boots still on. Wouldn't be the first time he'd slept with his boots on, and probably wouldn't be the last either.

A timid knock on the door interrupted his self-disgust. "Yeah?"

Amelia pushed the door open. "Do you need some help getting out of your boots?"

He sat up. In the dim glow of the single lamp on the nightstand, her loosened hair shimmered like a halo around her face. "Yeah, I do."

He held a foot up to her. She straddled his leg and presented her bottom to him. The calico pulled tight over the soft curves of her be-hind while she struggled to pull his boot off. As she tugged on the boot, her bottom wiggled in a most suggestive manner. Colt knew this wasn't a deliberate attempt at seduction on her part, but it didn't change the fact the tenuous hold he had on his desire was strained to the breaking point.

The first boot dropped to the floor.

"Damn, Amelia...turn around."

Startled, she dropped his foot and whirled. He grabbed her wrist and pulled her onto the bed with him. Before she could scramble away, he pinned her under him. Her face was flushed and only inches from him.

"I just kissed you in the kitchen and made an interesting discovery. I like kissing you. I don't know if you know it, but you are one fine-looking swatch of calico. Take my other boot off, but not the way you pulled the first one off or I am not going to be responsible for my actions."

Her eyes widened and her mouth formed a perfect O. He rolled off her, wincing with the motion. Amelia scrambled from the bed and backed to the door. He lifted his still-booted foot. "My other boot?"

Wordless, she crossed the room to him. She gripped the toe and heel and pulled, dropped the boot to the floor, and then bolted to the door. To his amazement, she paused in the doorway. "Can I tell you something?"

He nodded. "Amy, you can tell me anything you want."

She fidgeted with a pleat on her skirt, balling the fabric between her hands, not saying anything.

"Amy?" he prompted.

"I don't think I liked being kissed like that," she said from the doorway, and then fled. The door closed with a soft slam that spoke more of her flustered state than anything.

"The hell you didn't like it, Amelia McCollister," he murmured after a moment. "We both liked it too damn much."

AMELIA UNDRESSED SLOWLY in the darkened room. She tingled all over with the remembered contact of his firm, muscular body. Deep inside her, that ache she realized had never been present until Colt's arrival in her life, throbbed. Her hands trembled as she unbuttoned her chemise.

She pulled her nightdress over her head and slipped into bed with Jenny. Jenny thrashed her arms as if to push Amelia away, and then stilled. Amelia stared up at the ceiling. What was it like to share a bed, every night, with a man? Troubled, Amelia flopped onto her side and curled an arm under her head.

She tried to recall anything Momma ever told her about what happened between a man and a woman, but there hadn't been any conversations like that. She had never doubted her parents loved one another. She couldn't count the times she had seen them kiss, but those kisses hadn't been anything close to the kiss Colt Evans had given her. The kisses she had seen her parents share fit more into the category of a "peck on the cheek."

Had her parents kissed differently at night, behind the privacy of their door?

Jenny rolled over and slipped her slender arm around Amelia's waist. Her warm breath stirred the hair across Amelia's cheek.

Amelia gritted her teeth. This was foolishness. Someone like Colt would never think to stay in a place like this. That was like wishing for the moon. She could hear Daddy telling her to get her head out of the clouds. Forcing her musings away, Amelia began to recite the chores needing to be done at first light. Gather the eggs, feed the chickens, milk the cows, feed them, fix breakfast for Saul and Jenny and Colt...

Colt. There he was again, large as life, invading her thoughts.

Chapter Eight

The stifling heat of the last few days finally broke during the night. A gray, cold, drizzling mist accompanied by a fierce northwesterly wind heralded the new day.

At least Saul would be happy, Amelia thought, as she tossed a seasoned log onto the banked coals of the stove. He wouldn't have to water the garden today. Amelia wrapped her shawl tightly around her shoulders, shivering with the mournful sound of the wind seeping through the chinking in the house. Another job to be done before winter set in.

She opened the door, gasped with the cold, and raced from the house to the barn. Angel whickered, as if scolding her for being so late with his breakfast. Captain roosted on Buttercup's back and the two cows lowed in impatience.

"I'm hurrying," she said. "You don't even need milking, Dolly."

"Did you check the kitchen, Amy?"

Startled, she whirled to the doorway. Mist beaded Colt's hair and shirt, shimmering like so many glittering, twinkling diamonds.

"Milk's already there. You overslept, and I could hear them hollering." He walked into the barn, a few chickens following in his wake. "The other cow's gone dry. That one there," he said, nodding toward Buttercup, "is going dry. Even if you introduce them to a bull, you're going to need a milk cow or two until they calve."

"You milked the cows? With one hand?"

"I milked seven when I was a kid every morning and every night. Believe me, I got good at it." A grin creased his face. "It took a little longer than if I'd used two hands, but I got the job done. Milk is in the kitchen," he repeated, "covered with a clean towel. Didn't know what you wanted to do with it."

"Thank you." She picked up the hayfork and speared a flake for the cows. She wished she didn't instantly respond to his nearness. He made it impossible to think, made her heart pound as if she had run forever, and left her feeling like a giddy, giggling schoolgirl. She was a grown woman of nearly nineteen, for heaven's sake. Most girls her age were already married, and several of them already had children.

Colt stepped closer to her and took the hay-fork from her. "You aren't paying too much attention this morning. I've already fed them all too."

She scanned the mangers, feeling foolish. Was she this scatter-brained because of him? Amelia shut her eyes. Yes, she was this way because of him and the way he had kissed her. She had tossed and turned most of the night, unable to find a way to soothe the ache deep in her core. She glanced at Colt over her shoulder and murmured, "Thank you."

"I just didn't know if you wanted the cows put out or not." He paused, sparing a black glare for Captain. "If that damned rooster attacks me again though, I'm going to put a bullet into his head and we can have him for supper, stuffed with dressing and served with gravy."

Her heart leaped into her throat. "You wouldn't dare shoot Captain."

"The hell I won't. He's got spurs he knows how to use damn well, and he about broke my legs beating me with his wings." Colt paused. His brows lowered, then rose, and he cocked his head at her. "You named a chicken?"

"I raised him from a chick." Amelia scooped Captain into her arms and cradled him protectively. In all his life, Captain had never raked her with his spurs, and he had never once beaten on her with his powerful wings. "Daddy found him out in a snowbank three winters ago. He was almost frozen solid."

"You named a chicken?" he repeated. Amused disbelief shaded his voice. A smile toyed with one corner of his mouth.

"Yes. Unlike you, I give the animals names."

His smile died and the amused glint vanished from the depths of his eyes. "You'd stop getting attached to them and giving them names if you had to shoot your own dog." Colt spun on his heel and left the barn.

Amelia dropped Captain, ignoring his angry cackle, and raced after Colt. She caught him at the door of the cabin. "Why did you have to shoot your own dog?"

He glanced at her, his face frozen into an angry mask. "She had been out hunting rabbits during the night and the coyotes got a hold of her. She crawled in and my stepfather made me shoot her and put her out of her misery. I was ten at the time. He wouldn't do it, said I had to. I was crying so much I couldn't see to do it and it took three bullets. He then told me that a man doesn't cry and if I really cared about that dog, I would have been able to kill her with one clean shot."

"Colt, I'm so sorry." She stroked his arm. "I can't imagine what your childhood was like."

"You don't want to imagine it." He pulled away from her and thrust his hand into the pocket of his trousers. "I'm going to send Saul into town for some supplies. I have got to have some coffee, or I'm going to consider brewing up the roots of those chicory plants you've got growing in the garden. And you need something to reinforce the chinking in places. I could hear the wind whistling through the cracks."

Amelia shook her head. "I haven't had any additional butter I can take into town to trade with Thom Burlington at the mercantile. I don't have any money either."

"I've got money, Amy. There's a small leather pouch in my saddlebags with about two hundred dollars in it."

"I can't accept your money. How will I ever repay you?" If she accepted his money, would that make her a kept woman? And, what would the biddies in town have to say about, if they knew?

"Repay me? Who nursed me? Who's been feeding me and keeping a roof over my head? Way I see it, I owe you." Colt dragged his hand through his hair and stared off into the misting rain. "May as well put some of that money to some sort of good use. I think I'll go with Saul into town. He can drive a wagon for something other than to take Jenny to church, can't he?"

COLT FOLLOWED SAUL into Burlington's General Store and Mercantile. The rich aroma of leather, liniment, and spices overwhelmed him. It had been ages since he had been in a general store. He maneuvered around barrels of staple goods, gardening implements, and tables stacked with bolts of fabric. Several people stepped out of his way, backing away without meeting his gaze. He stopped at a glass-fronted counter. Its shelves were filled with large, clear glass jars of penny candy.

The sudden silence in the warm, fragrant building grew.

He should have worn his revolver. He was vulnerable without it. Undressed, even. He had debated with himself the wisdom of going into town without his revolver. However, he had promised Amy, and he intended to keep that promise to her. He didn't want to give the wrong impression to Saul either.

Someone whispered, "That's him. That's Colt Evans."

Another voice, this one feminine, asked eagerly, "Is that the man Amy has at her house? He's good-looking, if you don't mind his reputation."

Colt slowly turned, and the whispers ceased. A tall, portly man wearing a heavy canvas apron, obviously the shopkeeper, eyed Colt and then wrapped up his conversation with a taller black-headed man. "I'll get that stuff on out to the Rocking Bar M first thing in the morning, Drake. If you're going by your brother's place, will you let your sister-in-law know I've got that order in for her?"

The other man said, "Not a problem, Thom. I'll let Alli know." He caught sight of Colt and Saul. He nodded at Colt, and said, "Hello, Saul. You going to be out looking for a job this fall at roundup time?"

"You bet, Mr. Adams," Saul said. "Amy said I could ride for your brand."

"Good. I can always use an extra hand at roundup. I'll see you out at the Rocking Bar M, then, in about a month." Adams nodded again to Colt and walked out the door.

The shopkeeper approached Colt. "I'm Thom Burlington. How can I help you?"

Colt glanced around the mercantile and noted that Saul had gravitated to the back wall and the display of gleaming rifles. "Need a few things, starting with a pound or two of coffee beans."

Burlington whipped a pad of paper from the depths of the apron's pockets and pulled the pencil from behind his ear. He licked the end of the pencil nub, and suggested, "Give me your list and we'll get it filled."

Several customers shot sullen glares in Colt's direction. "Don't you have other folks that were here before me, that need their orders filled first?"

"Yeah, but I figured—"

"You figured wrong." Colt searched for Saul. The boy stared up at one of the rifles on the back wall, his expression full of longing. "I'll just go keep Saul company and take a look at the rifles while you wait on the folks that were here before me. I'm not in any hurry. Unless you want me out of your store in a rush."

Burlington shook his head. "No, not at all. Soon as I can, I'll get to you and Saul there."

Colt was all too aware of the buzzing whispers. He felt several pairs of eyes boring into his back. Setting his jaw, he joined Saul at the back wall of the general store to inspect the gleaming Winchester rifles lined up like so many tin soldiers.

JENNY RACED FROM THE door to Amelia, and tugged on her sister's hand, pulling her across the kitchen.

"Wait a second, Jenny. I have to pull this cake from the oven or it's going to burn."

Jenny bounced impatiently. Amelia slid the cake onto the table to let it cool. It seemed to be done. A fork inserted into it came out clean. That was how Momma always checked them. "All right, let's go see what's got you all in a dither."

She pulled the door open. Even in the gray, misting twilight, she could make out the wagon. The horse had already been unhitched and put in the barn where yellow lantern light spilled onto the muddy ground through the open door. The wagon's bed was lumpy and covered with a heavy tarpaulin. Two milk cows were tied to the back. A yap from the barn brought Amelia's head up. "What in the world...?"

She took Jenny's hand and led her to the barn. Saul spun around, a small, floppy-eared, red and white puppy cradled in his arms. Colt pushed his hat back. "Looks like we've been caught before we can break it to your sister, Saul."

Jenny raced to Saul and caressed the puppy's head. The puppy wiggled and lapped its bright pink tongue on Jenny's chin and whimpered. A delighted smile wreathed Jenny's face.

Amelia glanced from Saul, Jenny, and the puppy to Colt. He lifted his shoulders wincing with the motion. "Boy's gotta have a dog to grow up with," he said, as if that settled the matter.

"Mr. Burlington was giving them away." Saul handed the puppy to Jenny. "Don't hold her too tight," he cautioned. "He said this one was the runt of the litter and no one was going to take her. She's a beagle-dog. Colt says they make good rabbit dogs."

Amelia had to look at the floor to hide her smile. She controlled her features and lifted her gaze to Colt. "Thom Burlington tells everyone that. Every litter is full of runts that he says no one else will take."

"It's true, Amy." Saul stroked the puppy's domed head and let her floppy ears trail through his fingers. "She was the only one left and he said if no one wanted her, he was going to have to shoot her."

Saul's words brought back the memory of Colt's bruised voice telling her he'd been forced to shoot his own dog. She snapped her gaze back to Colt's face.

"Boy's gotta have a dog to grow up with," he repeated, holding her gaze.

For a long moment, Amelia kept her silence. It was another mouth to feed and things were precarious as it was. Then with a mental shrug of her own, she held her hands out to Jenny. Jenny handed her the wiggling, warm, chubby bundle. Amelia cradled the puppy and smiled as it snuggled under her chin. "What was her name, Colt?"

"We haven't named her yet," Saul said. "Please say we can keep her, Amy. Please. She's not going to be a big dog so she won't eat much, and we can teach her to hunt rabbits so she'll earn her own keep, and I promise I'll take care of her."

Amelia, not taking her gaze from Colt's face, repeated, "What was her name?"

Colt's expression softened. "Baby...she was the runt too." His voice had a ragged edge to it.

Amelia slid the puppy's warm, silken ears through her fingers. "Hello, Baby," she murmured.

"I can keep her?"

Amelia glanced down into Saul's eager, hopeful face and nodded. He let out a war whoop and danced around for a moment before he raced to the barn door. "Wait until you see what's in the wagon, Amy."

"Saul." An undertone of warning growled in Colt's voice.

The boy's shoulders slumped. "It's a surprise, for your birthday tomorrow. Well, part of it is, anyway."

Amelia was startled now. "You remembered my birthday, Saul? How sweet of you." She set the puppy down. Baby scampered around the barn, her nose to the ground.

"She will make a good rabbit dog," Saul said. "Look at how she's sniffing around."

Baby squatted. Colt's laughter rang and the horses jerked their heads up in surprise. "I think she was sniffing for another reason than looking for rabbits in the barn." He dropped his hand onto Saul's shoulder. "Let's put the cows up for the night and get the other stuff out of the wagon. Miss Jenny, will you please catch the dog and bring her into the house?"

"A dog in the house?" Amelia tilted her head. "I don't think that's a very good idea. Dogs should stay outside."

"She's too little to stay in the barn by herself for now," Colt said.

Before she could argue any further about a dog in the house, Jenny caught Baby into her arms and fled the barn, effectively ending any further protests from Amelia.

Amelia watched as Saul and Colt worked under the tarp, their attempt to keep her birthday surprise a secret. Saul handed two cured hams out and Colt carried them to the smokehouse. Saul carried a bag of coffee into the house before rushing back out to the wagon. He ducked back under the tarp and pulled out a fifty-pound bag of flour. He struggled to lift it, and then smiled his thanks up to Colt when the man helped boost it to his young shoulders.

"I'm going to help Colt chink the house for the winter," Saul announced, even though he staggered under the weight of a bag of cement mix he toted to the barn.

Lastly, Colt hefted a ten-pound bag of sugar and a flour sack of other items and carried them into the house. "Don't know where you want all this stuff, but Saul and I figured you and Jenny could have fun putting it away."

She stood in stunned silence as Colt set items on the table. Cork-topped glass bottles of cinnamon, paprika, black pepper, thyme, ginger, and allspice, bottles of vanilla, lemon and almond-oil extracts, hair ribbons, and several bars of French-milled soap. Colt picked up a pair of bright blue ribbons and compared them to Jenny's dark hair. "That should do nicely," he said.

Jenny took the ribbon from his fingers and tied them around her braids.

Amelia stared at the bounty on the table. She couldn't keep track of the cost of everything he had brought into the house, and she had no idea how she was ever going to repay him for his generosity. "Colt, what is all this?"

"You going to tell me you don't need these things?" Defensiveness shaded his voice and darkened his eyes, as if afraid she would reject the items.

He must know she couldn't. "No, I'm not going to tell you that."

He pulled a box of bullets from the bag and handed them to Saul. "These are yours."

"Colt." Amelia's heart stuttered and fear snaked through the pit of her stomach.

Saul clutched the box to his chest, his gaze darting from Amelia to Colt.

A gun? In her house? No, she would not stand for that. Not after what those instruments had done to her family, had done to her and Jenny and Saul.

Colt turned to Saul. "Go on out to the wagon and bring the Winchester in. May as well get this over and done with."

"Colt Evans." Amelia bit his name out through clenched teeth. "I will not have that thing in my house."

"For heaven's sake, Amy, how can I teach him to hunt if he doesn't have a rifle?" Colt rubbed the back of his neck, his expression as set as the granite slopes of the mountains towering in the western horizon. "Boy's gotta have a rifle and a dog if he's going to hunt rabbits."

Saul came back in the house, a Winchester rifle in his hands. In the lamplight, the barrel glinted with bluing and the wooden stock gleamed with a rich, burnished glow. How could something so beautiful be such a thing of death? Amelia whirled around.

Jenny stood frozen in the middle of the room, her eyes wide. The color had vanished from her face and her mouth opened and closed as her breath came in terrified pants. Before Amelia could stop her, the girl shoved her way past Saul and ran out into the dark, damp night.

Amelia paused long enough to shoot her words at Colt. "This is why I don't want any guns in my house."

"Damn," Colt breathed. "Stay here, Saul. I'm going to help your sister find Jenny."

He ran out the door, shouting the girl's name. After he shouted a second time, Colt shook his head. The kid wouldn't talk. How could she answer him?

Amelia emerged from the henhouse. "She isn't there. I'm going to try the barn."

The barn door stood open to the night. Colt caught Amelia's arm at the elbow.

"I'll check the barn. This is my fault. I should have asked you before I bought the rifle for Saul."

"Saul should have said something to you." Her voice rose in worried frustration. "If he had, we wouldn't be looking for a terrified seven-year-old now. And he knows how I feel about him picking up a gun."

"He's only twelve himself, Amy. He's not going to turn shootist because he's got a Winchester." Colt forced himself to keep his voice even. "He probably also knew if he told me, I wouldn't have bought it."

Colt trudged through the mud to the barn.

He lit a lantern and searched the warm, quiet building. He found Jenny in Angel's stall, knees drawn to her chin, arms wrapped around her legs. She was shaking with silent sobs. He hung the lantern on a nail and let himself into the horse's stall.

Colt sank next to Jenny in the clean straw. She looked up at him, her eyes welling with frightened tears. He slipped his arm around her and she dropped her head to his side, her tears dampening his shirt. "Aw, Jenny, I'm sorry. I didn't know."

She sniffled and wiped the back of hand across her nose. Angel nudged the girl, his warm breath rustling the bright blue ribbons. Colt pushed the gelding's head away.

"Amy said you saw your momma and daddy killed by some very bad people." He stroked her back, trying to calm her hiccupping cries.

Jenny lifted her head and nodded, memories darkening her eyes. Her lower lip quivered, and more tears spilled down her cheeks.

"Jenny, not everyone who carries a gun is going to hurt you." He caressed her slender arm. "Learning to hunt is something a lot of boys do. It's part of growing up."

She shook her head vehemently, and then buried her face against his side. Her arms snaked around him and hugged him tightly, her slender frame shuddering.

With a finger under her slender chin, Colt tilted her face up. The tears tracking her face and welling in her eyes burned against his heart hotter than a brand. "Do you think I would ever let anyone hurt you?"

Those huge brown eyes searched his face, and then, slowly, she shook her head.

He drew a deep breath. "Do you think I would give Saul a rifle if I thought he was going to hurt you or Amy with it?"

Again, she slowly shook her head. He brushed her bangs from her forehead and tugged slightly on one of her long pigtails. "You know, Miss Jenny, when I came here a few days ago, I was wearing a gun."

She swallowed and nodded.

"Are you afraid of me or scared I'm going to hurt you?"

There wasn't a second of hesitation before she shook her head. Colt folded her into his side again. "I promise, Miss Jenny, so long as I'm here, no one will hurt you or Saul or Amy. I swear that to you."

Her thin arms tightened around his waist and Colt's throat clenched. He sat with her for a long moment, the weight of her head against his ribs filling him with a protectiveness he hadn't felt in a long time. He slipped her long braid through his fingers.

"You know what, Jenny?"

She shook her head against his side, her tiny hand catching his in the sling. Her fingers tightened around his palm.

"A man could get real used to living in a place like this with a couple of kids like you and Saul. That used to be something I dreamed of having...a couple of great kids, a beautiful wife like your sister, a small ranch with a few head of cattle. I used to dream about it so much, I had the floor plan for the house all laid out in my head. I could almost feel the sun on me as I watched it sinking behind a mountain range in those dreams."

Jenny pushed back from him, and her brows lifted. She might not be able to speak but he could translate the silent query.

"I don't know what happened to those dreams." He smiled and brushed the last of her tears from her cheeks. "I guess, somewhere along the line, I realized someone like me will never be able to settle down and have those dreams come true."

She shook her head.

"No, what? No, I'll never be able to settle down..."

She shook her head again. The blue ribbons danced and shimmered in the lantern light. Rain falling from the roof pattered to the ground in a soothing rhythm. The horses shuffled in the stalls and the cows contentedly munched hay.

"I should see to making those dreams come true." *Here.*

She bobbed her head and a smile darted over her tear-streaked face.

"Wish I could, Jenny." Colt eased a deep breath in. He dropped his head to the wall behind him then canted his gaze toward the child. "But that gun I wore isn't going to let me."

Her brows lowered.

"I've done some really bad things. I will always be looking over my shoulder. And if I stayed here to try to make those dreams come true, you and Saul and Amy could be hurt because of the things I have done. I've done some really bad things," he repeated.

She shook her head again.

"Yeah, Jenny, I have." He drew another deep breath. "I'd better get you into the house and take the tongue lashing I know is coming." Colt stood, holding his hand down to Jenny. When he straightened and turned toward the aisle, Amelia stood silently a few feet away. Tears glistened in her eyes.

Colt brushed a hand over Jenny's head. "Go on into the house. And tell Saul to give that puppy a bowl of water."

He waited until Jenny left the barn before he said, "Well, go on. Have your say. I should have asked you before I bought Saul a rifle, and I should have warned Jenny before she saw it. This is all my fault, and I overstepped my bounds as a guest in your home."

"Yes, you should have asked me first." Her heart was breaking for the wistful tone she had heard in his voice when he told Jenny of his dreams. Hidden beneath his harsh exterior was a man who just wanted what every other man wanted, a home, children, a place he knew he could be safe. And he had said she was beautiful. "Colt, I didn't know..."

"How much of that did you hear?" Ice formed in the air with his tone of voice.

"All of it. I came into the barn when I heard you tell Jenny you were sorry, that you didn't know." She took a step closer. "I heard all of it, Colt."

"Yeah, well, don't dwell too much on it. They're just dreams. I won't be staying too much longer." He walked to the door.

"Colt." He stopped, his back still to her. Amelia plunged on, before she lost her resolve. "You don't have to leave if you don't want to. There have been others who walked away from the life of a shootist."

"I told you, they're just dreams, Amy. Something we all have to learn is that part of being a grown-up means we realize dreams are only that—dreams." He glanced over his shoulder. "I grew up a long time ago. And walking away doesn't work. Sooner or later, no matter where he hides or how much time he puts between him and yesterday, a shootist's past finds him." He strode out of the barn without a backward glance.

"You gave those dreams up only because you didn't have a choice," Amelia murmured. She looked at Angel and shook her head.

"How do I convince him he has a choice, now? Daddy had the same choice to make and he walked toward those dreams he had."

SAUL STOOD IN THE KITCHEN, his face set in stubborn lines. Jenny was clinging to Baby, and Colt leaned against the kitchen counter, nursing a steaming cup of coffee.

"She's my puppy. Colt, tell her Baby is my puppy!"

Amelia shut the door on the cool, damp night. "What is going on in here?"

"Jenny wants to take Baby to bed with her." Saul's voice rose into a wail. "She's my puppy, Amy."

Amelia shot a glare at Colt. "Why haven't you said something?"

"Do I look like I want in the middle of this?" He set the cup down. "I tried to work out a compromise with both of them, but neither one is budging."

Amelia sighed. It was as if their conversation in the barn had never taken place. "Saul, Jenny goes to bed a full hour before you do. Let her take Baby to bed with her and when you go to bed, I'll get Baby for you and you can have her."

Jenny shook her head, her blue ribbons gleaming in the lamplight. She clutched the puppy to her chest, forcing a grunt from Baby.

"Jenny, we are not going to argue this," Amelia said. "Baby is your brother's dog. You can take her to bed with you. But when Saul goes to bed, I will get Baby and he can have her for the rest of the night."

Jenny shook her head and cast a pleading gaze to Colt. He threw his hands up into the air, raising the one in the sling as high as he could. "Don't get me in the middle of this, Miss Jenny. You had your chance for a compromise."

Amelia hissed, "Coward."

"Amy, she's my puppy, not Jen—" Saul's wail ended mid-word when Amelia rounded on him. "Okay. Jenny can take her to bed with her. But I get her when I go to bed. She's *my* puppy, Jenny."

Jenny set her mouth in a stubborn line and again shook her head. Too well, Amelia knew that glint in her eyes. She had her mind set and neither heaven nor hell was going to budge her.

Amelia glared at Colt. "You solve this. You created this problem when you brought that puppy here."

His brows lowered. "Me?"

"Yes, you, Colt. I am going to wash the dishes. It's your problem to resolve." Amelia turned her back on the three of them.

While the water heated, Amelia watched Colt with Saul and Jenny. Jenny sat on his knee, the puppy in her arms. Saul stroked the puppy's head, nodding at whatever Colt was murmuring in a low voice.

Amelia dropped the dishes into the heated water and scrubbed them clean. Colt announced, "We've got it all worked out, Amy. Jenny will take Baby to bed with her tonight, and tomorrow, Saul can have her." He sounded pleased with himself. "Of course, Saul and I have to go back into town and find Jenny her own puppy."

"What?" Amelia shot a startled glance at him. "Another puppy? Another mouth to feed?"

"Or a kitten if we can't find a puppy, which might be a better pet for a young lady anyway," Colt said. "You don't have to feed a cat, because they earn their keep by mousing and ratting."

"Oh, I give up," Amelia muttered, sinking her hands into the hot water.

"If you can have a pet rooster named Captain, Jenny can have a puppy or a kitten."

She had to admit he did have a point about cats catching small varmints. And she had made a pet of a rooster. She felt, though, that she should protest at least one last time. "I swear all three of you were in cahoots about this the whole time, Colt."

"Girl's gotta have a kitten, that's all there is to it," Colt said it as if it were etched in stone somewhere, never to be altered or defied.

AMELIA WHISTLED SOFTLY for Baby. Saul was sprawled on his bed but Baby was nowhere in sight. She peeked into Jenny's room. Like Saul, Jenny was sound asleep, her features relaxed and peaceful. Yet there was still no sign of Baby. Where had that puppy gotten to?

Baby had to go outside once more before Amelia could go to bed for the night. On a hunch, she eased the door open to her room.

Colt was sound asleep, flat on his back. A small red and white bundle snuggled into his side, safe within the protective curve of his arm. Colt's upper arm pillowed Baby's head.

The puppy's tail thumped on the mattress and Colt's arm tightened, pulling her closer into the safety of his side. Baby's tail thumped faster and harder on the mattress. In his sleep, Colt drew a hand slowly down the puppy's back.

Amelia crossed her arms over her breast and leaned her head against the doorjamb, smiling. Her heart seemed to swell, and a soul-deep warmth washed over her. Not for all the money in the world would she have stepped into the room and taken that puppy from the safety of Colt's arm. She tiptoed to the bed and pulled a blanket up over them.

Baby's black nose emerged from the blanket and she sighed.

"Good night, Baby. Good night, Colt," Amelia whispered, and pulled the door shut.

Chapter Nine

Amelia stood for a long moment, staring. Disbelief and amusement vied within her and she couldn't hide her smile. Saul, Jenny, and Colt sat on a glider swing at the edge of her herb garden and all three were grinning from ear to ear. Baby gamboled in the sagebrush and scrub grasses near the house, chasing grasshoppers.

The misting rain of the previous day had given way to bright sunshine and a cool breeze. The dark slopes of the Medicine Bow were more sharply defined in the crystal-clear air, seeming to be closer. Meadowlarks celebrated the sunshine with their liquid trilling, matched with the happy chirruping of several small brown sparrows. Drops of water glistened in the sunlight, casting a myriad of tiny rainbows throughout the small herb garden.

"Happy birthday, Amy," Saul said.

Colt moved over a little on the seat. "Try it out."

Wordless, Amelia sat down. Saul kicked and set the glider in motion. Amelia smiled at Colt. "Thank you. This is very nice."

He nodded. "Happy birthday."

A moment later Colt craned his head to the road approaching the house. His eyes narrowed and his expression froze even as he came to his feet. Amelia twisted around on the seat, and spied Marshal Taylor riding toward them.

She stood and pulled Jenny off the glider. "Take Baby, go on into the house, and get cleaned up for dinner." She gave Jenny a hug. "Thank you, Jenny. I was getting a little cross when you wouldn't let me out of the house all morning, but now I know why. The three of you had a very nice surprise for me."

Taylor arrived before she could send Saul to the house. The marshal drew rein on his black gelding, nearly on top of Colt. He tipped his hat to Amelia, but his gaze was fixed on Colt. "You were in town yesterday, Evans."

It wasn't a question. Amelia moved next to Colt.

"Yeah." His voice wasn't as icy as the last time, Amelia suspected, because Saul stood a few feet away, watching them with wide eyes and bigger ears.

"You bought a rifle and rounds," the marshal noted.

"Yeah." Colt's voice was quiet.

"It's my rifle, Marshal," Saul said. "Colt's going to teach me how to shoot."

Taylor's eyes narrowed and his jaw tightened. "Surprised you didn't buy him a revolver. That's your weapon of choice and you seem to be fairly proficient with one."

The sarcasm in the marshal's voice sent a chill skittering up Amelia's back.

"I don't want a revolver." Saul scuffed the damp ground with the toe of his shoe, not looking anywhere but at the ground. "Not anymore."

Colt didn't say a word, but the air thrummed with his restrained anger. He seemed carved of marble.

Taylor's gaze slid momentarily to Amelia. "You know about this, Amy?"

Amelia nodded. "Yes, Saul and Colt told me last night when they got home." She dropped a hand onto Saul's shoulder. "Why don't you go into the house and help your sister set the table for dinner?"

"But, Amy—"

Colt snapped his head around to Saul and leveled a cold stare at him. Saul heaved a sigh and shuffled to the house. He closed the door with more force than necessary, and Amelia winced.

"You got a reason to be out here, Marshal, or you just passing this way and decided to drop in?" With Saul in the house, Colt's acrid sarcasm returned.

"Where was Colt last night, Amy?"

"I was—"

"I asked Amy." Taylor cut him off. "Where was he last night?"

Amelia glanced from Colt to the marshal. "I went to bed about midnight. Colt was here then, asleep. I woke up at six and the three of them were already awake. Jenny had to keep me in the house until Saul and Colt said I could come out." She gestured to the new glider. "They were setting the glider in the yard."

The marshal jerked his head at the glider, his unforgiving gaze leveled on Colt. "You managed that with your arm in a sling?"

"Yeah, I did. With Saul's help. What's this all about, Marshal?"

"So, there were at least five-and-a-half hours when you can't account for your time last night." Taylor leaned an elbow on the saddle horn. "Unless you want to tell me you were sleeping the whole time."

"I get the feeling that if I said I was, you wouldn't believe me anyway."

"You're right on that score." The black gelding took a step forward, forcing Colt and Amelia to move back. "I've got a dead man in town, shot with one bullet through the heart, and two of Deb English's doves swear they saw you in town, around three in the morning."

Amelia's heart wrenched. She shook her head. "Two women from a brothel say they saw him there?"

"I wasn't there, Amy." The words sounded forced out and Colt was pale under his tanned complexion.

"Now, I'm thinking," Taylor went on, as smooth as silk, "if you can manage, even with Saul's help, to get that glider swing up, you can manage to saddle a horse, spend a few hours with a couple of soiled doves, and even shoot a man dead with your arm in a sling."

Amelia stiffened. Taylor's voice had the quality of granite, just as hard and unyielding. The marshal dipped his head to Colt's arm secured in the sling. "That the hand you shoot with?"

"No." Granite clashed on granite in Colt's response.

"One shot, through the heart, quick and clean. That's how you like to do your killing, isn't it, Evans?"

Colt shook his head. "Marshal, you want to make sure Amy tells me to hit the road, fine, you go on and get nailed to the counter and tell her I was in a brothel with a couple of fancy girls last night. But don't add to the lie and tell her I killed a man when I didn't. And don't come here asking her where I was with the expectation that she'll lie for me, because I won't let her do that." Icy anger gave depth to his voice. "I don't know who did kill that man, but it wasn't me. I've got enough I'll answer for to the Almighty, don't add any more that I ain't done." He turned to Amy. "I wasn't there, Amy. I never left the house last night."

She searched his face, aching at the desperate pleading of his expression. "Hold your hand out, Colt."

"What?"

"Hold your hand out," she repeated. Her heart clenched in fear and the hope he wasn't lying.

He held a perfectly steady hand out to her. Without hesitation or doubt, she took his hand into hers. "He wasn't there, Marshal."

Taylor jerked his head back, and then slowly straightened in the saddle. "Now, how do you know that, Amy?"

"I know. He wasn't there last night."

Taylor tugged on the horse's reins and backed away from them. "No one saw the shooter this time. But I'm patient. I don't like people being killed in my town, and I will find out who did it. The question then will be if you still rate a new rope with me, Evans."

He kicked his heels into the black gelding's sides and was gone.

Colt pulled his hand free of Amelia's grasp and punched a leg of the glider frame. He spun around. "I wasn't in town at three in the morning."

"I know that."

Her conviction rocked Colt. "How the hell do you know that? What made you so certain all of a sudden?"

The intensity of her smile was enough to dim the sun. "You don't have the shakes," she said.

Colt shook his head. "You remembered that?"

"Yes." She knit her brow. "What did he mean by rating a new rope?"

Colt stared off into the pine-blackened slopes. He squinted against the sunlight glittering on the white granite of the peaks above the tree-line. "It means when he finally gets around to figuring out how to convince the people of this town to lynch me, he's going to add a final insult by using a rope that's already been used to hang another man." Bitterness added a biting taste to the words. "Supposed to use a new rope for any man condemned to die by hanging."

"He's not going to hang you," Amelia said, and placed her hand on his arm.

He studied her small hand. "Yeah?" He met Amelia's gaze before tilting his head in the direction Taylor had taken. "Tell him that."

Amelia smiled again, a new depth and intensity to those bluebonnet eyes. "I think I will tell him that and a few other things too."

"AMY, I DON'T THINK Colt's been honest with us."

Amelia glanced down at her younger brother. At least he had stopped sulking over not being allowed to drive the wagon into town that morning. "What makes you say that, young man? That's a terrible thing to say about anyone."

"I just think he's pretending that he isn't really a shootist."

"Why do you think that?" Her heart climbed into her throat, making it hard to swallow.

"Amy, I'm not stupid. Marshal Taylor thinks he is—why else would he have come out to the house yesterday after that man was shot?—all the people in church were talking about him, and when we were at Burlington's, I heard someone say he was. Is he? I think he is, even if Kyla says her pa told her he isn't."

Amelia shook her head. No matter how she answered Saul, it wouldn't be truthful. "Really, Saul, that's one of the most ridiculous things you've asked in a while." She reined the horse in outside of Burlington's General Store.

"I'm just telling you what I think." He stood up, grabbing Jenny's hand.

Amelia caught Saul's arm before he bailed from the wagon. "You keep an eye on your sister." She handed him two coins. "Take her over to Mr. Milton's candy store. There's a penny for both of you."

Saul helped Jenny from the back of the wagon.

"Where are you going?" he asked.

"I'll be right down the street at Marshal Taylor's office."

"Are you going to talk about Colt?" Saul's head tilted back, and his eyes narrowed in what she could define as suspicion.

"What we talk about is none of your business, young man. But so you don't get any more ridiculous notions, Dolly and Buttercup both need to have a calf. I need to talk to Marshal Taylor about that." And she had other more important things—things that had nothing to do with getting Dolly and Buttercup bred—to discuss with him.

Amelia strode down the boardwalk, nodding to polite greetings. Mrs. Hamilton and Mrs. Porter stood outside of Wes Carr's butcher shop with their heads close together. When Amelia approached them, they ceased their conversation and gave her cool nods. Amelia returned the greeting but continued walking.

As Amelia passed, Mrs. Porter murmured to her friend, "Reverend McCollister must be turning in his grave. Amy harboring such a dangerous man."

"Her mother would be mortified," Mrs. Hamilton said. "Why, I've heard, he sleeps in her bed."

While I sleep with Jenny! Amelia ground her teeth to keep silent. She straightened her shoulders, and marched past the two matrons. *The devil take you, Donnie Morris. The only way either of them could know that is if you told your mother, and she proceeded to tell the whole town. And while Daddy might be turning in his grave if he knew, it wouldn't be because Colt is dangerous.*

Taylor's horse, tied to the hitching rail outside of the marshal's office, dozed in the warm afternoon sunlight. Amelia pushed the door open and stormed in.

"Amy." Taylor pulled his feet from the desktop and rose. "Is everything all right?"

"No."

Taylor lifted his gun belt off the coat-tree behind him and began to buckle it around his waist.

"You don't need that, Marshal Taylor." Amelia leaned over the marshal's desk and braced her palms on the desktop. "I know Colt wasn't in town the other night, regardless of what those...those women may have said."

Taylor returned the gun belt and crossed his arms over his chest. "What makes you so certain?"

"Colt told me that every time he's forced to kill a man—"

"Forced?" The disbelief in Taylor's voice grated like sandpaper.

Undaunted, Amelia repeated, "Forced to kill a man, he gets the shakes. He said he has to drink until he passes out for several days because he can't sleep otherwise. He didn't touch a drop of whiskey last night, and when I checked on him—like I check on Saul before I go to bed in Jenny's room—he was sound asleep. He can't sleep after he's been forced to kill a man."

Taylor expelled a breath. "And you believe him?"

"He's given me no reason to doubt him." She straightened and tugged at the front of her dress. "Marshal, the only lie I know for certain he's told is to tell Saul that he isn't the famous shootist Colt Evans, that he just has the same name as that man."

Taylor's arms dropped. "I would have thought—"

"You thought wrong if you thought Colt would tell Saul he is a shootist. No more than you would tell your own daughter he's a shootist." Taylor's expression shifted from disbelief to something she could only define as uncomfortable. Amelia shook her. "How could any man want a young, impressionable boy to think that killing others is something to be emulated? Colt said being a gunfighter isn't living, it's more like just surviving."

Taylor raked his hands through his graying, sandy-brown hair. "Amy, when Jenny was born, your parents asked Rachel and me to look after all of you should anything happen to them. Your father was one of my closest friends, so I take that promise I made to him damn serious. Colt Evans is just trouble—trouble for you and Saul and Jenny."

"Have you seen him with Jenny?" Not giving him a chance to answer, she plunged on. "He is so good with her and she adores him. Marshal, I know Colt wasn't in town two nights ago. I know, deep in my heart, Colt isn't the gunfighter the whole world sees. He's just a man who had to pick up a gun when he was thirteen to survive."

The marshal's jaw clenched. "You're infatuated with him."

"Now that sounds like something my father would say to me. You aren't my father and you don't have that right to say those things to me." Amelia flung her head back. "No, Marshal, I'm not infatuated with him. Infatuation is what I felt for Donnie Morris. This is different."

Taylor walked to the windows at the front of the jail. For a long moment, he kept his back to her. When he finally turned, his face was set in harsh, uncompromising lines. "I'm going to sound like your father again. Has he done anything to you?"

Heat seared Amelia's face. "That is none of your business."

"I thought so," the marshal breathed. "Amy, I can't say this enough. That man is trouble. He's going to bring you nothing but heartache. Send him on his way and marry Donnie Morris."

"No." Amelia shook with her audacity. All her life she had done what she had been told, never questioning any authority. "I have had to be both mother and father to Saul and Jenny for the past seven months. I had to grow up overnight, become an adult, and make adult decisions. I have no desire to marry Donnie Morris, nor will I send Colt on his way. If he wants to leave, I won't try to stop him, but I will not make him leave."

"You think you're in love with him?"

"If what I'm feeling for him is love, then yes, I'm in love with him." Amelia held her hands out, palms up. "I just know that Colt Evans is a good man. He has a good heart, with a conscience that tortures him every time he is forced to kill another man. I also know Jenny adores him and Saul looks up to him."

"Saul looks up to a cold-blooded killer, a man no better than the men who killed your parents. He's lower than those men. He kills because he can. Your parents were robbed when they were killed."

"How dare you compare Colt to those animals!"

"I dare because he is lower than them. He isn't forced into killing. Finish growing up, Amy, and see him for what he is. He's a cold-blooded killer."

"So was my father, and you respected him. You called him your friend. But before your friend was Phillip McCollister, the *Reverend*

Phillip McCollister, adored and loved as a pastor to his flock, my father was known as Brimstone Phillips." Amelia marched over to him. "Unless you have a warrant for Colt's arrest with conclusive proof he shot and killed that man the other night, don't you ever come back to my home. Is that clear enough?" She punctuated her words with a finger jabbed at Taylor's chest. "Don't you ever come back."

Stunned with her own daring, Amelia backed away from Taylor, spun on a heel, and dashed across the room.

"Amy!"

Amelia flung the door open and rushed headlong into Rachel Taylor, nearly toppling the smaller woman. Blinking back angry tears, Amelia murmured, "I'm so sorry," and turned to flee across the street.

Rachel grabbed her elbow. Her brow furrowed as she scanned Amelia's face. "What's wrong, Amy?"

Amelia shook her head. She shot a glance over her shoulder at the marshal's office. "Nothing, Mrs. Taylor. Please, I have to find Saul and Jenny and get home."

Rachel released her. "Is everything all right out at your place?"

"Why does everyone in this town assume that something is wrong at my home?" Amelia waved at the buildings and the citizens going about their business. "Why does everyone in this place have to assume because I have an injured man at my home that there is something wrong? Why can't people understand that injured man is no danger to me or to Saul and Jenny?"

"Maybe because that man is a shootist, a known killer," Rachel suggested gently. "And maybe I assumed such a thing because you flew out of Harrison's office as if something had upset you terribly." A grin crossed the other woman's elfin features. "Should I go box my husband's ears for something he said to you?"

"Yes," Amelia muttered. The mischievous smile on Rachel Taylor's face and the mental image of the tiny woman boxing her tall, imposing husband's ears took the edge from her anger. She sighed. "No, you don't need to box his ears. Your husband is only doing what he thinks is best." Amelia glanced across Federal Avenue.

On the other side of the dusty street, Mrs. Porter and Mrs. Hamilton stood staring at them. Amelia's hands balled into fists. Anger and frustration boiled out in her words. "Did you ever do anything you knew was the right thing, even though everyone else around you was telling you it was the wrong thing to do?"

"Yes, actually, I have. There was a time when I was the topic of gossip in Federal. Harrison too. But I did what I knew in my heart to be the right thing, Amy, and I have never regretted it for an instant." Rachel took Amelia's clenched fist into her hand. "If your heart tells you it's the right thing to do, listen to it. Hold your head up, look everyone else in the eye, and dare them to stop you. And Federal is like any other small town. By next week, those two old hens over there will have something else to gossip about."

Tears sprang into Amelia's eyes. "Thank you for understanding."

Rachel smiled. "I think you'd be surprised just how much Harrison understands too."

DR. ARCHER'S BUGGY stood in the yard when Amelia returned home. "Stay here," she said to Saul and Jenny. She leaped from the wagon and raced to the house.

Archer met her as she rushed onto the porch.

"Colt?" she asked in a breathless rush.

"Colt's fine." He smiled and patted her arm. "I just came out to check on him. I made him lie down because changing the bandage wore him out. Pain can do that." Archer set his black bag on the low railing. "What happened to make that wound break open? He's awfully tight-lipped about it."

"Donnie Morris shoved him into the doorjamb after I slapped him."

Archer's brows shot up. "You slapped Colt and then Donnie—"

"No, I slapped Donnie. He said something inappropriate, and I lost my head and slapped him." Amelia dropped her gaze. "I shouldn't have done that."

Archer cleared his throat. "So, Donnie took his temper out on Colt. Lucky Donnie's still walking." He picked up the bag. "I'll be back in about a week and we'll see how that shoulder's healing. By the way, that was a good idea, putting his arm in a sling. It has to be a bit more comfortable for him."

"Dr. Archer." Amelia caught his arm before her resolve faded. "Saul and Jenny haven't seen Nathan and Molly in some time. Would you mind taking them home with you, and I'll come and get them later this evening?"

Archer tugged the ends of his mustache. "Folks are already talking, Amy. You sure you want to be here alone with him for a couple of hours?"

Rachel Taylor's words echoed in her head. *If your heart tells you it's the right thing to do, listen to it.*

"You don't trust him either?"

Archer shook his head. "It's not Colt I don't trust. It's the course of nature that worries me the most. Putting two attractive young people together in a situation where they can be alone is dangerous. It could have lasting implications."

Amelia's face burned. "I need to talk to him, and it is rather hard to do that with Saul and Jenny here. I'm asking you to do this favor for me as my friend, not as my doctor."

Archer was silent for a long moment. He cleared his throat again, shifted his bag from hand to hand, and tugged at the collar of his frock coat. "Amy, I—"

"Please don't lecture me. I've already been lectured by Marshal Taylor today. People in this town seem to forget that I'm nineteen, and most girls my age are already married. And Momma and Daddy aren't here anymore. Whether or not I wanted to, I had to become an adult that day."

"You remind me of Rebecca." The doctor tugged lightly on the sleeve of Amelia's blouse. "This isn't a good place to wear your heart."

Amelia drew a deep breath. "Dr. Archer, everyone is telling me to marry Donnie Morris. Are you going to tell me that too? They're all telling me to send Colt on his way. That he is nothing but trouble for me and Saul and Jenny. A few years ago, I remember folks saying you got away with murder when you were found not guilty after your first wife died, yet no one told Rebecca that you were nothing but trouble for her."

Archer's gaze moved to the distance.

Amelia knew she had scored a point. She had been old enough to hear the gossip about how troubled Dr. Archer's marriage to Rebecca was at first, and the whole town had buzzed for weeks over Dr. Archer's arrest and trial. Amelia quelled her guilt for reminding him. "Colt is not trouble for me or Saul or Jenny. And I don't want to marry someone like Donnie Morris."

At long last, Archer nodded and peered down at her. "This is against my better judgment, and will have every tongue in town wagging, but I'll take Saul and Jenny with me. Rebecca and I can keep them overnight. It'll give me an excuse not to go into the office in the morning. Mrs. Porter has an appointment, and I swear that woman has a mighty grist of imagined complaints."

"Thank you." For one moment, she hesitated, wondering if this was the best course of action. Then Rachel's words echoed in her again and she lifted her chin, squaring her shoulders. Her heart was telling her this was the right thing to do. Now, she just had to summon the courage to tell Colt what she wanted to say and find the words to say it.

AMELIA WAVED TO JENNY and Saul as they rode away in Archer's small buggy. When she walked into the cabin, Colt stood by the table, watching her intently.

For a moment, Amelia stood motionless. Then she flung herself at him and wrapped her arms around his neck.

Colt caught her with his good arm. His deep chuckle washed over her, warmer than the heat of the July sun. "What's this all about?"

Amelia shook her head, unable to voice her emotions. For just a second or two, she relished the strength of his arm around her waist, the warmth of his shoulder under her cheek, the sound of his voice and the scent of him, a blending of bay rum, talc, and soap. "You washed your hair," she murmured, refusing to lift her head from his shoulder.

"It was a little difficult one-handed, bending over a bucket at the hand pump, but I couldn't stand it another minute." Colt eased away from her. "Now, what's this all about?"

Amelia dropped her head, uncertain of where to start or even how to begin.

He caught her chin in his palm, fingers splaying over her cheek. With gentle pressure, he tilted her head up to him, and forced her to meet his cool, gray gaze. "Amy?"

"I've been thinking." She backed a step away. There was a curl to the ends of his silver-shot black hair she hadn't seen before. He was dressed in another of her father's shirts, and the white sling wasn't such a contrast to the gray material. The color deepened the gray of his eyes to a shade that made her think of the underside of a towering thunderhead, heavy with rain.

She forced her attention away from the depths of his eyes, tried to gather her scattered thoughts, and repeated, "I've been thinking."

"Obviously. Want to tell me what you've been thinking?"

She licked suddenly dry lips and wished her mouth didn't feel as parched as an arroyo in August. "I think, when you kissed me, I was wrong when I told you I didn't like being kissed like that."

"How were you wrong?"

She dropped her gaze and trailed a fingertip along the edge of the table, riding the bumps and ridges of the hand-hewn pine planks. Now that the moment had arrived, she couldn't find the words she had rehearsed in her head all the way from town. A huge lump seemed to be lodged in her throat.

"Amy?"

"Does being grown up mean really having to give up dreams and never letting those hopes be more than dreams?" She lifted her face to him.

"What are you getting at?"

He hadn't moved, yet Amelia sensed he was poised somehow. "I don't know, Colt, what I'm trying to get at. I was raised to be a good, obedient girl. I was raised not to talk back or question my elders. Yet today, I told Marshal Taylor off. I just sent Saul and Jenny home with Dr. Archer, and I don't care what anyone in town will think when they hear we've been here, all alone for a night."

He tilted his head, and one brow rose in slow degrees.

"For as long as I could remember, I was raised to marry someone like Donnie Morris. But I don't want to be married to someone like Donnie Morris. I don't know anything about the things a husband and a wife do, but I know that when Donnie Morris kissed me"— she drew a deep breath—"when he kissed me it wasn't anything like when you kissed me."

Colt dragged his hand through his hair, thoroughly disheveling it, but didn't speak.

Amelia glanced away from him for a moment. "I don't know what it is, but ever since you've been here, I can't stand to be away from you. Whenever you're near me, I have butterflies in my stomach, my heart races as if I've been running a long, long way, and I know I like the way you make me feel. I know you've only been here for a day more than a week, but I also know I could never even think of kissing someone like Donnie Morris again. I don't think anyone will ever make me feel inside the way you make me feel."

Colt's jaw dropped as if she had hit him across the back of the head with an axe handle.

"I'm not asking you to stay, Colt." She lowered her gaze to the table. "And I'm not even asking you to kiss me again, because you probably don't want to. I know I'm not pretty."

Silence reigned in the cabin for the space of a heartbeat. With one finger, Colt tilted her head. "Don't you ever say that again."

"I'm sorry, but I just wanted you to..."

He pressed a finger over her lips, stilling her words. He shook his head, amazement and awe lining his lean features. "Don't you ever again say you're not pretty. Not where I can hear it. As to wanting to kiss you...Amy, I have been wanting to do a whole hell of a lot more than just kiss you."

Colt brushed the back of his hand along her jaw and curled his fingers around her neck. Amelia stepped closer as he pulled her to him. His thumb lightly rose along her jaw, tilting up her face.

The butterflies had returned, fluttering into her breast. Her heart raced and her hands trembled. A shock of hair fell across his forehead. With trembling fingers, she pushed it back onto his head. It felt like the most natural thing she had ever done. She trailed her fingertips down the side of his face, tracing the strength of his jaw.

Sunlight slanted into the small cabin through the still-open door, bathing Colt in the long rays of the setting sun. Amelia couldn't breathe for the tenderness and awe in his expression. His eyes told her that she was something to be treasured, something beautiful, and fine. This was a totally new sensation, heady and exhilarating, and her throat tightened.

Colt shook his head. "This isn't right, Amy." His voice was rough.

Her heart felt as if it was being squeezed. He didn't want to kiss her again, despite what he'd said. Tears stung her eyes.

As if he read her thoughts, he pulled her into his embrace, and stroked her back. "It's not right. You deserve so much more than a few stolen hours. It shouldn't have to be this way for you."

Amelia slipped her arms around his waist and pressed her cheek to the width of his uninjured shoulder. "If all we have..."

"No. I want more than a few hours, Amy. I want to know that maybe those dreams I gave up aren't gone forever. I'm tired of constantly looking over my shoulder. I'm so damn tired of surviving. And you are worth so much more than that. You don't deserve that kind of life, and you don't deserve a man who can't be committed completely to you because he's always looking over his shoulder."

Colt broke away from her, his chiseled features lined and haggard. He shook his head and that shock of hair fell over his brow again. She ached to brush it away.

"I don't want a few stolen hours, lady." His voice grew rougher. "I want to be able to come to you and know it's going to be for the rest of our lives."

"Then stay. Stay here with me and Saul and Jenny. Stay and learn to dream again."

"I wish to God I could."

Frustration added an edge to her voice. "Why can't you? I'm offering you a chance to put your past behind you, to make a new li—"

"My past is the very reason I can't stay, Amy. Don't you see that? I will always have a past, and I will always be waiting for it to come riding over the horizon, waiting for the bullet that has my name on it to find me." He turned from her, his shoulders slumping. "And I don't want my past ever finding me here, because I don't want you hurt by the things I've done."

Chapter Ten

C olt sat on a granite boulder high atop a ridge, staring down at the small cabin. Smoke curled from the chimney, which meant Amelia was awake and had started breakfast. The early morning sunlight took the chill of the night from the land and beat down on his back, warming him.

He pulled his gaze from the house to settle on a hawk rising into the brilliant azure dome. The raptor screamed at regular intervals, Colt knew, to try to scare some small game into bolting from a hiding place. The bird of prey circled lazily, soaring higher and higher until it was little more than a tiny speck of black and its cries were whisper quiet.

The faint, acrid scent of burning tobacco made Colt look around but he didn't see anyone. Any man trying to get the drop on him wouldn't be smoking. Colt allowed himself to relax and remain seated on the granite boulder. He shut his eyes. Did Amelia know what she had offered him? Not just herself, not just her heart, but the chance to finally stop looking over his shoulder, to maybe make a life for himself.

What kind of a fool was he for refusing her offer? No, he wasn't a fool, but he also wasn't a blackguard or a conscienceless cad as those damn dime novels Saul read made him out to be. What kind of fool was he to even hope he could accept her offer and put his past behind him? He knew better.

He smiled at the irony of it all. All those years he'd been packing iron, dodging his past and dreaming of hanging up those guns, he never would have imagined something like this would be offered to him. And his dreams of a house in a small mountain valley, a couple of kids, a few head of cattle...he had never really thought about a wife until the other night in the barn when he talked with Jenny. He knew having kids most of the time involved a woman's contribution, but a woman like Amelia?

Ladies like her had never looked at him as a prospective husband. Oh sure, a few of those respectable ladies had shot him sidelong, encouraging glances, especially once he had finished growing and filling out. The one time he'd made the mistake of thinking those encouraging glances meant anything more, the "lady" had made it abundantly clear he had merely been a way to satisfy an itch, and that was all. He had steered clear of respectable ladies ever since.

He never would have dreamed that a woman like Amelia would look at him in any manner other than disdain or pity. That she regarded him with open, undisguised love rocked the foundations of what he thought he knew of humanity.

"Sitting out in the open without a gun is a good way to get yourself killed when you're a shootist."

Taylor's voice forced Colt's eyes open. He shook his head. "If you were trying to sneak up on me, you didn't succeed, Marshal. I could smell your cigarette from a ways off." He fixed his gaze on the small cabin on the valley floor. Taylor could so swiftly re-establish Colt's long-held beliefs of the smallness and pettiness of humankind, and this morning, he didn't want to believe that of anyone.

"If I was trying to get the drop on you, I wouldn't have been smoking," Taylor said. "If I wanted the drop on you, I've got it because you're not wearing a gun. I never thought I would see the day that the notorious Colt Evans would be caught without iron."

"I promised Amy as long as I was here, I wouldn't wear my revolver." He sent a sidelong glance in Taylor's direction, forced to squint at his silhouette in the early morning sun. "So, I have to ask,

Marshal, have you made it your personal responsibility to ride shotgun over me?"

Taylor walked closer, leading his black horse. "It is my responsibility to look out for Amy and Saul and Jenny."

"I'm not going to do anything to hurt her or those kids."

Taylor nudged his hat back and then leaned a shoulder against his massive black mount. "Did it ever occur to you, that just being here could hurt them? How long, Evans, before your past shows up and they get caught in the crossfire? Or does that even matter to you?"

"What if my past never shows up?" Colt bent over and plucked a long stalk of grass. He twirled it between his fingers, and rose to his feet, glancing around for the marmot angrily scolding the intruders on his mountaintop.

The plump rodent was perched on another boulder, chattering in a shrill voice. The animal's coat gleamed with a yellow-gold cast in the early sunlight. The moment the creature realized Colt had spied him, it dove into the safety of its burrow.

"Evans, she's an impressionable young girl. She thinks she's in love with you. Leave now, while she can still let you go. Before she gets more than she bargained for. Give her a chance to marry the right man."

"The right man..." Colt snorted. He dropped the stalk of grass and pulled his hand through his hair. "Isn't that Amy's choice, not yours?"

"You're a shootist, with a seemingly deserved reputation." Taylor straightened, dropped one of the black's reins and walked closer to Colt. "What kind of a future can you promise her? It isn't going to matter when you hang those guns up. You are always going to be a shootist."

Colt rounded on a heel, crunching granite gravel and grit under his boot. "What kind of a future can anyone promise her?" He forced away his anger. Taylor was only repeating the same conclusion he'd reached himself. "Marshal, what the hell did you say to her yesterday?"

"What I'm telling you." Taylor jerked his head in the direction of Amelia's home. "You're trouble for her and the best thing she could do is send you packing, as soon as she can."

"Well, I need to thank you." He dipped his head in the direction of the small cabin, mimicking Taylor's gesture. "It ain't often I get an offer like the one she made me yesterday afternoon. No commitments, no promises..."

"You son of a bitch." Taylor's hand dropped to his revolver, faster than Colt would have imagined the lawman could move. For one moment, he wondered just how tight Taylor walked the edge between lawman and outlaw.

"Don't slur my mother." Colt lifted his own hand from his side. "I'm unarmed. Most places, that'd be considered murder."

"Not shooting something like you it wouldn't be." Taylor's hand remained on the grip of his revolver. "It would come along the lines of doing my civic duty."

Colt refused to snap up the marshal's bait. "I also turned down her offer, tempting as it was."

Something shifted in Taylor's expression. "I find that hard to believe."

"Believe it or not, it's the truth. I didn't take her up on that offer." Colt stared down at the cabin again. The breeze switched, carrying the scent of pine smoke from the chimney of the cabin. "She does deserve more than what she offered me."

"My God, you have feelings for her." Taylor swept his hat off his head. "I'll be damned. I would have thought the only person you could ever care about was yourself."

"Why does it come as such a surprise to you that I could care for someone like Amy? Regardless of what I am, I still—" He broke off, shaking his head. "Never mind, Marshal. I don't think someone like you would understand it. Everything is black and white to you, isn't it? It's cut and dried, and there's no room for negotiation."

"What is there to negotiate? You're a shootist, a killer. She's an impressionable, vulnerable young woman who thinks she's in love with you. What kind of a future could you ever give to her? What kind of a life would she ever have with you?" Taylor tossed the lead rein over the saddle horn and mounted. "Evans, I'll say it again. Leave. Let her have a long, happy life with someone who has a future. If you care at all for her, care for her enough to walk away. She deserves better. You said it yourself."

THIS IS WHAT A MOUSE pinned down by five hawks had to feel—the panic, the fear, even the inability to move. As the members of the Federal City Ladies of the Society for the Preservation of Christian Morals encircled her, Helen Morris placed a hand on Amelia's shoulder. "We are just very worried about you, dear."

Amelia's stomach ached with twisting knots. She gestured in the direction of the stove. "Ladies, I can make a pot of coffee, and I have some chocolate cake."

Before any of the women could respond, the back door flew open.

"Amy, it looks like a damned convention out in the yard. Where did all those buggies—" Colt halted and nodded at the five women standing around the table. "Ladies."

Dressed all in black again, with the contrast of the sling against the dark fabric and a day's worth of beard stubble covering his cheeks and chin, he appeared every inch the dangerous gunfighter the whole town had decided he was—even without his revolver strapped to his thigh.

Mrs. Porter drew herself up, looked Colt up and down, and then stepped forward. "Mr. Evans, I am Mrs. Porter. This is Mrs. Hamilton."

Thin, eagle -beaked Mrs. Hamilton peered at Amelia first and then Colt over the edge of her wire-rimmed glasses.

"This is Mrs. Ames."

Portly, short and wheezing, Mrs. Ames snuffed and turned her nose up with Colt's cool smile.

"And this is Mrs. Black and Mrs. Morris."

Colt slipped his hand into the back pocket of his denims. "Donnie Morris's mother?"

"Yes, I'm Donnie's mother. I was just telling Amelia how disappointed Donnie is with her."

Amelia had never seen so much devilment fill a grown man's expression. Colt's smile wouldn't have melted butter. "I'll bet he's disappointed with her, especially after he left here wearing her handprint on his face. It did clash with that dandified striped suit of his. If I were you, I'd go home and wash his mouth out with soap for whatever he said to Amy."

"Colt!" Amelia sank into a chair at the table and wondered if she could crawl under it and squeeze through one of the razor-thin cracks of the floor.

Mrs. Morris huffed. "Well, I never—"

"That's Donnie's whole problem. You obviously never did teach him how to talk properly to a lady. Hopefully, that highfalutin school for teachers back in Indiana will. Somebody's got to do it."

"Mr. Evans!" Mrs. Porter slapped a small book onto the table. "We are very concerned for Amelia and her well-being and safety. We have come out here to warn Amy of the consequences of living in sin with a man, and especially with a man of your ill repute."

Colt lifted his brow and chuckled. "Last I heard living in sin required certain acts to be performed." He sent a sidelong glance at

Amy, dark amusement glittering in his eyes. "But then, aside from Mrs. Morris, I don't know if any of you ladies would know what those acts might be. Do I need to tell you what some of them are?"

Every member of the morality committee flushed a different shade of red. Mrs. Hamilton's mouth formed a shocked circle and her eyes widened behind her glasses. Amelia sank deeper into the chair, her face on fire. Breathing was impossible. She risked a glance at the cover of the small, paper-bound book. The title leaped up at her: *The Devil's Own Desperado: or The Life and Times of the Notorious Shootist and Killer known as Colt Evans. A True Tale of Lawlessness and Degenerate Behavior.*

Mrs. Porter pointed a finger at the dime novel on the table. "Are the allegations made in this...this...this book true?"

Colt inclined his head to the book in question. "I wouldn't know. I've never read the thing." He crossed the room to the coffee pot, lifted it, but set it down without pouring out a cup. He leaned against the counter and crossed one ankle over the other.

"This says you carry a gun with pearl grips," said Mrs. Porter, sounding more curious than outraged. "And that the barrel is notched for every man you've killed."

Colt laughed. "Pearl grips? No, ma'am, just plain old walnut. I can go get my weapon if you'd care to verify that fact. And why would I notch the barrel of a perfectly good revolver? Those notches would be a place for rust to start and I don't want to have to get a new gun. I rather like the one I have. Besides which, any shootist worth his salt knows you notch the grip, not the barrel."

"The book intimates that you have had carnal knowledge of every dance-hall girl and soiled dove from Denver to Austin." Mrs. Morris sounded as if she were choking. "And that you gamble."

"Yes, I do gamble. My game's poker. I think most of the others are stacked pretty well to the house, but I win more than I lose when I play poker. Unless someone is dealing off the bottom of the deck, but that's another story. Now as for the other"—Colt lifted his un-injured shoulder—"a man ain't got that much time to have carnal knowledge of every dance-hall girl and soiled dove from Denver to Austin. Hell, there's got to be a thousand of them." His voice grew ragged with laughter. "But there was one dance-hall girl down in Waco...when she danced..."

Amelia lifted her head as Colt trailed off, his gaze fixed on something far away. She glared at him as jealousy twisted her stomach.

"Mr. Evans, this is no laughing matter." Mrs. Black's voice grated in Amelia's ears. "This is a very serious matter. Amy is...was...a proper, well-mannered, Christian young woman. For you to be here, living under her roof, and the two of you living in a state of sin..."

Colt pushed away from the counter. "Ma'am, my mother tried to raise me to respect my elders, but if any of you say anything more about Amy's morals or virtue, I will say something that I wouldn't want my mother to hear." Colt advanced a step on the tiny woman. "Amy is not living in sin. As I said before, that would require that certain acts be performed. She still is a Christian young woman. The fact she let you old biddies in here is proof of that. She should have bolted the door and told you to go away."

All five members of the Federal City Ladies of the Society for the Preservation of Christian Morals gaped as Colt stalked to the door and opened it. "I suggest you all leave now. And try to remember that not everything in print is the gospel truth."

The ladies filed past Colt, each of them pulling their skirts to themselves, as if afraid of contamination. Mrs. Morris marched out last, and then pivoted, her mouth opening.

"Not one more word, ma'am," Colt said. "Please leave now." He closed the door before she could speak.

Amelia dropped her head into her hands again. "Oh dear," she whispered, remembering Mrs. Porter's many quivering chins, Mrs.

Hamilton's eyes widening behind her glasses, and Mrs. Morris left speechless. "Oh dear."

"I guess I didn't handle that right, did I? It's just that when I walked in here and saw all those old bats clutching their Bibles to their chests, and you looking as if you'd just been thrown to the wolves, well...hell...it's probably high time someone told them off."

Amelia slid her elbows along the table and leaned forward, her head on her hands. Her shoulders shook with silent laughter.

Colt stroked her back. "Amy, I'm sorry. Don't cry. I'll go catch them and apologize to them."

"No." She sat up and let the laughter have full voice. "Helen Morris was so angry, and she couldn't get a word in edgewise...Oh, Colt, I've never seen her at a loss for words."

A sheepish smile crossed his face. Amelia's heart twisted. How could she have grown to care for someone as much as she cared for him in so short a time? How had he managed to so fill her heart and her life in a little over a week?

"So, you're not mad at me?" He seemed for all the world like a chastised boy hoping for a reprieve.

"A little." Amelia stood, and crossed her arms over her breast. Her heart beat rapidly. "What was her name?"

He wrinkled his forehead. "Whose name?"

"The one you said you knew. The girl in Waco." Jealousy was a terrible thing, Amelia decided. It made her heart ache.

"The girl in Waco?" Devilment danced in his eyes. "Oh, *her*. Her name was Consuela. A waist so tiny a man could span it with his hands, long black hair, dark eyes, and when she danced..."

Amelia choked and turned from him. It shouldn't hurt. It had happened long before she ever met him.

Colt grabbed her arm and spun her around. The teasing expression was gone. "She took me in for a little while after my stepfather threw me out. She was a dance-hall girl, yes, but I never touched her."

Amelia studied his face, and then forced the words out. "How many women have you known?"

"As in the biblical sense, 'known'?"

She nodded.

"That's a little personal, isn't it?" He sighed and shook his head. "Not as many as those dime novels have written. I haven't been a saint, but I'm not putting notches on my gun belt either. Don't ever believe what's written about me in those things. If there is anything you want to know, ask me, Amy."

She glanced at the thin, paper-bound book Mrs. Porter had left on the table. Drawing a deep breath, Amelia asked. "How many men have you killed, Colt?"

He cupped the side of her face and tilted her head up. "Four, and I regret killing three of them."

Amelia's heart constricted with the icy fury in his eyes. "Why not the other one? Taking a life is wrong."

"Not that one." He dropped his hand. He walked across the room and knelt beside Baby. The puppy thumped her tail on the floor when Colt fondled her ears. "He deserved to die."

A shiver whispered over her at the tone of his voice. "No one deserves to die, Colt."

"That one did." He rose slowly. "My stepfather, Jackson Hayward, killed my mother. I came home one day, and my mother was dead. Maybe it was an accident, I don't know, but they argued and fought all the time. He never laid a hand on her that I know of, but the screaming and shouting was brutal enough. She had fallen from a second-floor balcony onto the flagstones outside their bedroom. It was my twelfth birthday." Colt's eyes closed and his head bent, as if he shouldered an immense weight. "He said no one would notice if one more 'whoring Mexican bitch' was dead."

"Colt." Amelia was certain her heart was shattering into a thousand small pieces. His pain sliced through her, became her own.

"I don't ever regret killing him. He figured when he threw me out, he'd never see me again, and he could lay claim to everything that was my mother's. He was more than surprised when he saw me in Waco, seven years later." Colt lifted his head, meeting her gaze, his mouth curled in a bitter parody of a smile. "He married her for the money and for a six-thousand-acre ranchero in the Rio Grande bottoms. He was the one who first taught me to fast draw and the one who started telling people how fast I was. Don't get me wrong, he never once touched me, but that was only because I was beneath his notice."

Her father once told her that anytime she meant to teach someone else a lesson in meanness, not to be surprised if the pupil learned the lesson too well. "Your mother was Mexican?"

It would explain his complexion and why he appeared to have spent a lot of time in the sun without a stitch of clothing. He wasn't tanned, it was his natural coloring.

Colt stiffened and his eyes narrowed. "Her great-grandfather was granted a large ranchero by the Mexican government for his services in the Mexican Army. When Texas declared its independence from Mexico, her grandfather sided with the Texans. She was a Texan and an American, who just happened to have Mexican blood."

"You loved her very much, didn't you?"

The tension left his shoulders and his expression softened. "Yeah, I did. And she was a lady, down to her very core."

Amelia nodded, and then picked up the small, flimsy book. Grabbing a towel, she wrapped it around the hot handle of the bottom door on the stove and opened the door.

Colt held his hand out. "Don't do that yet. Let me see that thing."

Puzzled, she closed the stove's door and handed the book to him.

He opened it and flipped through the pages. His brow rose and he snorted with laughter. "I didn't kill Lester Biggs. The damn fool got drunk and shot himself in the leg. He died a few days later of blood poisoning. Hell, I wasn't even in Cheyenne that day."

Amelia peered at the page, trying to read the print upside down. "How can you be so certain where you were that day?"

"I know. I was in Abilene. I won Angel in a poker game."

Amelia allowed herself a small smile. Colt had taken to using the name she'd given his horse. It was a small step, to be sure, and a long way to admitting that he could leave his past behind, but it was a step, just the same.

"I sure wasn't in Cheyenne, and Biggs wasn't there either when he shot himself and died. He was in Deadwood." Colt shook his head.

Amelia took the book from his hand. She skimmed the pages, and then asked, "What about Omaha? It says you killed two men in a saloon brawl there."

"Omaha? I don't think so. Never been to Omaha, I know that for certain." Colt crossed the room, kicking the latch on the bottom door of the stove. "Toss that in here, now."

"Oh my, this is interesting reading." She pointed to the book. "I didn't know that about you. I'm willing to bet you didn't know it either. According to this, your uncle taught you to be a gunfighter." Amelia giggled. "And being an outlaw runs in your family. Your uncle was a notorious Mexican *bandito*."

"Do they just make this up out of whole cloth? Please tell me there is nothing in there about my mother."

It was always better to tell the truth, or so Amelia had been told. "I saw a mention in it that she was an actress."

"My mother was a what?" Colt closed his eyes, a pained expression crossing his face. "I'm glad she's dead and can't read that about herself. She didn't think highly of anyone who took to the stage or performed in the traveling troupes. She'd have my hide if she were alive and knew that was being said about her."

"So, which notorious Mexican *bandito* was your uncle?" Amelia teased, hoping to ease the sting.

"You're really enjoying this, aren't you?" Colt leaned against the wall, a slow grin tugging the corners of his mouth. "Well, they've got that all wrong. My uncle wasn't a Mexican bandito. He was an Apache war chief."

"Oh really? Which one?" Her heart began to thunder at the new glint in Colt's eyes and a delicious heat stole through her.

"Cochise. I'm sure you've heard how much the Apaches liked to take beautiful white women as captives." His brow rose and that grin widened. "If you haven't heard, I can tell you...you would have been quite a prize for any Apache male. You would have become the favorite, and it would have taken a lot of horses to ransom you."

"How many?"

Colt's smile faded and his voice softened and deepened. "If my uncle really were an Apache, and if I were living with them and had taken you captive, I know there aren't that many horses on the face of God's green earth to convince me to give you up."

Amelia dropped her gaze to the flimsy book in her hand. She tossed it into the banked coals of the stove. "That Colt Evans never existed. The only Colt Evans I know, contrary to what that horrid little book said, is the son of a Texas patriot and pioneer."

"Did you see anything in there about Brimstone Phillips?"

For a second, Amelia's breath caught in her throat. "Who?" she finally asked, hoping that Colt hadn't noticed her hesitation.

"Oh, no one...just a shootist that I heard tell of all the way down in Texas."

SAUL AND JENNY BOTH stood, arms folded, mouths set in firm lines. Amelia glanced at Colt, hoping for some support from that quarter. Once more, he was taking the coward's way out. He lifted his brows and smiled with a boy's roguishness.

"It's already an hour past Jenny's bedtime," Amelia protested.

"Dr. Archer said it's going to be a total eclipse tonight. I want to see it." Saul nudged Jenny with an elbow. "Don't you want to see it too, Jenny?"

Jenny nodded.

"We can all go outside and sit on the glider and watch it. Please, Amy?" Saul added, "Dr. Archer is going to let Nathan and Molly stay up to see it."

Amelia scanned the room. Even Baby had sided with Saul and Jenny. She sat between them, her soulful eyes fixed on Amelia's face, tail thumping the floor. Amelia was outnumbered. Sighing in defeat, she threw her hands up. "Okay, you both can stay up to watch it, but I don't want to hear one word of grumbling tomorrow about how tired you are."

"No, ma'am, not one word," Saul promised. He grabbed Jenny's hand. "Come on, let's go out now and watch the moon rise." They raced out the door, Baby bounding behind them.

Colt's deep laughter filled the cabin. "Amy McCollister, you made that too easy for them."

"And you were no help at all." Amelia wagged her finger under his nose. "The least you could have done was point out that Dr. Archer said the eclipse won't start until ten and won't be total until almost midnight. Do you know how difficult it will be to make Saul get out of bed in the morning if he stays up that late?"

Colt caught her hand. "Let them have this little victory," he said. "They'll be sound asleep before the thing even starts. They're both dog-tired. I'll bet they stayed up most of the night, giggling and whispering with the Archer kids."

"Not Jenny," Amelia said. "I don't know what I would do to help her get past what she saw, to hear her talk again."

"Jenny makes herself understood very well. If the sawbones thinks she'll talk again, she will." He brushed his hand over Amelia's cheek, a soft smile warming his eyes. "I wish I was the cad that book said I was. I'd have no qualms on taking you up on that offer you made me yesterday."

Fire blazed in her veins with his slightest touch. "The offer still stands, Colt."

"I know," he whispered. He released her hand and took a step back. "And for the same reasons I stated the other night, I'm not taking you up on that offer. God knows, I want to. But you deserve better than what you're offering. You sell yourself way too short, lady. You deserve so much more than a few stolen hours."

JENNY WAS SNUGGLED into Amelia's side, a quilt draped over her, sound asleep. On a blanket spread out on the ground, Saul lay on his back, mouth open, arms flung out to his sides, sleeping deeply. Amelia traced out familiar constellations in the dark sky and counted several shooting stars blazing across the velvety blackness.

The rich aroma of brewed coffee announced Colt's return. He eased onto the glider. "I told you they'd be asleep before it even started."

Amelia smiled. A full moon rode in glistening glory across the inky firmament, the earth's shadow just beginning to nibble at its rounded face. The prairie was bathed in the soft silver light of the moon's glow. She tilted her head again to the night sky.

Stars glimmered and danced in the dark expanse. In the distance, a wolf howled and was answered by another. From her position safe between Amelia's feet, Baby rumbled a low growl.

Colt blew across his coffee. "Never bothered to see an eclipse until now."

"It's almost a pity Jenny and Saul fell asleep." Amelia ran a hand lightly over Jenny's head. "They're going to be disappointed in the morning when they realize they slept through it, after what they went through to talk me into letting them stay up this late."

Colt chuckled softly, his smile brilliant in the silver moonlight. "Hell, Amy, they didn't work too hard."

It should be against the law for any man to do to her senses what Colt Evans did with a simple smile. She shifted uncomfortably on the glider, a now familiar ache settling deep in her. She clasped her hands on her lap to hide their tremble.

Colt set his coffee cup down. He leaned closer and caught a tendril of her hair. Letting it slide through his fingers, he murmured, "We shouldn't be sitting out here in the moonlight on a warm summer night, Amy."

Her heart leaped. Moonlight lent a silver cast to his gray eyes and shaded the hollows of his face with midnight. The pale light glistened on the silver strands of his hair and deepened the black to pitch.

She leaned closer and traced the slant of his cheek, and then slipped her trembling fingers through his hair. His breath caught. Emboldened, she trailed her fingertips down the side of his neck and pressed her palm against his chest. She explored the planes of his shoulder, the heat of his body branding her palm through the chambray of his shirt.

He pulled her to him. His mouth slanted over hers as he wound his fingers through her loose hair, cradling her head. She parted her lips to the demanding pressure of his mouth. Amelia stiffened for a moment when his tongue plunged into her mouth, but then his heat consumed her and the ache in her became a ravenous need.

Timidly, she met the bold, possessive thrusts of his tongue with her own. Colt groaned and crushed her to his chest.

Jenny stirred in her sleep, and Amelia and Colt pulled apart. Amelia was gasping as if she had been running for miles. Colt whispered, his voice ragged, "I think we should get Jenny and Saul into the house and into bed."

Amelia nodded, unable to meet his eyes. Colt brushed the back of his hand along her cheek, setting her heart racing faster.

"Don't make the same offer you did, Amy, because I don't have the strength anymore to turn it down, and then I would have to live with that, and so would you."

Chapter Eleven

Amelia stared out into the dark night, not seeing anything. Her hands had still trembled when she pulled on her night rail. He said not to make the same offer, because he wouldn't be able to turn it down anymore. She pressed her fingertips to her lips. Did she dare go to him? Could she not dare? What if he turned her down again, despite his words earlier? She didn't know if she was interpreting this right, and what if she was? Would she truly regret spending the night with him?

If she let this opportunity pass, if he left, she would never know. The thought of spending the rest of her life married to someone like Donnie Morris, someone who didn't reach deep inside of her and stir her to life was terrifying. She knew, deep in her heart, she would wonder all her life.

And if she did go to him, would she then spend the rest of her life regretting it? Would she forever compare every other man to Colt? She retreated from the window with a sigh. She would compare every man to Colt, regardless of what happened between them. Whether or not Colt stayed, there would never be any other man for her.

He wasn't a gunfighter. He was a thief, because he had stolen her heart. She turned and walked quietly from Jenny's small room.

Her steps carried her to the closed door of his bedroom. She knocked lightly and without waiting for a response, pushed the door open.

A single lamp danced with the breeze stealing in the window, bathing Colt in the dim, flickering yellow light. He stilled, his fingers on a button of his black shirt. The shirttail had been pulled from the waist of his trousers. Amelia closed the distance between them. "I don't want anything more than right now, Colt," she said.

"Amy, don't do this to yourself. Don't do this to me. I can't turn you down because I'm not that noble or that strong." His voice sounded pained. "My God, Amy, do you know..."

She pressed her fingers over his lips. "I don't want anything more than this. I'm not asking you to stay, I'm not asking for anything from you but just this moment." She lowered her hand to his shirt and opened the front, button by button.

His quickening breathing with each parted button stoked the fire burning in her, until it blazed as an inferno. When she had opened the shirtfront, she stood on tiptoe and pressed herself to his chest and reached behind his neck to untie the sling. Colt groaned and he trembled. "Amy..."

The ragged timbre in his voice told her the effect her actions were having. It was like throwing lamp oil onto a raging forest fire. She slipped her palms under the soft-spun cotton and ran her hands over the muscled contours of his chest and up to his shoulders. She forced herself to slow when her fingers brushed the heavy bandage on his left shoulder.

The shirt slipped from his shoulders and fell to the floor with a nearly silent rustle of cotton. "Now your boots," she murmured, pushing him back to the bed.

He collapsed onto the thick feather mattress, falling onto his back. Amelia turned, and straddled one leg and then the other to pull his boots off. She dropped the last one to the floor and straightened.

Colt sat up and held his hand up to her. Amelia took it, and gasped when he pulled her onto the mattress with him. He fell back, rolling onto his uninjured shoulder, his face inches from hers. He lifted his left arm and winced.

"Colt?"

"It doesn't hurt very much anymore." He stroked her cheek, pushing the loose hair from her face. "My God, Amy, you are beautiful." He caught the ribbon lacing her night rail and pulled the bow. He slowly unlaced the garment, his eyes molten silver. He paused the ribbon only halfway pulled loose.

His gaze dipped to the partially opened neckline. Amelia's breath caught and quickened when he trailed his fingertips over the swell of her breasts. His breath escaped him on a long, slow sigh. He bent his head to her throat.

Amelia gasped. She shifted on the mattress as he trailed a burning path along her collarbone and nuzzled her nightgown off her shoulder. He pulled the ribbon loose, opening the night rail to her waist. She slid her hand across his back and muscles rippled and flowed under her palm.

Colt lifted his head and took possession of her mouth. He pushed the nightgown further off her shoulders and then dragged his palm over her until he cupped a breast in his hand. The pad of his thumb brushed over her nipple and Amelia arched her back, pushing into his palm.

She was on fire and yet everywhere he touched her, he branded her.

He ceased his tender torment of her breast and slipped his arm around her back. The feel of his hard chest crushed against her breasts sent another jolt through her. The tight curls on his chest grated deliciously against her skin. She pushed her hand through his hair, and clutched a fistful of that thick, silver-shot black.

Colt rolled onto his back, never breaking the contact of his mouth on hers, his arm holding her to his chest. Amelia shivered with the cool breeze through the window when he dragged her night rail down her back, and she slipped her arms from the sleeves.

His hand roved down her back, cupping her bottom and pressing her to him. Amelia whimpered, the ache in her core growing. She dragged her palms up his sides. He was all hard muscle and sinew.

Colt tugged and pulled her night rail down further, moving only slightly away to tug the material past her hips. He pulled his head back, breathing heavily. His gaze slowly slid down her.

His expression blanketed Amelia in warmth. Awed reverence. They were the only words she could find to describe the way he looked at her.

He slipped her night rail the rest of the way from her. "My God," he breathed. "Tell me this isn't a dream."

"It's not."

Colt slid his palm along her arm, rounded her shoulder and cupped her chin. He brushed the pad of his thumb over her lower lip. "Oh, God, Amy..."

Further emboldened, Amelia ducked her head, pressing her mouth to the base of his throat, and trailed her fingertips down his chest. He flinched when her light, roving touch crept down his flat stomach and his breathing grew ragged.

Amelia pushed herself back. She tugged at the top button of his denims. Colt sucked in his breath in a hissing sound. His hands closed around her waist, and then dragged up to her breasts. He cupped her, thumbs encircling her nipples. She parted another button with trembling fingers.

He pushed her into the mattress, and his tongue flicked against her throat, his teeth grazed and nipped her collarbone. Amelia struggled to keep her mind on the simple task of opening a button.

Another button opened.

She gasped as his hot mouth slid down her breast. The jolt searing through her when his mouth fastened on her nipple made her arch up to his mouth. His tongue lashed at her, teasing until she nearly sobbed.

Another button separated. Colt caught her hand in his and guided her to the waistband of the trousers. He slid her hand under the waist and pushed the material from his hips.

His hands seemed to be everywhere, caressing her breasts, cupping her bottom, skimming over her stomach. Instinctively, she writhed and arched up to him, but his hand dipped no lower.

He returned to her mouth, his tongue again invading and retreating. His hand skimmed down her stomach, and his fingertips brushed through the thick curls hiding her womanhood. Her sobbing, wordless plea was lost under his mouth. Helpless, she arched to his hand.

His fingers slipped lower and found her opening. She pushed up into his palm, desperate to find release from the pounding ache coiling into her.

"Easy, Amy. We've got the whole night."

He parted her, stroked her, his fingertips flirting with her, tormenting. Amelia couldn't think anymore. All she could do was feel. Sensations washed over. His mouth hot against her throat, his teeth nipping her chin, his hand sliding over her breast, his fingers caressing and stroking the sensitive flesh at the entrance to her. She tossed her head from side to side, his name a litany. His thumb encircled the small nub, and his fingers stroked her, never entering her, until she was quaking and crying with need.

He shifted slightly on the mattress, pressing the length of his member against her hip. She turned, needing to touch him as he touched her. She cupped the weight of him in her hand. A part of her registered that she had found something of him not muscled.

Colt stilled when she curled her fingers around the length of him. "God, don't, Amy."

Startled, she pulled her hand back, and stared up into his face. The heat in his eyes and the raw need on his face seared her.

"Don't. If all we've got is right now, tonight, then by God, I want the whole night." His voice was ragged. "I want the whole damn night."

She trailed her fingers up his length and reveled in the full-bodied tremor that raced over him.

His fingers slipped along her slick entrance again. "I want the whole night to touch you, to make you burn. I want the whole night to feel you, and to make you wet." His tongue flicked her breast. "To hear you crying my name." His finger slid fractionally into her. "To make you feel like this."

Amelia's arms encircled him. She pressed her head back into the mattress and arched into his questing finger.

He withdrew, and then, slowly, slid his finger further into her. He retreated again, and then with the same maddening deliberation returned. Amelia clung to him, capable only of experiencing the new, overwhelming sensations.

His actions pushed her to the brink of some wide chasm and when she tumbled over the edge, she knew she had shattered into hundreds of glittering, shimmering pieces. Colt lay next to her. Slowly and with a touch no heavier than a down feather, he trailed his fingertips along her flinching stomach, and traced circles on her breasts.

She entwined her fingers with his, and ran her other hand over his broad, firm chest. She brushed her thumb over the small nipples hidden within the thick, black curls. She smiled when he responded. Would he gasp for air, as she had, if she pressed her mouth to him, and encircled that small nipple with her tongue?

Amelia pressed her mouth to him, flicking him with the tip of tongue. A hissing breath escaped him and another tremor rippled across him. She trailed her mouth to the hollow of his throat. His pulse raced frantically under her lips. She traced the curve of his ribs, marveling at the muscling of his flat stomach. The back of her hand brushed against the swollen, heated length of him. Colt caught his breath. With the same light touch, she trailed her fingers down his member. He bucked into her fingers, a choked groan breaking from him.

Another smile curved her mouth. Colt caught her in his arms and pulled her level with his face.

"Amy, look at me."

"I am," she whispered, her gaze moving down the length of his body. "You're...you're beautiful."

His eyes shut for a moment, but his face was lined with awe. His eyes snapped open, and the heat in those gray depths seared her. "Amy, we don't have to do anything but what we're doing. I won't leave you empty, but, you're..." He shook his head. "Damn it, Amy, you've never been with a man. You're still a virgin. We can do what we're doing, and when morning comes, you'll still be a virgin."

"If you want the whole night, I want more than just this."

He groaned. "Do you know what you're offering me?"

She nodded. "All of me, my heart and my soul."

He crushed her to his chest, her face pressed into his shoulder. His fingers pegged her bottom, dragging her against him. His length pressed against her stomach, hot and throbbing. He parted their bodies and returned to his exploration of her.

When Amelia was certain she was going to lose her mind with his torment, he rolled her onto her back and rose over her. The end of his manhood pressed at the opening to her innermost region. There was a bright flare of pain when her maidenhead gave way. Amelia sucked her breath in as she felt herself stretching to accommodate all of him.

Colt's expression twisted and he was perfectly still in her. "I'm sorry," he grated out. "I didn't want to hurt you."

The pain had already receded, replaced with a new aching need. Amelia lifted her hips to him. He groaned again and then began to move in her. His hands lifted her to meet him.

Amelia clung to his back, her nails digging into him. Every thrust of his body into hers stoked the need building in her. When her release came, she tightened convulsively around him and a moment later, felt Colt spilling in her.

Breathing heavily, he collapsed on her. The weight of his body was comfortable, secure. She pressed her lips to his neck, tasting him, and smoothed her hands down his sweat-slicked back.

Colt slid off her and collapsed onto his back. He gently gathered her into his arms, with her head on his chest. His heart thundered in her ear.

Feeling braver than ever in her life, Amelia slid her hand down his body, and stroked him. It was an erotic, intoxicating sensation, his velvety soft skin slick with the mingling of her moisture and his release. He began to stir under her ministrations. She murmured, "It's not morning yet."

Colt's deep laugh echoed in her. "You are a wanton, do you know that? At least let me catch my breath."

IT WASN'T QUITE DAWN when a fierce pounding on the door jolted Amelia from Colt's arms. She fumbled in the darkness for her dressing gown and dragged it on. She scooped the blanket from the bed, wrapped it around herself, and padded to the kitchen door.

She paused long enough to strike a match and light a lantern. She lifted the wooden bar from the door and opened it. Joshua Taylor, the fifteen-year-old son of Rachel and Harrison, stood on the small porch. "Miss Amy, Pa said you told him he couldn't come out here again, so he sent me. There's some kind of trouble in town."

A shiver cascaded over her. Without being told, she knew it had to involve Colt.

"What kind of trouble?" Colt asked from behind her. Amelia sank against the width of his chest, grateful for the strength in the arm he coiled around her waist. She lowered the lantern onto a hook next to the door.

"Silas Kirk sent one of his girls out to the ranch. He said to tell you there's some man in the Thirsty Dog Saloon been bragging all night about how he's going to kill you."

Amelia's hands flew to her throat. "Josh, why hasn't your father arrested him?"

"Ain't no law against bragging, Amy," Colt said. He released his light hold of Amelia's waist and stepped back. "Tell your father I'll be into town shortly."

"Yes, sir." Josh stared wide-eyed at Colt. "He figured you would, so he's waiting for you. Said he'd be at the livery, most likely."

Josh paused on the top step of the small porch. The admiration in his expression reminded Amelia of the way Saul looked when he first thought Colt was a notorious shootist. "Mr. Evans, he also said to be careful." The boy sprinted down the steps, mounted his father's large black gelding, and rode into the night.

Amelia spun on a heel to Colt. "Why are you going into town?"

Colt buttoned his shirt, wincing as he moved his shoulder. "For a couple of reasons. One, I don't want whoever it is coming out here looking for me. Two, men in saloons talk a lot, so he'll know where to look for me." He shoved the tail of the shirt into his trousers. "Three, I am not going to take a chance you and those kids get caught in the crossfire. Four, Taylor wants me in town for the reasons I just listed. You really think he sends that kid out every time some hot-headed drunk starts bragging he's going to kill someone?"

Amelia shook her head. "I doubt it."

"So do I." He stood on tiptoe and reached into the back of the cabinet and withdrew his revolver and holster.

Amelia's heart froze in her throat as he slipped the leather around his hips and buckled it. She couldn't stop the small gasp of fear for his safety when he bent and tied the bottom of the holster just above his knee. Nor could she help noticing how narrow-hipped the holster made him appear. Buckling on that contraption created a man she didn't know. His expression seemed carved of granite, tinged with a mockery that added a deadly, determined glint to his eyes.

She stopped him before he walked out the door. "Are you going to put your arm back into a sling?"

"Not for this, Amy." A thin smile, devoid of amusement, skimmed his lips. "The last thing I want to do is look like I'm at a disadvantage. Sometimes a reputation keeps the other man from drawing. If I'm wearing a sling, he's going to think he's got an advantage. I don't want to have to kill anyone."

"Be careful, please. Come back to me."

He smiled, but the warmth never reached his eyes. They were as cold as a mountain lake slumbering under a January freeze, and they reflected nothing back at her. She had seen that look when he first arrived, and it had frightened her then. Now, it terrified her.

"Be careful," she repeated.

"Yes, ma'am."

COLT REINED ANGEL IN at Morris's livery and swung off the gelding. The livery was less than a city block from the Thirsty Dog. He had to give Taylor credit. The man had given him the advantage of walking to the saloon, rather than riding up and announcing his arrival to the would-be Johnny Quick Draw. Colt wondered again just how close to the line between law and outlaw the marshal had walked.

"You constantly surprise me, Evans."

Colt dipped for his revolver but halted the motion when he realized who had spoken. "That's a good way to get yourself killed, Marshal."

"I figured you'd stay the draw, so I also figured you wouldn't kill me." Marshal Taylor materialized from the deep shadows of the livery and paused on the boardwalk. His badge caught a thin ray of light as the moon emerged from the eclipse. "You're not going to kill that braggart in Silas's saloon either. Not tonight."

"He draws on me, I sure as hell am going to try." Colt looped Angel's drop-rein over the hitching post.

"No, you're not." Taylor leaned a shoulder onto a post. The flare of a match briefly illuminated his face as he lit a cigarette. He flicked the match away and gestured to the roof of Greenburg's Feed Mill. "There's a man on the roof of that building there. His name's Ben Hauser. He's my foreman and a town deputy."

Without turning Colt inclined his head a little to the roof of the feed mill, acknowledging the deputy. "Yeah."

"Yeah. If that drunk in the saloon insists on calling you out, get him out in the street and Ben will take him down. You're not going to kill him."

"You are?" An indistinct chill whispered across the back of his neck. "Or rather, your deputy is?"

Taylor shook his head. "Nope. Just going to bring him down, wing him most likely. You just make sure Ben's got a clean shot and you won't even have to slap leather tonight."

Colt laughed. "Hell, Marshal, what's stopping your deputy from putting a bullet into my back?"

Taylor pulled a drag off the cigarette and then studied the glowing end. "Not a damn thing. The only thing keeping me from shooting you, or letting you get shot, is I'd have to face Amy and she thinks she's in love with you." He took another drag. "Against my better judgment, I'd say you've got feelings for her. I would have put even odds on you not showing up tonight."

"I wouldn't do that. I don't want them coming out to Amy's looking for me." Colt flexed his fingers. "Regardless of what you think about me, I won't do anything to put Amy or those two kids in danger."

"Then start thinking real hard about moving along, Evans. I'm good friends with Silas Kirk and Silas was another man who counted Amy's daddy as a good friend." Taylor pulled a last long drag off the cigarette before he flicked the glowing butt into the street. "Had this tomfoolery been going on at the Golden Eagle, we wouldn't have known about it until the glory hound showed up at Amy's place. Hiding at the McCollister homestead won't stop your—"

"Let's get this over." This wasn't the time or the place to debate whether or not his past would come for him. Having Taylor tell him what he already knew didn't make it any easier to hear. Colt walked down the center of the dusty avenue, mentally cataloguing the buildings, weighing each corner, nook, or alcove in the event of a gunfight in the street.

The clock on the tower of St. Mark's Episcopal Church chimed the three-quarter hour. Nearly four in the morning, but loud piano music and drunken laughter spilled onto South Street.

Taylor went into the saloon, calling out, "Going to have the church ladies here again, Silas, if they find out I got dragged into town in the middle of the night."

Silas shrugged. "They're here most of the time, protesting and complaining about my business, even though I keep it clean. Wouldn't be anything new, and I might think they've given up on leading me to salvation if they didn't show up at least twice a week."

Colt paused on the boardwalk, letting his eyes adjust to the light inside the saloon. He shoved the swinging doors open and took a second or so to note where everything and everyone was, just as he had done out on the street.

A saloon girl hung on the neck of a drunken cowboy seated at a poker table. Three other men sat with an inebriated wrangler. Another scantily dressed woman leaned over the railing of the second floor and gave Colt a quick smile and a wink. One girl slunk further into the deep shadows at the back of the room, as if not wanting to be seen. Colt looked away. Taylor was at the other end of the teakwood bar, already in a conversation with Dr. Archer and some drunk in a fancy black frock coat. Taylor must be expecting gunfire if he'd dragged the doc into town at this hour of the night.

Another group of cowboys sat around a table in the back of the room, the poker chips on the table attesting to a large haul for someone that night. The piano player was murdering some tune on an off-key upright.

A heavyset, balding man stood at the bar. He spat onto the floor and thumped his glass on the teak counter. "Gimme another one, and then I'm riding out to find him."

Colt leaned an elbow onto the bar. Silas glanced at him, but Colt shook his head, motioning him away.

Silas said, "Mister, from what I've heard about Colt Evans, he's not a man to be trifled with. I've heard tell he's killed fourteen men, and some say he's about the fastest man alive on a draw."

Colt raised his brow. The total kept going up. Did the gossips just add one for every year he'd been packing iron?

"He ain't as fast as everyone says he is," the drunk slurred. "I've seen him draw. He can be beat. And he can't be accurate every time."

"You think so?" Colt asked in a voice he kept cool.

The balding drunk wobbled around to him. "Yeah, I do. I can beat him."

Colt glanced at the man's holstered gun—a heavy, much older Navy revolver, black powder, if he knew anything about guns. He picked up a match from a shot glass on the counter and stuck it in his mouth. He chewed on the small piece of wood, and then said, "I don't think you can outdraw me, mister. Not with that antique. And, I haven't missed. Yet."

The heavyset man's jaw dropped. The color drained from his face as if someone had pulled the plug from a bathtub. "You're Colt Evans?"

At the words, conversation in the saloon died, and silence rippled out from the bar. Even the piano player's hands stilled on the keyboard.

"Yep." Colt splintered the match between his teeth, sparing a glance at Taylor. "Who are you, so the Marshal can notify your next of kin in the morning?"

"Jedadiah Fox. Look, I was just shooting off my mouth, Mr. Evans. Me and Donnie was talking today and he said you was practicing and you weren't hitting your target every time, and then a man gets too much to drink and starts thinking he's something he ain't." Sweat rolled off the man's balding head and he wiped it away. "You know what happens when a man starts to drinking."

Donnie Morris...so the little celluloid duck actually did have a bit of grit to him. Not a lot, but enough to lie to try to get his competition out of the way. "Actually, I've made it a point never to drink before I decide to call someone out to a gunfight. You might want to remember that."

"Mr. Evans, I wasn't really going to come out to that girl's place. I don't know when to stop yapping, or so my wife says."

"Then, I'll offer some advice, Mr. Fox. Listen to your wife when she tells you to stop yapping." Colt dropped the match to the floor and let his gaze sweep around the silent room, allowing his glare to linger on a few men. "You tell anyone who wants me, I'll be found in town." His gaze locked on Taylor. "You tell anyone looking for me to stay the hell away from the McCollister place, because I'll kill any man coming out there looking for me."

Taylor touched the brim of his hat, dipping his head, and resumed his conversation with the drunk and the doctor.

Colt turned on his heel and walked to the doors. A hissing intake of breath on the other side of the room alerted him. He dropped his hand to his revolver and spun into the saloon. The weapon was cleared of leather, cocked, and aimed before he had completed the turn.

Jedadiah Fox lowered his only half-drawn gun into its holster and stared down the barrel of Colt's revolver.

Colt straightened and eased the hammer home, but kept his revolver aimed at the other man's chest.

Taylor grabbed the balding man's gun and slid it down the teak counter to Silas and positioned himself between Colt and the coward in the same smooth motion. "Put it away, Evans."

Heart slamming against his breastbone, Colt eased the revolver into its holster. He sucked in a harsh breath and then offered a curt nod to Taylor. "Mister, the last man who drew on me behind my back ended up dead."

"It's your lucky night, Jed. You get to sleep this one off in my jail." Taylor guided the shaking Fox across the floor. The marshal paused at Colt's side. "You're a hell of a lot faster than even I gave you credit for. Cooler too. Most men would have fired."

"Most men don't live by a gun, Marshal."

Taylor's mouth curled up in a cold smile. "And most won't die by it either."

Chapter Twelve

Amelia couldn't sit at the table waiting another moment. If she did, she would go insane with the fear and tension pulsating through her. She had traced the red and white squares on the table cover until her fingertip numbed with the repetition.

Was this what it had been like for her mother every time that knock came in the middle of the night? Before Daddy hung up his guns, left Brimstone in the past, and became the Reverend Phillip McCollister? Was that the reason that even after Brimstone was left in the past, Daddy moved them so many times before he settled in Wyoming? Did he finally think he was far enough away that he and his family could be safe?

She bolted to her feet and paced the room, twisting her robe in her hands. At the window, she peered into the gray-shrouded dawn. The birds were twittering sleepily to themselves as the night gave way to daylight. A light fog banded sections of the landscape, shifting and altering in the light breeze.

No one approached up the road. Hugging herself, she forced away the thought that Colt might have been hurt or even killed. If Marshal Taylor was there, surely, he would make sure there was no gunfire. Surely, he would make sure that Colt and the other man didn't get hurt.

Her heart stammered to a halt. Taylor had said he would have to decide if Colt rated a new rope to be hung with. Was this a plan to put Colt into a situation where he would be forced into shooting another man so the marshal could hang him?

No! Thinking like that was only going to increase her tension and panic.

She had known Marshal Taylor almost her whole life. He had been the marshal when Momma and Daddy moved to Federal and she knew he wasn't that kind of man. Despite his recent rush to judgment concerning Colt, she knew Marshal Taylor to be a fair and decent man. She could not envision him entrapping any man.

She had to stop pacing, had to stop the terrorized sensation crawling over her, had to find a way to stop her insides from quivering with nauseating fear.

Amelia slipped into Jenny's room and dressed in the ever-lightening gray. She let herself out of the house and made her way to the barn. With shaking hands, she lit a lantern and banished the shadows into the deeper recesses of the warm, quiet building. Angel's empty stall hit her as hard as a mule kick to her stomach. She shivered, as much with the sight of the empty stall yawning at her as from the chill of the night air.

She wasn't going to worry. He had promised he would be careful. *Just like he was careful when he was shot by someone days before he rode in here?*

Gritting her teeth, she seized the milk buckets and her stool. The dairy cows blinked at her, as much in surprise as from the light of the lantern. "I know," she crooned. "I'm early."

She settled on the stool and pressed her head into the first cow's flank. The animal shuffled a little to the side. Amelia rubbed her hands together. "Sorry, I guess my hands were colder than I thought."

The barn cats gathered around the milk bucket, Jenny's little kitten at the front of the group. Amelia aimed a stream at the kitten, hitting her in the face. The cat pawed her face and daintily licked the cream-rich milk from her paws.

The clop of a horse's hooves in the yard forced Amelia's head up. She raced to the doorway. Angel was slowly walking toward the barn. In the saddle, Colt held his arm pressed tightly to his side.

Amelia ran to him and caught Angel's reins. Wincing, Colt swung down. Sweat beaded his forehead, despite the chill of the predawn breeze.

"Are you all right?"

He nodded. "I should have taken the sling with me so I could have worn it on the way home. My shoulder is pounding all the way into my head."

He took Angel's reins and led him into the barn. Methodically, he lifted the stirrup. Amelia stepped between him and the gelding. "I can do that. Go on into the house and sit down. I'll be right in to start a pot of coffee for you."

Again, he nodded. Amelia searched his face before he turned from her. Colt walked to the doorway and paused to glance over his shoulder.

"Go on in. I'll be right there," Amelia urged, as she tugged on Angel's girth. She removed Angel's bridle, settled it over the saddle horn, and lifted the saddle. The horse let loose a long, sputtering breath. Despite herself, a smile tugged Amelia's mouth. "If that was thank you, you're welcome."

She scratched his poll and then left the barn.

Colt sat at the table, his arm held securely in the sling. His eyes were shut, his head bent to his chest.

The rich aroma of coffee permeated the cabin.

"I said I would start the coffee when I came in," Amelia said, more harshly than she had intended.

He pried one eye open. "Figured I was capable of making a pot of coffee, Amy."

"I better go wake Saul and Jenny and then start breakfast." She walked past him, halting when he caught her wrist.

"I didn't kill him, Amy. I didn't even shoot him." His eyes were dark with old memories and his face lined with a weariness she had never seen before. So much pain and loss haunted his eyes, aging him years.

"So, your reputation prevented a shooting this time."

He shook his head, letting go of her wrist. "No. Taylor intervened."

"I see," Amelia whispered, not sure she did.

"Amy, Taylor kept me from being shot in the back."

She gasped. A new fear twisted in her. Maybe he never could walk away from who and what he was. She shoved that thought away. Daddy had walked away and left his past far behind him.

Colt could hang up his gun any time he wanted. He would be safe here. The fact Marshal Taylor had prevented him from being shot in the back was proof of that. And, given enough time, the people in Federal would see that he wasn't the horrible man those dime novels proclaimed him to be.

Colt rose and crossed to the perking coffeepot. He poured a cup and blew across the rim before sipping from the steaming brew. "I'm going to go out later this morning and check the fence lines where you're pasturing those milk cows."

"That's Saul's job." Amelia set a pan on the stove and spooned in bacon grease. "Will eggs be all right for breakfast?" This near to him, her skin tingled with heightened awareness. His presence filled the kitchen until she felt as if she couldn't breathe.

"Does that mean you don't want me checking the fences?"

His tone lifted the hairs on the back of her neck. The lines of his face were set in granite, his eyes icier than any glacier clinging to the peaks of the Medicine Bow.

"I'm sure Saul will appreciate you checking the fences for him."

He set the cup on the counter and braced himself on his good arm. "You didn't answer me. Do you want me to check the fences or not?"

"Your shoulder hasn't healed yet." The aroma of horse, leather, and bay rum drifted from him, sending her senses reeling. She dropped her gaze to the hand emerging from the white sling. Memories of him plying her with those long, elegant fingers brought an uncomfortable heat to her face and made her inner core clench. She forced herself to look away from him.

The grease sizzling in the pan and the muted song of the birds in the small bush outside the window filled the silence between them.

Colt caught her chin in the palm of his hand and her breath hitched. Her skin tingled anew as he caressed her cheek.

"I want more, Amy."

She couldn't back away. The stove blocked her retreat. "Saul and Jenny will be awake any moment."

He shook his head, releasing her chin. "That's not what I mean, right now." He rubbed the back of his neck and closed his eyes for a moment. "I want to stop looking over my shoulder, and I want to stop being Colt Evans, gunfighter. I don't know if I can, though. Hell, I don't think you believe I can. When do you plan on telling Saul the truth? That I am the Colt Evans he first thought I was? I don't think either one of us have thought this through. But I want more than just one night, Amy. I want to hang up the hardware."

Amelia's heart stuttered and she chewed on her lower lip. He was right. She hadn't thought this through. "I'll figure out a way to tell Saul that we haven't been totally honest with him. But you don't have to leave, Colt. I've told you that before. I will never ask you to leave here."

"I know." He turned from her and stared out the window. Captain crowed loudly from the henhouse. "Even when everyone else in this two-horse town is telling you the best thing you could do is tell me to saddle up and ride on, even when my own better judgment says I should do that before you or the kids get hurt by my past, I know you'll never ask me or tell me to leave." He shook his head again and shot a glance at her over his shoulder. "I want to try to stop being the shootist everyone thinks I am."

Amelia caught her breath with the anguish darkening his eyes and twisting his mouth into a pained half-smile.

"What kind of a lowdown cad does that make me, Amy? What kind of man am I, that I'm willing to risk your safety and the safety of those two kids just so that I can grab at a dream? Kinda puts me onto the short side of decency, doesn't it?"

"It doesn't make you any kind of cad, Colt." She brushed her hand down his back. "Daddy came out here for a dream. He came out here to be the minister of the Methodist church, but he also came out here because he wanted a safe place to raise his children, someplace where a man's past didn't matter."

Colt turned back to her.

"I was seven, almost eight, when we came out here. Daddy's dream was to have a safer place to raise his children, have a place of his own so he could raise a few head of cattle, sit and watch the sun set. He dreamed of sending Saul to college and me and Jenny to finishing school and he dreamed of leaving his past, Brimstone Phillips, far behind him."

"Brimstone Phillips?"

Amelia nodded. "Daddy stopped being Brimstone Phillips when Saul was born. He left Brimstone in the past. Even when he and Momma were killed, no one took any credit for killing Brimstone Phillips. Instead, everyone mourned the senseless death of Reverend Phillip McCollister. And he never stopped dreaming, Colt. Never."

"His dreams never had the potential to put you in danger. Mine could."

Amelia shook her head. "Boy's gotta have a dog, girl's gotta have a kitten, and a man's gotta have a dream or two." She gestured to the window. "This place, Daddy said, the West, is a place to dream. A man can have big dreams out here, he said. And out here, no one can stop a man from making those dreams a reality because no one asks who you are or where you came from, only what you can do."

"I don't need a big dream made reality, Amy. Just this one." Colt sighed. "I'm going out and check on those fences. I need to get my head clear." Colt opened the door and his spine stiffened. "Damn early for company."

"What?" Amelia peered over his shoulder and couldn't suppress a sigh. "Donnie Morris."

Colt shook his head. "If you want to send Saul out with breakfast for the both of us, I'll be following the south line."

Before Amelia could stop him, he left the house. Colt walked to the gleaming black buggy, his gaze running over the handsome bay in the traces. The animal was a damn fine piece of horseflesh. Donnie sat in the seat, not moving as Colt approached him. Colt glanced over his shoulder at the cabin. Amelia stood in the doorway, but out of earshot.

Donnie stammered, "You're still alive?"

"You're surprised or disappointed?" Colt propped one foot on a spoke in the front wheel.

"Neither. But I was worried about Amy and the kids because I heard there was some trouble at Silas's place a few hours ago. I heard you were involved."

Anger growled deep in his chest. "Trouble you started."

Donnie gulped. "Jed and I were just talking."

"Morris, the next time you talk to some drunk who thinks he can call me out, I hope you try to talk him out of it. I almost killed that man because you lied to him."

"I thought maybe if he showed up, Amy would realize the kind of danger she's in because of you."

Defeat slammed into Colt. It was a dream. That was all it was, and he knew it. No matter how he grabbed at it, he could never catch it or ever have a hope of holding onto it. He could never stop being a shootist. Not until a bullet ended his life. And probably then, he'd spend all of eternity with a marble slab over him proclaiming to the world that he had been a shootist. He took a step back from the buggy, gesturing to Donnie. "Come down from there, Morris. I need to talk to you."

Donnie blanched whiter than milk and his Adam's apple bobbed against the tight celluloid collar circling his throat. He climbed down from the buggy and Colt grabbed the man's arm and dragged him to the barn.

Inside, Colt turned on a heel and said, "Listen to me. Neither one of us deserves that woman, but at least you don't have a past that could show up at any time. So, I'm going to tell you to do something and I hope to hell you do it. Marry her and marry her damn fast."

Donnie's jaw dropped. "Is there a reason I need to marry her fast?"

"Don't be an idiot." Colt leaned closer to Donnie. "No, there's no reason, other than if you don't, I might start to think I can. Marry her, Morris, and treat her right. Because if you marry her and don't treat her right, you'll answer to me." Colt spun Donnie to the house and gave him a slight shove. "Go ask her, and this time when you talk to her, try not to be wearing her handprint when you're done."

Colt didn't wait to see Donnie walk to the house. He couldn't bring himself to watch that, knowing when Donnie left the house, it would most likely be to start wedding plans. Colt saddled his gelding and made his way quickly away from the cabin, heading to the southern fence of the small farm.

AMELIA WAITED FOR DONNIE on the porch. He doffed his bowler. "I heard there was some trouble in town last night and I came out here to see that you and the kids are okay."

"We're fine, Donnie, thank you." She pulled the collar of her dress shut. "It is a little early to be out, though, isn't it?"

"Yes, but I was worried about you."

Amelia stared at him. She couldn't even recall what the kiss he had stolen from her a year ago had felt like. She dropped her gaze to his hands, curled around his bowler. The thought of Donnie touching her in the same manner as Colt twisted her stomach.

Donnie cleared his throat. "I came out for another reason, Amy. I've thought about it, and I was all wrong the other day. So, I came out to ask you to marry me before I have to leave for Terre Haute in a week. Will you marry me?"

Startled, Amelia shook her head. "Marry you? No, Donnie, I can't do that."

"Why not? I'm asking you to marry me, and I don't care what—if anything—you and he have done. I won't hold it against you. You're a pretty woman and I've heard some of the women in town saying that he is handsome, in an unpolished sort of manner, so I could understand if—"

"But I would hold it against you, Donnie," Amelia interrupted. She wondered which women in town were talking about Colt's looks. And what had made Donnie start telling her she was pretty? She sighed and gazed in the direction Colt had ridden. "I would hold it against you that you aren't Colt. Don't you see that?" She turned back to him. "I can't marry you. When I get married, I want to marry a man I love."

Donnie's face grew red and his voice hardened. "I suppose you think you're in love with him."

Amelia nodded. "Maybe I said the wrong thing. Donnie, you and I have been friends for a long time, but I don't love you. My parents loved each other very much. I want to be married to a man that I love."

"Even though I would never hold it against you, would never throw it in your face that you let him—"

"Yes, you would hold it against me, because you do now. But I want you to know something. I didn't let him do anything, Donnie." Amelia squared her shoulders, not in the least ashamed of what she and Colt had shared a few brief hours before. "It was more that he let me." She nodded to Donnie's horse and buggy. "Maybe it would be best if you left now."

Donnie turned on a heel, and then pivoted back. "He's a killer, Amy. He's a shootist with a past and a reputation he'll never get away from. One of these days, someone is going to be here to settle an old score with him. Then where will you be? No one in this town will have anything to do with you then, because you've chosen to bed down with a drifting, cold-blooded killer. I'm not stupid. I heard from Josh Taylor that you were parading around the house in only your nightshift with him here. It doesn't take a lot to guess what else has happened."

"And I'm sure you'll tell your mother what Joshua told you, so she can tell everyone in town." Amelia curled her hands into fists. "Please leave now, Donnie."

AMELIA SCRUTINIZED the thick, black thunderheads gathering along the spine of the Medicine Bow. Distant lightning flickered through the clouds, glaring off the sugary-white mountain crests. Faint thunder growled in a low undertone. The sound lifted the hair on her arms and a chill skipped over her skin.

"Saul!"

The boy ran from the barn.

"Saddle up and go get Colt. He was down by the arroyo, checking the fencing. It's going to be a bad one and I don't want anyone out with this rolling in." Amelia spun around, looking for Jenny. Hopefully, the young girl hadn't heard that first, faint rumble.

Amelia cast another worried look to the sky. The clouds were blacker, more towering, sweeping out in an anvil. An anvil forged of darkening clouds meant to hammer the ground. It was going to be bad. Even the meadowlarks had fallen silent in the face of the approaching storm.

She had to find Jenny.

When Colt and Saul rode in a few minutes later, the wind had risen to a mournful howl. Dust swirled in the yard, carried aloft on whirling vortices. Lightning snaked from the clouds into the mountains and the thunder's voice had grown louder. Amelia searched frantically for Jenny in the eerie, green-yellow light.

Saul led both horses into the barn, his worried gaze on the advancing black clouds. Amelia grabbed Colt's arm. "Did you see Jenny when you rode in? She was out picking blackberries."

Colt shook his head. "She'll be back. She's a smart kid, Amy." He tilted his head at the wall of clouds. "She's not going to stay out in that."

"No, she won't come back. She's terrified of thunderstorms. She clamps her hands over her ears and runs." Amelia turned to the advancing storm and sucked her breath in on a frightened gasp.

The clouds seethed in a mass of greenish-black, writhing and twisting into each other. Lightning ripped through them and forked brilliant, harsh spears into the foothills. A wall of dark rain swept out from the front edge of the anvil-shaped clouds like a black curtain. A few raindrops carried forward by the wind splattered into the dry ground, raising tiny dust puffs.

Colt twisted around to the roiling sky. "Saul, get over here." He grabbed Amelia's arm, and shoved her toward the house. "I'll go look for Jenny. Are you sure she isn't in the house?"

"I've looked twice. She's not there. I was going to check the barn again."

"Get in the root cellar, both of you." Colt caught Saul's shirt when the boy rushed by him, his voice almost a shout over the fury of the rising gale. "Don't you let your sister out of that cellar until the storm is long gone. Is that understood? Don't you let her out of there."

Saul nodded. Amelia paused in the doorway. "Please, Colt, be careful."

Colt forced himself to grin at her. "I'm always careful. That's why I'm still alive."

He waited for Amelia to usher Saul into the root cellar and pull the door shut before he returned to the barn. Colt debated saddling up Angel. A nearby lightning strike speared into the ground, causing him to jump with the instant crack of thunder. No, Angel would be terrified out in that, just as Jenny had to be.

He grabbed a slicker from a peg inside the barn door and pulled it on as best he could in the howling winds, hindered by his sling. He made his way up into the hills around the house, shouting for Jenny over the deafening thunder and roaring winds.

So far, it hadn't started to rain, but Colt knew that was a temporary reprieve. He shot another glance skyward and flinched. The black curtain of rain sweeping out from the base of the roiling thunderheads marched relentlessly nearer. Damn, he wouldn't be surprised if the storm dropped down a tornado. He'd seen skies like that too many times in Texas, and they often brought violent, whirling death with them.

The breath of icy drops touched his face a second before the heavy rain reached him. It fell in hammering sheets, pushed into horizontal waves with the ferocity of the wind.

"Jenny!"

The lightning was all around him, spearing the ground with flashes of blinding light. Thunder snarled and barked. It was as dark as the hour after sunset.

Where would Jenny run to?

He scanned the top of a large granite outcropping with the next flash of lightning and caught his breath. Jenny was crouched atop the huge monolith, under the scant protection of a gnarled ponderosa pine growing from a split in the granite. Colt shouted, "Stay there, Jenny. I'm coming up to get you."

If she heard him, Jenny didn't respond in any manner. He scrambled up the rain-slicked rock. He lost his footing and slid back, tumbling to the base. His knee felt as if it was on fire, and his injured shoulder screamed at him. Gritting his teeth, ignoring the pain, he started up again.

Jenny stared at him as he reached the summit of the tall outcropping. Her eyes were wide with terror, and she had her hands clamped over her ears. She cowered on the granite slab, rocking to and fro. Not sure if it was tears or rain streaking her slender, pale face, Colt knelt in front of her. "It's going to be okay," he shouted over the wind and the rain. "I'm going to get you off this rock and get you back to the house."

He pulled her to her feet. Her mouth opened in a silent shriek and she flung herself away from him. Her feet slipped out from under her on the treacherously slick granite and she fell heavily onto her back.

"Jenny, sweetie, it's only me. It's Colt. Sweetie, look at me." Colt grabbed her chin, forcing her to look into his face. "It's only me, Jenny. No one is going to hurt you. Jenny, it's okay."

She pressed her hands over her ears and shook her head vehemently. Colt let go of her chin.

"Jenny, we have to get home. Take my hand, Jenny. I'll take you home."

Colt glanced around in startled shock when a chunk of ice shattered on the granite. "Jenny, we don't have time to argue this. Take my hand, now."

More ice pelted the pinkish-gray granite and hammered into Colt. Jenny winced as a large hailstone hit her head. Colt grabbed Jenny by the waist and flung her over his shoulder. She kicked and flailed, struggling to get free.

The hair lifted on the back of Colt's neck as he raced to the edge of the monolith. Cradling Jenny against his chest as best he could, he flung himself down the granite.

The sky split apart and the darkness flared with white-hot light. Even as Colt shut his eyes against the brilliant flash, the old pine Jenny had cowered under burst apart. Flaming branches flew past him, extinguished just moments later by the downpour. Colt risked a glance over his shoulder as he slid down the granite on his backside. Only a splintered trunk remained of the pine. The flames sputtered in the rain and wind.

He darted under what little shelter the outcrop provided just as the skies began to dump hailstones the size of goose eggs. He set Jenny down and shoved her into the scant protection of the overhang. The icy rain and the hail hammering into his back and arms forced a gasp of pain from him. The only manner to shelter her small form was with his own body.

Every clap of thunder sent a shudder through Jenny's slight body. Her ragged breathing racked her as well. Even if he knew what to say to her to calm her fears, he wouldn't be heard over the thunder, the roar of the hail pounding into the ground, and the screeching winds. Instead, he just held her and tried to shelter her.

He dropped his gaze to the gravelly ground. Discarded cigarette butts littered the ground under the granite overhang. Colt's stomach clenched and a new chill crawled over his skin.

Someone had been on the hilltop. Had spent a lot of time there.

Colt craned his head over his shoulder but couldn't see much further than five feet through the blinding torrents of rain and hail. He didn't have to. He knew what he would see if not for the rain. This hilltop provided a clear view of the small home where Amelia and Saul were huddled in the root cellar.

Had it been Taylor? Colt discarded that notion. No, Taylor approached from the town of Federal. This was the other side of the tiny farm. This was the side of the approach he had taken, so many days before, injured, and nearly out of his head with delirium.

Colt tightened his arm around Jenny and dropped his cheek to the top of her dark head. He shut his eyes, refusing to let his sudden heartache and anguish find an outlet. Someone other than Taylor had been observing the house, and judging from the pile of butts, had spent a good amount of time doing it.

He had no idea how long he and Jenny had been crouching under the outcrop before the hail stopped and the rain lessened. In time, the lightning faded, and the thunder receded in the distance. Colt straightened and pulled Jenny out from under the granite.

She seemed totally drained. He lifted her again in his good arm. She flung her slender arms around his neck and dropped her head onto his shoulder. Colt forced a cheerful tone to his voice. "Good thing we're not too far from the house. I don't think I could carry you all the way back."

Jenny's grip around his neck loosened, her form as limp as a rag doll against him. The warm and evenly measured intervals of her breathing assured him she had fallen into an exhausted sleep.

AMELIA STOOD JUST OUTSIDE the doorway, watching for them. When she spied Colt coming to her, Jenny cradled in his good arm, she couldn't stop the tears of relief breaking from her.

She rushed to Colt across the muddy yard. Blood trickled in a wide path down the side of his face. "What happened?"

Colt handed Jenny to her and wiped the blood from his scalp. "Hail."

"Are you all right? Is Jenny okay?" Amelia demanded as she led the way to the house.

"She's fine, Amy. I got pelted pretty good with the hail, but I'll live. I made sure she was safe."

Colt followed her to the room she and Jenny shared. He hesitated in the doorway as she slipped Jenny into bed and pulled the blanket up over her.

"She's not going to catch a chill, being in those wet clothes, is she?"

"I don't want to wake her." Amelia pulled another blanket up over the child and tucked it in around her. "Come on into the kitchen and let me see how bad you got pelted."

Colt sank into a chair at the table. "I feel as if I've been run over by a freight train."

Amelia tilted his head back and wiped the rest of the blood from his face. She carefully lifted his matted hair to peer at the damage. "That is going to be a good-sized knot on your head, but I don't think it will need stitches."

"It was a hell of a big chunk of ice that hit my head...and my back...and my arm." He smiled at her. The sudden warmth pooling in the depths of his eyes matched the heat coiling through her. Her stomach knotted and her heart pounded a maddened triplet. She licked suddenly dry lips and stepped back.

"What did you say to Donnie this morning?" she asked, trying to ignore the way her body responded to his nearness.

"Had a man-to-man talk with him, something he needed pretty bad." Colt raised his hand to his head and touched the still-oozing gash. "Never knew ice could hurt so much."

"Stop trying to change the subject." Amelia wet a clean washrag under the hand pump, and then pressed it gently to Colt's head. "I don't know what you said to him, but he came in here all sweating and red-faced and asked me to marry him."

Colt turned his narrowed gaze to her. "What answer did you give him, Amy?"

Chapter Thirteen

Colt waited for her answer with his heart in his throat. Telling Morris to marry her had been the right thing. She had herself convinced that Colt's past wasn't going to matter, that it wasn't going to show up someday and put her and Saul and Jenny into harm's way. As much as he would like to hope and dream it wouldn't, he knew better. The drunk in town full of liquored-up bravado had proved that beyond any doubt. The cigarette butts he'd seen less than an hour ago on the ridge further drove that point home. They were proof that someone had been keeping close tabs on him, and he was willing to bet whoever it was had something to do with the Matthews clan.

His past was going to show up, sure as the sun would rise in the east. It was high time he stopped dreaming and well past time Amelia stopped clutching at straws.

Amelia pulled the cool rag away from his head. "I think it's stopped bleeding. At least I don't have to try to stitch it or put turpentine on it to stop the bleeding."

"Now you're trying to change the subject." Colt caught her wrist. "What did you tell him, Amy?"

She studied his face for a long moment and then smoothed his hair away from his brow. "I told him no. I told him I would not marry him because I don't love him."

Colt exploded to his feet. "Damn it, Amy, why'd you tell him that? He'd make a good husband for you and a damn sight better father than I ever could to Saul and Jenny." He leaned closer to her.

"You don't love him...what the hell does love have to do with anything?"

She paled but didn't back away from him. Her shoulders stiffened and her chin tilted up. "I told him that because he's not the man I want to spend the rest of my life with. He's not the man I want to be the father of my children. He's not the man I want to sleep next to every night of my life. And he's not the man I love. That's what love has to do with all of this."

"I'm a shootist, Amy, a gunman. Do you know what that means? It means that every man I've killed has a family wanting to avenge his death. Maybe not all of them will try, but I know of one family that will. One of them already did try." Colt leaned closer, his face inches from hers. "It means that someday, someone will show up here, looking for me with a loaded gun, hell bent on killing me."

"You can stop being a shootist any time you want." Her chin jutted stubbornly at him. "Any time you want, you can hang that gun up and never pick it up again. Others have done it. It can be done. I'll live with the chance your past will come back for you."

Colt grabbed her shoulder and shook her. "You are a fool, Amy. I can't give you what he can. I can't promise you tomorrow."

"Neither can he, and he can't give me what you can. I love you, Colt."

She could have hit him across the head with an axe handle and it would have had less effect on him. She looked up into his face, those soft, blue-bonnet eyes shimmering with an emotion he'd never expected to see from any woman.

"The thought of any other man touching me or holding me or doing any of the things we've done leaves me feeling cold and empty. I don't want to marry Donnie Morris. I don't want to marry anyone but you."

Taylor had been right, and that knowledge was worse than a red-hot poker in Colt's gut. She loved him, and unless he could make his past vanish, he wouldn't be the only one looking over his shoulder. If he stayed, Amelia would be forced to look over her shoulder too, waiting for the specter of his past to rear up.

What a choice it left him. Hurt her now, so she'd have a chance to heal and move on and learn to love someone else. Or stay around and hurt her—perhaps with a crippling hurt—later.

"I'm not the marrying kind, Amy. You don't love me. You just think you do."

She shook her head. "Then don't marry me, but don't leave either. I won't stop loving you, Colt Evans. I love you."

"No, you don't. You're infatuated with me and with the dream of being able to change who I am and what I am." He caught her chin in his hand. "You can't change those things. Yeah, I carry a Bible in my saddlebags, because it's the only thing my mother ever gave me that Jackson Hayward didn't steal from me. Just because I carry it, sure as hell doesn't mean I live by anything in there. I'm a gunman, Amy, a shootist, and nothing will ever change that fact."

"I told Amy you were just pretending not to be a shootist. You really are a gunfighter," Saul's awed voice announced from the doorway.

Amelia whirled around. For the space of a heartbeat, she kept her back to Colt. Then her shoulders rounded, and her head bowed. She turned back to him, her face pale. Her eyes had a bruised quality to them.

Colt forced himself to look at Saul. "Saul, go outside for a few minutes, please."

The admiration on Saul's face twisted like a dull, rusty blade in Colt's stomach. "Will you teach me to shoot your gun?"

"Go outside, Saul," Colt repeated through clenched teeth.

"Wait until I tell Kyla I was right. She thinks she knows everything, just because her dad's the marshal." Saul ran away from the doorway.

Amelia took a step away from Colt. "You knew he was there, didn't you? You know how infatuated he is with men like Earp and Masterson and you made sure he knew you're just like them. How am I ever going to tell him that isn't a life for him?"

"Amy, I didn't know he was there." Colt held his hand out to her, but she slapped it away. "I didn't know he was there," he repeated. "Do you really think I want any kid, especially that boy, to ever to pick up a gun?"

"I don't know what I think, right now." Welling tears thickened her voice. She pivoted from him, her back ramrod straight, her shoulders squared and unyielding.

Colt raised his hand to her stiff back, and then dropped it to his side without touching her. He clenched his fist. "Tomorrow, I'll take Saul out hunting, make sure he knows how to properly fire the rifle. Then I'll leave. Marry Donnie Morris. He's a better man to be a father to Saul than I could ever be."

She was as silent as the woods on a bitter winter's day. He paused in the doorway, trying one more time. "Amy, I didn't know he was there."

If his words had any effect, she didn't reveal it.

AMELIA JERKED A WEED from the herb bed, pulling up a mint plant along with it. Colt had to have known Saul was in the doorway. Why had he done that? Why had he deliberately played into Saul's infatuation with killers like Holliday, Earp and Masterson?

She shook her head, seizing another weed poking through the muddy yellow ground. With a hard tug, she separated weed from soil. She had said she would find a way to tell Saul the truth. Instead, Colt had deliberately let it be known. Now, Saul could hold Colt up as an example.

No matter how many times Colt told Saul that carrying a gun was no way to live, there would be no stopping the boy. He wanted to pick up a gun, and she knew why. More than once, Saul had told her he wanted to find the people responsible for killing their parents and make them pay.

From the corner of her eye, she spied Colt walking to the barn. Her heart twisted. For the past few hours, he had been as silent and resolute as the granite slopes rising around the small valley. Yet there was something in his stiff back and frozen expression that said her angry accusations had wounded him.

Maybe he hadn't known Saul was there. Maybe his only reason for telling her to marry Donnie and his refusal to admit a man could change who and what he was lay in his belief that it wasn't possible. Somehow, she just could not envision Colt encouraging Saul to pick up a gun. But how could anyone other than Colt encourage Saul not to choose that life?

Amelia rose. She tried to brush the clinging mud from her knees but surrendered to the notion the mud wasn't going to be removed until she washed the garment. More laundry. She straightened, thrusting the thought from her mind, and walked to the barn.

The wisp of a curry brush over Angel's coat filled the air. Colt's quiet murmuring to the horse snaked into Amelia's heart.

Amelia stopped a few feet from the horse's stall. "Have you seen Saul?"

Colt shook his head, keeping his back to her. "Not for about an hour. I thought he said he was going to go down to the creek to try and catch a few fish. He said the fish bite pretty well after a rainstorm. Wouldn't listen to me that they bite better before, not after."

"Have you talked to him?"

Colt set the curry on the edge of the stall door. "I tried." He shrugged. "I don't think I got through to him. Amy, I can't say this enough. I'm sorry. I didn't know he was there. The kind of life I lead isn't a life I would want for anyone, but especially not for Saul."

"I know that. I know you would never want him to pick up a gun." Amelia took a step closer.

"Amy, I have to leave. I have a past. We've both been denying that truth ever since I got here. I'm not a good example of clean living, and I'm not the marrying kind."

For a moment, Amelia chewed the inside of her lower lip and studied the floor at her feet. She forced herself to look up. "I thought...I thought maybe you found a place to make those dreams you told Jenny about reality," she finally whispered, and turned away.

The stall door banged against the wall a second later. Colt grasped her elbow and spun her around. He caught her chin in his hand and pressed his open mouth to her lips. His hand slipped around the back of her neck, his fingers cradling the base of her skull, and his tongue probed her closed lips.

Fire raced through her and a sudden sob of hurt and need caught in her throat. She wrapped her arms around his waist, clinging to him and drinking in the heady, intoxicating taste of him.

His tongue invaded her mouth, stroking hers. Amelia's womb clenched with the feel of him, the taste of him, the scent of him.

When he withdrew from her, his eyes were nearly black, and his chest heaved. "Don't you think I'd stay if I could? The thought of you in another man's arms, of any other man touching you, kissing you, and loving you is agony, Amy. But the thought of you or Saul or Jenny getting hurt when—not if—when my past shows up is tearing me apart."

She drew a steadying breath and backed away on trembling knees. "Don't I have a say in this decision?"

Colt threw his head back and stared at the ceiling for a moment. Then he dragged his hand through his hair. "Oh, God," he murmured, anguish thickening his voice. He lowered his gaze to her. His agony found an echoing emotion in her. She had never felt this kind of pain in her life, not even when she found her parents' bodies on the road to Federal.

He shook his head, while trailing the back of his fingers along her cheek. "I'm not going to take that chance with you. I can't. And if you're really honest with yourself, you'll admit you don't want to take that chance either, not with Saul and Jenny's lives at stake."

Colt lowered his hand and walked away from her. Amelia watched him leave the barn through a haze of tears. She wanted to call his name, beg him to stay, tell him it didn't matter that what was in his past could come back to haunt him. But she knew it did matter. She wasn't the only one affected by her decision. She had to think about Saul and Jenny.

Colt paused on the small porch of the cabin and leaned his head against the roof support. The pain in his soul hurt worse than the bullet hole in his shoulder ever had. Yeah, he could stay and see Amy or the kids or all of them get hurt when someone from his past came gunning for him. Or he could ride away, not look back, and be secure in the knowledge it would only take a matter of hours for the town's gossip mill to circulate the information he'd ridden off. Hell, he could make sure the town gossips knew he had ridden away from the McCollister place. That wouldn't be all that difficult to do. Riding off would assure safety for Amy, Saul, and Jenny. Ridicule and scorn for sharing a bed with a gunslinger could be survived. A bullet might not be.

Even though his head said riding away was what he needed to do, his heart argued this was where he was supposed to be. Colt ruthlessly quelled that voice and muttered, "A gunfighter with a conscience. Thought that was a commodity you couldn't afford, Evans."

He shoved the back door open, his conflicting emotions tangled and jarred.

A telltale double click made him whirl to the side and drop into a crouch. His hand instinctively went to his thigh. Only his revolver wasn't there.

It was in Saul's hand while his gun belt hung loosely around his hips. Colt stared across the kitchen floor at the boy, the distance made even more miniscule over the barrel of blued metal.

"Saul. Put the revolver down, now." Colt's heart hammered painfully against his breastbone. He never liked being on the receiving end of a revolver, especially in the hands of a novice. Knowing how smooth the trigger on his weapon was only heightened that discomfort. Colt swallowed, trying to force his heart from his throat.

Saul jerked the gun belt up as it slid down his legs. "You're going to teach me how to be a fast gun like you, right, Colt?"

Colt didn't move, but his heart sank with the boy's nearly monotone demand. "Saul, aim that gun at the floor. It's loaded."

"Not until you promise to teach me how to be a fast gun. I'm old enough to handle a gun." Saul brought his other hand up to the butt to steady the revolver. "It's a single-action Peacemaker, isn't it? Not like those double-action ones that Smith and Wesson make."

Colt straightened slowly. "Yeah, it's single-action. Now, do what I said and aim it at the floor, Saul."

Jenny walked into the kitchen and froze as still as a marble statue. Her dark-eyed gaze darted from Saul and the gun in his hand to Colt's face. Saul raised the muzzle and pointed it at Colt's chest. "Not until you promise to teach me how to be a fast gun—"

Colt stiffened when the barrel came level with his heart.

"—then, I promise, I'll put it down. I want to be a gunfighter, Colt. I want to find the people who killed Momma and Daddy and make them pay."

Colt's heart wrenched. "Saul, only Jenny knows who killed your parents and she isn't talking about it. I'm not going to teach you how to be a gunfighter. I will not let you be like me. Making other people pay isn't your job or mine. That's Marshal Taylor's job." He took a step closer to the boy. "Hand me the gun, son."

Saul shook his head. Something hardened in the depths of the boy's eyes, sending a corresponding chill through Colt. "Someone killed Momma and Daddy and they've got to pay."

"I'm not arguing that, Saul. I agree with you. Someone needs to hang for what they did to your parents." He took another step forward. "But when you start trying to mete out justice through the barrel of a gun, it isn't justice." Colt closed the distance by another step, Jenny's terrified, blanched face visible in the corner of his eye. "It's revenge and it means someone else is going to come looking for you for the same reason."

"Marshal Taylor can't find them."

"I know that." Colt froze when Saul pulled the hammer back another click. "But that also means you don't know who killed your parents. Give me the gun, Saul."

Saul shook his head, his eyes narrowing, and backed a step away. "If you won't teach me, I'll find someone who will."

Jenny shook her head, tears rolling down her slender face.

"Oh, my God," Amelia croaked from the doorway. Colt didn't risk a glance at her. He never took his gaze from Saul's pale, sweating face. Was that how he had looked, the first time he held a gun on another man? "Saul, you don't want to spend the rest of your life looking over your shoulder, wondering when the bullet with your name on it is going to find you."

"They have to pay," Saul said, but the hardness began to ebb from his expression. He dropped one hand to hitch up the sliding gun belt, and then steadied the wavering revolver with both hands.

"Yes, they do have to pay for what they did. But you can't be the one to demand that payment. That's what a judge and jury are for, when Marshal Taylor finds them." Colt held his hand out to Saul. "And killing the people who took your mother and father from you will not bring your parents back to you. If you kill the people responsible it's only going to kill something deep inside of you. Believe me on that."

Saul wavered. Colt took another step toward the trembling boy. "Saul, my mother was killed when I was twelve. When I was nineteen, I killed the man I believed murdered her. I pushed him into slapping leather so there could be no question of who drew first, but it didn't bring her back to me. Now, every time a man thinks he can make a name for himself by killing me and I'm forced to kill him, it takes something out of me. My mother didn't raise me to be this kind of a man."

Amelia's muffled sob knifed through him.

"Your mother and father didn't raise you to be a killer. Your father was a preacher-man, a man of God. Do you think he'd want you to take another man's life?"

"No." Saul's voice was a pained whisper.

Jenny shook her head vigorously.

"I know my mother wouldn't be proud of what I've become. I'm not proud of who I've become. Do you think your mother would be proud of you if you took another man's life?"

Saul shook his head. "No, she wouldn't."

In a whisper, Colt repeated, "Let me have the gun, Saul."

Saul lowered the revolver, gripped it by the cylinder, and then turned it butt end to Colt. He met Colt's gaze and extended the weapon.

Colt took the gun, thumbed and held the hammer all the way back and then squeezed the trigger to ease the hammer down. He set the gun on the floor and bent to gather the shaking boy into his arms. He ignored the flare of pain when he moved his shoulder to hold the boy to him.

Saul's arms slid up around Colt's neck and he began to sob. "I just want them to pay for what they did. I just want them to pay."

"I know you do, Saul. I know." He smoothed Saul's tousled hair. He bent his head into the curve of Saul's shaking shoulders, his eyes closing. God, what was going to happen to this boy? What kind of a man was he going to become? Could Donnie be the kind of father Saul needed?

A small hand gripped Colt's shoulder. He lifted his head. Jenny stood behind Saul, one hand on her brother's shoulder, the other on Colt's. Tears spilled from her dark eyes, slipping down her cheeks. Colt opened the circle of his arms and pulled Jenny into his embrace.

A moment later, Amelia said in a ragged voice, "Saul David Mc-Collister, how could you do that? How could you scare Colt, me, and your sister like that? You know I don't want you to pick up a gun, and yet you did. After what happened to Momma and Daddy, you can just pick up Colt's gun, point it at him, and—"

"Let it go, Amelia." Colt rose and dropped his hand onto Saul's shoulder. "Saul and I are going to go out to the woodshed and have a man-to-man talk, aren't we, son?"

Jenny tugged on Colt's sleeve. She shook her head. She glared at the revolver on the floor, shook her head again, and then studied Colt's face.

Colt smiled. "I promise I won't kill him, Miss Jenny. But Saul's got to realize there are some things you just don't do."

Jenny flung her arms around Saul's waist.

Saul extracted himself from her hold. "It's okay, Jenny. I've got it coming to me. I shouldn't have touched Colt's gun, and I was wrong to point it at anyone. I'll go get Daddy's razor strop."

Colt stopped him. "I'll get it. Go on out to the woodshed, Saul."

He waited until Saul slowly walked from the house and pulled the door shut before he went to the bedroom. The shaving equipment was set out on the old chest of drawers. He picked up the strop and pulled it through his fingers. His stomach sank as he realized what he contemplated doing.

Amelia cornered Colt in the bedroom. "Are you really going to take the strop to him?"

The razor strop dangled from his fingers. "Nope. But he can sit out there for a few minutes and sweat. That's not going to hurt him, and it will give him time to think about what he did and what he wanted me to do."

"How am I ever going to raise him by myself?" Amelia reached for his arm.

Colt turned from her, ignoring the pain in her expression. He paused in the bedroom door. "You've got a good foundation to start with, Amy. Your parents did a good job during the time they were here. And you're doing fine so far. The fact he thinks I'll teach him how to kill another man should be more than reason enough for you to tell me to leave."

Saul lifted a tear-streaked face when Colt walked into the woodshed. Silently, Colt pushed the door closed, and Saul dropped his gaze to the floor. Saul's hiccupping cries were the only sound and Colt allowed the silence to weigh on the boy, knowing from experience how painful that void could be. At long last, Saul whispered, "I'm sorry, Colt."

Colt studied the top of Saul's head, the hitch of his slender shoulders with his unsteady breathing. "Look at me, young man."

Saul tilted his head up. "I'm so sorry," he whispered, the words thickened with tears.

"So am I. Do you have the slightest idea what seeing you with that gun did to Jenny? Or to Amy?"

Saul shook his head. "I didn't think. And you and Amy kept saying you weren't that Colt Evans..."

The lie hung in the air.

Colt sighed. "That was a mistake on our part, but we did what we thought was best for you and Jenny. Saul, you're almost a man. You've got to think of the other people around you. What in the name of heaven made you think I would teach you how to be a fast gun? Or that I would even consider teaching you how to kill another man?"

Tears slid down Saul's pale face. "I just wanted—"

"I know what you want to do. But it ain't happening. I will never teach you to shoot with the sole intent to kill someone. That isn't going to bring your parents back to you. Nothing can ever do that." Colt dropped the strop and sat on a pile of cut wood. "Do you remember when I told you that most gunfighters die young? And those that don't spend the rest of their lives looking over their shoulder, waiting for the bullet to come that'll end their life? What makes you think I want that kind of a life for you?"

"But you're good and you're fast. I can get as good as you are with a gun."

"I was shot because I'm not good enough or fast enough anymore. You either get real fast and real accurate in a hurry, or you die in a hurry." Colt slammed a fist into the wood next to him. "Being a gunfighter is not living...it's merely surviving. It's not the life I want for you. I know for certain it isn't the life your sister wants for you. Do you understand what I'm saying?"

"I think I do." Saul nodded, misery evident on his face before he dropped his gaze to the floor again. "There's always going to be someone faster and better."

"Yeah." Colt caught Saul's chin, and tipped his tear-wet face up. "You're a better man than this. Your sisters deserve a better man than one who lives by the gun. I want your promise you will never pick up a gun with the sole intent to kill another man, and that as long as I'm here, you will never ask me to teach you how to shoot with that idea."

Saul nodded again. "I promise."

Chapter Fourteen

L ong before dawn, the sound of far distant thunder woke Colt from a troubled sleep. Rain tapped on the roof and pattered to the ground, splashing onto the sill of the open window. The dampness created a chill that bore the unmistakable scent of winter snow.

The relief cascading through Colt was almost crippling.

If it was raining, he couldn't teach Saul to use the rifle, and until he did that, he was staying with Amelia. He wouldn't leave until he was certain the boy knew how to properly load and fire the rifle.

At most, teaching Saul to properly fire that rifle would take a day. Saul was a smart kid, caught on fast. The toughest part would be learning when not to fire, but that could only come from experience and Colt wouldn't be there to help him with that.

Colt sighed and got out of bed. He crossed to the window and pulled the curtains back, staring out into the rainy night. Nothing moved in the damp darkness, other than the few stunted trees bending to the wind's will.

He leaned against the wall next to the open window. Far distant lightning flickered across the blackened skies, briefly illuminating the room. Huge, distorted shadows danced across the walls and splashed over the bed.

A shiver, not entirely from the damp chill, crept over his bared chest. Colt pulled the window down, shutting out the cool breeze and the damp scent of the earth. A few large raindrops pattered against the pane and slid slowly down the glass.

He returned to the bed and sat on the edge of the mattress, still shivering, and absentmindedly drew Baby's silken ears through his fingertips. The puppy snuggled closer to him, her tail thumping on the mattress. Colt lay back and Baby rested her head on his chest.

The puppy whimpered when Colt drew his hand down her back. He crawled under the blankets again and nestled her into his side. Slowly, his shivering subsided, and he began to drift off to sleep.

Let it keep raining. Let it rain for days and days. As long as it's raining, I can't take that boy out and teach him to hunt. Let it keep raining.

He fell back to sleep with that prayer echoing in his head.

"AMY, STOP SNAPPING at them." Colt rose from a chair at the table. "We've been cooped up in this house all day because of the rain, but that isn't their fault. They're normal kids and they're going to play inside if they can't be outside. It's not like they've broken anything."

Amelia turned to the stove, her shoulders sagging. "I know and I'm sorry. I'm just on edge, I guess."

Colt caught Saul's shoulder, and pointed him in the direction of the doorway. "Run out to the barn and dig around in my saddlebags. You'll find a deck of cards in there. Bring them in here. I'm going to teach all three of you a couple of card games."

Amelia glanced over her shoulder and Colt's heart stammered with the puzzled expression on her face. "What kind of card games can you teach two children?"

"Poker." Colt forced a grin to his face and damned his aching heart. "They're not going to turn into riverboat gamblers or become disreputable citizens if they know how to play poker, Amy."

"I don't know, Colt." She smoothed her hands down her dress. "It's gambling and I know Momma and Daddy wouldn't have approved."

"It's that, or else we sit in this house staring at one another until we start snapping again." Colt took the towel from her hands and dried the dishes she had just washed. He put them on the shelves over the dishpan. The routine of dishwashing had become as familiar and comfortable as if he had been doing this his whole life.

At least, until he left, he could dream this could be the rest of his life.

"What are we going to use in the place of money?" Amelia asked.

Colt dropped the dishrag, pulled open a cabinet and drew out a tin of crackers. "This. And the one with the most crackers at the end of the evening wins. It means the rest of us have to wait on that person hand and foot the next day."

She smiled. "I have the feeling, Colt Evans, that we will be waiting on you tomorrow."

Her smile tightened around his heart, but he grinned at her. "I think that was the whole plan when I suggested this."

Jenny came into the kitchen and Colt tossed the dishrag to her. "Wipe the table off, Miss Jenny, if you please. I'm going to teach you and your sister and Saul how to play poker."

Jenny's brows lowered and she shot a glance at Amelia. Amelia smiled at her and Colt laughed. "Why do I have the feeling she is going to have a heck of a run of beginner's luck?"

Jenny wiped the table off, put the towel on the hook by the sink and then returned to the table. She plunked down at a seat. Saul pulled the back door open, pausing when Colt barked, "Wipe your feet."

Saul scraped his shoes on the small rug at the door, adding, "Yes, sir," even as he complied. The boy dropped the cards onto the table. "What game are we going to learn?"

"Poker," Colt said, pulling a chair from the table and turning it around. He sank to the seat, only to rise up again. "My hat...gotta have my hat to play poker."

"Your hat?" Amelia met his gaze across the room. "You've only worn your hat once or twice since you've been here."

"I also haven't played poker since I've been here." He grabbed the hat from the peg next to the door. "And not one word about it not being polite to wear a hat indoors." He settled the hat onto his head, pushing the bill back. He resumed his seat and shuffled the cards as best he could, hampered by the sling.

"Rules are simple." Colt set the cards down. "A pair is good. Two pair is better than that. Three of kind beats two pair. A straight beats three of a kind, and a flush beats a straight. A full house—which is three of a kind plus a pair—beats a flush. Four of a kind is almost the best you can do, unless you get a straight flush."

"Colt? What did you just say?" The confusion in Amelia's voice matched the expressions on Saul and Jenny's faces.

He grinned, doling out twenty crackers to each of them. "I'll explain as we play."

Jenny picked a cracker up and nibbled it.

Colt shook his head. "Can't win that way, Miss Jenny. If you eat your crackers before we tally up the winnings at the end of the night, they don't get counted."

Jenny put the cracker atop the small pile in front of her. Her dark eyes sparkled, and her smile twisted into Colt.

"Okay," he said in a tone he forced into lightness, "first hand is going to be easy. Five-card stud, with nothing wild. I deal one card down followed by four cards face up. After each card, we place bets, and it's going to cost everyone a cracker to even get into the game. For this first hand, I'll deal them all up, so you can get an idea of how to play."

Amelia chuckled. "He didn't tell you what the stakes in this game are," she said to Saul and Jenny. "When we're all done playing, whoever has the most crackers wins, and the rest of us have to be that person's servant for the day tomorrow."

Saul's eyes grew large. "You mean, if I win, I won't have to do any chores tomorrow?"

"That's about the size of it," Colt said, sliding a cracker into the center of the table. "Everyone ante up." Three other crackers joined Colt's. He slid the cards to his right to Jenny. "Cut the deck, my dear."

Jenny wrinkled her brow. Colt lifted half the deck and set it beside the bottom half. "That's cutting the deck. Trust everyone most of the time, but don't even trust your preacher if you're playing poker with him."

He restacked the cards. "Cut the deck, Jenny."

She lifted about four cards and placed them on the table. "Who taught you to make such whorehouse cuts?" Colt asked without thinking.

"Colt!" Amelia's shocked voice echoed in the sudden silence.

Jenny's smile was huge. Colt shrugged. "Sorry, Amelia. I spoke without thinking."

He dealt four cards, one to each of them. He glanced around the table, and realized he was memorizing how they all looked. Saul studying the deuce on the table as if he could make it a higher number just by staring at it, Jenny grinning at the ace in front of her as she realized she had the high card, and Amelia tracing the contours of the heart marking a corner of her king. Colt shook his head and forced another grin. "Beginner's luck...Jenny, you've got the high card on the table. What's it going to cost all of us to stay in this game?"

She pushed a cracker into the center.

Colt pushed his hat back. "Big spender, there."

He dealt the second set of cards, and still Jenny had the high hand with a pair of aces. Colt shot a sidelong glance at her. "Sure you didn't stack the deck when you made that cut, Miss Jenny?"

Jenny shook her head, her dark curls bobbing. She pushed another cracker out to the middle of the table.

With the third card, the best hand changed to Saul. His lowly deuce had become three deuces. Without any prompting from Colt, the boy pushed two crackers into the center. Amelia laughed. "You were saying something earlier about a big spender, Colt?"

Colt flipped his cards face down onto the table.

"I'm out," he said.

Jenny, Saul, and Amelia all regarded him as if he had lost his mind.

"Hey, I'm not quitting the game, just this hand. There is no way I can beat Saul's three of a kind, because the odds aren't good enough for me to get dealt a pair that would match one of the three cards I had." He flipped another card to Jenny.

"No help," he murmured, and then tossed one across the table to Amelia. "That's no help either."

Colt flicked a card over and dropped it onto the table for Saul. "Sh—oot," he finished, biting off the curse. He had dealt Saul yet another deuce. He grinned at Jenny and Amelia. "My suggestion is to fold. He's got both of you beat with what he has showing on the table. I can't deal him another deuce, but...neither one of you can beat him."

Jenny promptly flipped her cards face down. Amelia smiled at Saul. "Looks like you've won."

"I won?" Saul came out of his chair. "I don't have to do chores tomorrow?"

"Sit down," Colt said. "You won this hand, but we ain't done playing."

Colt gathered in the cards, and then pushed the pile of crackers to Saul's place. "Let's try five-card draw and go once around the table. You can drop three on the draw."

"What?" Amelia asked. "Will you please explain that to us in English?"

He shuffled the cards without looking at them. "It means I'll deal five, face down. Pick them up, make the best hand you can and discard what you don't need. I will then deal out a second round and you can take up to three cards."

When all five cards were dealt out, Colt dropped two of his own onto the table. Jenny's brow was knit with concentration. Then she placed one card on the table. Amelia stared at her hand, frowning. Colt chuckled. He had seen that frown before from a lot of beginning poker players, players he had won a lot of money from.

"If you aren't sure, Amy, remember pairs and three of a kind. Unless you've got a straight or a flush."

"What's a flush?'

"All the cards are the same suit. A straight means they're consecutive. Best hand anyone can ever have is a royal flush. That's a straight in the same suit with the face cards and ace."

Amelia studied her cards again, and then pulled out one and set it on the table. Saul dropped two. Colt dealt the second round of cards and said, "I never can win at this one. Don't know why I picked it."

The evening flew by, with the winning hands going more often than not to Saul or Jenny. At one point, Amelia said with a laugh, "You're stacking the deck so they win, aren't you?"

Colt smiled. "Nah, it's just beginner's luck."

Shortly, Colt was down to one cracker. Saul grinned. "I'll loan you a couple of crackers, Colt."

Colt laughed. "Great. Just what I need. A loan of a few crackers. Slide 'em on over here, kid."

Amelia stood, stretched, and glanced at the mantel clock. "Oh my goodness," she said. "It's after midnight."

Jenny and Saul looked up, their expressions stricken. Amelia sat down again. "We'll finish this hand, but then you two have to go to bed."

Jenny and Saul nodded. When the last hand went to Saul, he leaped up from his chair, proclaiming, "I won! I don't have to do any chores tomorrow."

"Okay, both of you," Amelia said. "Go get into your night clothes and get to bed. Saul, you are hereby relieved of all duties and chores for tomorrow."

"Yes," Saul whispered triumphantly. "No chores."

Colt stayed at the table, never taking his gaze from Amelia as she walked Jenny and Saul to their rooms. Jenny held Amelia's hand, and Amelia had her other arm draped over Saul's narrow shoulders. Everything Colt had ever hoped for, had ever dreamed of having was here within the walls of this small home. And a pile of cigarette butts on a ridge had shattered those dreams beyond repair.

Colt stood. An ache that started in the depths of his soul seared through him. He pulled his hat off and tossed it across the room to the hat rack. He pumped water into the coffeepot and set it on the stove, and then tossed a few pieces of wood into the belly of the stove.

Jenny padded into the kitchen. Amy had twisted her hair into her nightly braids. Jenny held her arms up to him. He swept her up and hugged her tightly. Jenny wrapped her slender arms around his neck and pressed a kiss against his cheek. A lump formed in his throat. Colt set her on the floor, ruthlessly quelling the stinging in his eyes.

He turned her toward her bedroom and managed, "You'd better head on to bed now, Miss Jenny."

She started to leave, paused, and smiled at him over her shoulder. As she disappeared into her room, Saul appeared in the doorway of his own. "Good night, Colt," the boy called. "Thanks for teaching us to play poker."

Colt nodded. "I just don't want to find out you're gambling at school. Your sister will have my hide hanging out to dry if you do that. I kind of like my hide on me."

Saul giggled and darted back into his room. Colt pulled the bubbling coffeepot off the stove as the rich aroma filled the house. He walked to the door and pulled it open, gazing out in the night.

The rain had stopped, and the temperature had dropped significantly. Colt stepped out onto the porch, shivering with a cold that came from within. A brisk wind scoured the velvety blackness, leaving the stars twinkling and glittering. The barest sliver of a moon rode low in the horizon, playing hide and seek among the thin remnants of the rain clouds.

How long did he have? Whoever had been on the ridge had been watching the house, and he wasn't about to make the mistake of thinking that it had nothing to do with him. He hadn't survived as long as he had by deluding himself. He had this night, maybe the next day because of the rain. He didn't know a soul who liked to be riding out in the rain, and even a man with vengeance on his mind preferred to remain holed up in bad weather. But now that the rain had ended...how long?

He surveyed the barn, shrouded in darkness. If he was lucky, he'd have the next day to take Saul out and teach him how to use his rifle. Then he had to saddle up and put the homestead behind him. He'd stop in town, tell the marshal and anyone else he saw that he was leaving, just to be sure no one would come looking for him at Amy's. He would leave a trail so obvious and so wide even a blind man could follow it, so that whoever had been on the ridge watching the house would come after him, leaving Amelia and the kids alone.

The lump in his throat threatened to choke him. Damn it, why had he let himself care?

Colt straightened and marched to the barn. He flung the door open, walked down the short aisle, and stared out the back doors of the barn into the darkness where the ridge and its pile of butts were.

"Colt?"

He turned around. Amelia stood in the doorway, holding her hand out to him. Against his better judgment, he held out his own. She closed the distance between them, and her fingers curled around his. He pulled her to him and rested his cheek against her hair as her body melted to his. She still smelled like rainwater and vanilla. He swallowed hard.

He felt her every breath, her every heartbeat. "Amy—"

"It's all here, Colt, everything you told Jenny you wanted. It's all here, if you want it." Her fingers, intertwined with his, pressed his palms to her waist. "Make a bet with me, Colt. Play me one more hand of poker. If you win, I won't say another word to try to stop you from leaving. If I win, you stay, or we leave with you. We can go somewhere that no one knows who you are."

He could as easily stop his own breathing as he could add a solid foundation for the hope shimmering in the depths of her eyes. With a groan of anguish, Colt pulled his fingers free of hers and stepped away.

"Even if I agreed to those terms..." He trailed off, unable to voice how much he wanted to stay. He knew if he told her, she would only try that much harder to keep him there. He moved over to Angel and shoved the horse's nose away from his shoulder.

"We want you to stay, Colt, all three of us. I know if you asked Saul and Jenny, they'd tell you the same thing." She hadn't moved, either closer to him or away. "You want to stay here, without having to worry about us because of who you were. Isn't that what you told Jenny you wanted?"

"Who I am, Amy. Not who I was." Colt raked his hand through his hair. "And those kids don't understand the risks involved. I don't think you fully understand the danger I have dogging my heels. Hell, Amy, let's get serious here. Not only am I a gunman, I'm a cad. I took your virginity. Most men want a virgin for a wife, not someone else's leavings."

Amelia flinched, and bright color stained her cheeks. "If you leave—"

"When." He couldn't allow her to draw him into a debate. He was already wavering.

"If you leave, there will be no other man."

Anger with himself and with her flared brightly. "You are the most stubborn thing I have ever met, Amelia. How many times do I have to tell you that I am not staying? I'm not good for you. I can't offer you a damn thing. No tomorrows, no promises, not a single moment beyond this one."

She moved toward him. "If you can't bring yourself to promise me anything other than this moment, then I'll have this moment and I will treasure it." She pressed her palm onto his chest. The heat of her hand seared him like a brand, and Colt knew he was lost.

Her arms slid around his neck and he was straining for her mouth. His hands moved up and down her back. A tiny mewling sound broke from her throat as he ravaged her mouth. She plucked at the buttons of his shirt and then he was tugging at what seemed to be thousands of tiny buttons of her dress, all suddenly much too large for the holes.

The dress slid from her and she was standing before him, gloriously nude. Some part of his mind registered that she had taken off her undergarments before coming out to the barn to seek him. He shrugged out of the sling and shirt, ignoring the dull pain flaring in his shoulder. He spread out his shirt and lowered her into the fragrant hay.

Her hands were at his waist, tugging the buttons of his trousers. He found her breast with his mouth and sucked her into him. Her gasp quenched the last of his resolve and he shoved his trousers down. His swollen manhood brushed against her sleek stomach.

She brought a trembling hand to his cheek, and then pulled him to her lips. "Colt, I want..."

He entered her, slowly, giving her time to adjust to him. Her body trembled under his and then she lifted her hips. He lost all control with that. He thrust into her, over and over.

Amelia whispered his name and rose to meet his every advance, her nails digging into his back. She was slick around him, tight and pulling him in deeper and deeper. Her cries stoked the fire burning in him and when she tightened around him and her high, thin cry echoed through the barn, he shuddered his release into her.

Breathing heavily, Colt rolled off her, his hand entwined with hers. He gently gathered her into his arms and stroked the length of her back. She was quiet, and after a moment, he realized she was crying on his chest.

The words to halt her tears stuck in his throat, words he wouldn't say because he knew he couldn't. He wouldn't make a promise he couldn't keep.

Chapter Fifteen

Colt motioned toward the large buck partially hidden in the copse of pine trees. The animal sniffed and tested the air before lowering his head with its massive rack to the summer-burnt grasses. Silent, Saul lifted the Winchester to his shoulder and sighted along the barrel.

"If you've got a clean shot, take it. Right behind his shoulder, in the middle of his ribs," Colt whispered. "One shot and we won't be chasing him all over the mountainside to finish him off."

The buck suddenly lifted his head, snorting. His large ears swiveled back and forth, and a moment later he bounded off into the safety of the dark woods, tail flipping up with a flash of bright white. A distant baying echoed under the crashing of the buck through the rain-soaked undergrowth. Saul lowered the rifle with a deep sigh, and then handed it to Colt.

Colt said, "I thought I told you to leave Baby with Jenny."

"I did," Saul said. "I even made Jenny promise to keep her in the house."

Colt's name sounded through the cool woods.

"Did you hear that?" Saul asked. "Someone is calling you."

"Yeah, I heard it." Colt stood and peered through the pines.

"It sounds like Jenny." Saul's face was pale.

"Jenny?" Dread coursed an icy path through Colt and settled heavily in his gut.

Saul pivoted and raced down the trail, toward the sound of his sister's voice. Colt ran after him. A moment later, Jenny emerged on the trail. Tears streaked her slender, dirt-smudged cheeks and her sobs tore from her. Baby barked and raced to Saul.

The look of terror on Jenny's face knifed through Colt. Without a word, he knew Amelia was in danger.

Jenny ran to him. Her slender arms slipped around his waist as she sobbed. Colt pushed her away. As much as he wanted to hold her and console her, instinct told him every moment counted. This time, he couldn't be a second too slow.

"Jenny, what's wrong?"

She opened her mouth, struggling to form words.

"Take a breath, Jenny. Relax, and then tell me. You can do this, I know you can." He smoothed the hair from her sweaty brow, wondering when he had grown to love this little girl so much.

"Jenny, what's wrong?" Saul demanded, pushing Baby away.

Jenny knit her brow and Colt motioned to Saul. "Don't rush her." He dropped to one knee, setting the Winchester on the ground at his side, and tilted Jenny's chin. "Take your time, sweetie, and you can do it. Tell me what's wrong."

The slender girl shuddered with the effort. "He...He...Help Amy."

It was enough for Colt. He grabbed the girl's hand and raced down the trail to the horses. He lifted Jenny onto Saul's horse, and then flung Saul onto the mare behind her. Colt scooped Baby into one hand and shoved her into Jenny's arms.

"We've got to get home," Saul said, his voice breaking.

"No, you don't. I'm going there. You hang onto your sister so she doesn't fall off, and ride like hell for town and get Marshal Taylor. You hear me? You ride like hell, Saul."

"Yes, sir." Saul kicked his mare, aided by Colt's slap to the horse's rump.

Colt pulled off his sling, slid the rifle into the saddle-boot and swung up onto Angel. He pulled the gelding's head toward the house and kicked him into a gallop.

AMELIA STRUGGLED WITH the two men who had invaded her home, terror giving her a strength she didn't know she had.

The taller of the two slammed his fist into her jaw. Stars rained across her vision and she fell to her knees. Before she could rise to her feet, they'd pushed her to the ground, her face pressed painfully into the straw of Angel's stall.

A length of rope bit into her wrists and one of the men pulled her up to her knees with his fist knotted in her hair. "You're a little spitfire, ain't you?"

Amelia twisted her head and bit his arm. He bellowed in rage. For her efforts, she received a vicious kick in the ribs. She tumbled deeper into the stall. The other man approached her, his tobacco-browned teeth exposed in a wide grin. "That wasn't real nice. You drew blood on poor Johnny, there."

Amelia fought to catch her breath, but each time she drew in air, her ribs flared white-hot. He grabbed her hair and slapped her. "Biting ain't nice."

"Colt will be back shortly," Amelia said, trying to stop the lurching of her stomach and the terrified racing of her heart.

He leaned closer to her. "We know Evans and the boy went out hunting, because they left an hour or so ago. Evans took a rifle, but he weren't wearing his gun. We're going to wait here for him and while we're waiting, you're gonna be real nice to me and Johnny, ain't you?"

"Leave her alone, Billy," Johnny said. "Once we're done with Evans, you can do what you want with her, but not until then."

Billy sighed, and then leered at her. "Anticipation will make it a lot better, don't you think? Sometimes, waiting is the hardest part."

Amelia gagged with the stench of his breath and the terror that nauseated her. "Colt will be back at any minute," she forced out.

"No, he won't." Still holding her captive with a fistful of her hair, Billy unsheathed the knife on his waist. "Ain't no harm in looking, is there, Johnny?"

"Keep your mind on what we gotta do for Mitch and Frank. I'm going outside to keep a look out for Evans."

Billy's leer widened. "Let's see what's hidden under all this calico."

Sick with terror, Amelia choked when the cold steel of Billy's massive knife brushed against her skin and the bodice of her dress fell open.

The sharp click of metal on metal froze the knife blade in midair. More frigid than a glacier, Colt's deep voice said, "Drop the knife, Billy, and step away from her."

Relief made Amelia's head swim. Billy lurched upright and dragged Amelia to her feet. In a movement so fast it barely registered with her, he pulled her in front of him and pressed the Bowie knife to her throat. "Drop the rifle, Evans, and I'll let her go."

"Not a chance, Billy-boy." Colt shifted his gaze to her, and then returned to Billy. "Let her go or I'll blow your brains out where you're standing."

His expression could have shattered steel, and in that moment, Amelia knew what every man who challenged Colt had seen over the barrel of his revolver. Icy gray eyes set in a frigid, slightly mocking expression promised a swift death.

"Let her go, Billy."

"I ain't stupid." Billy's voice broke. "I know as soon as I let her go, you're going to kill me."

The ice in Colt's eyes deepened. "I'm going to kill you. That's for damn sure. You can either let her go now, or you'll let her go when I take your head off with this rifle. Let her go and do one decent thing in your life before you die."

"You could hit her, Evans."

Amelia bit back a cry when Billy's knife dug into her neck. A drop of blood rolled in a heated path down the side of her throat.

"You really want to take the chance you'll hit her, or that I'll slit her throat before you can pull that trigger? You want to take that chance?"

"I squeeze the trigger and you're a dead man, Billy. Think you can really slide that blade faster than a bullet can travel fifteen feet?" Colt's voice hardened. "Where's Johnny? You never go anywhere without him. He's half your brains. The two of you can't operate without the other."

Amelia opened her mouth to warn him, but another harsh click of metal silenced her.

"I'm right behind you, Evans," Johnny announced. "Now, you do just what Billy there said, and you drop that rifle."

Colt's eyes narrowed and a muscle ticked in the length of his clenched jaw.

"Drop it," Johnny barked.

Colt lowered the rifle from his shoulder but didn't release it.

"Drop it, Evans, and kick it away from you, or I'm going to gut-shoot you through the back and then, while you're laying there dying, you can watch us with the woman."

"That's provided I don't shoot and kill you two half-brains before I go down." Colt slid his gaze for another moment from Billy's face to Amelia. His chest rose with the deep breath he eased in.

Billy dragged the knife further along Amelia's neck, forcing a frightened yelp from her. "Put the rifle down and kick it away, or I will slit her throat."

Colt released the pent-up breath. "All right, Billy." He lowered his hand to his side, the muzzle of the rifle pointing to the ground.

"Let her go, and you and Johnny can fill me so full of holes I'll look like a sieve."

"No, Colt," Amelia said.

His gaze returned to her face and he slowly leaned to the side, lowering the rifle.

Billy shoved Amelia away and reached for his revolver in what seemed to be the same motion.

Amelia fell to her knees, screaming Colt's name. He whirled to Johnny, dropping to one knee. The rifle barked and Johnny collapsed to his knees, a bullet hole over his heart. Even as that shot echoed, Colt dropped to the floor, rolled to the side and levered the rife.

Billy was drawing his revolver when Colt's shot hit him in the shoulder. The round spun Billy around, but he clung to the revolver. Colt levered the spent bullet and chambered another one.

Billy dropped to his knees. Colt scrambled to his feet and aimed the rifle at Billy's head.

"Drop the revolver, Matthews, or I'll blow your head clean off your shoulders."

"Shoot, you bastard. I'm dead as it is."

Amelia struggled to her feet, hindered with her hands bound behind her back.

"That shot wasn't fatal." Colt's voice crackled. Amelia had never heard anything so cold. "You'll live, if you drop that damned gun now. Drop it."

Billy's fingers uncurled and the revolver dropped to the floor with a dull thud.

"Push it far away from you."

Billy shoved the revolver away. Colt crossed the barn floor and kicked the revolver into an open stall. He pressed the muzzle of the rifle into the back of Billy's head. "Now the knife. Drop that too."

Billy dropped the knife. A small puff of dust rose as it hit the dirt. Keeping the rifle in the base of Billy's skull, Colt bent and picked up the knife.

He jerked his head at Amelia. "Come here, Amy."

Lightheaded with relief, Amelia flew across the barn to him. Though it felt as if an eternity had passed from the first shot Colt fired until Billy surrendered his knife, only seconds had ticked by.

"Turn around, honey, and I'll cut you loose."

Once the ropes fell from her wrists, Amelia wanted to fling herself into his arms. But she couldn't, not so long as he held the rifle to Billy's skull. Colt smiled briefly at her. "Go get a length of rope."

A sick dread sank her stomach into her shoes. "You're not going to hang him, are you?"

Colt chuckled, and some of the chill melted from his eyes. "You hear that, Billy-boy? You abused her, threatened to kill her, tried to kill me, and she's afraid I'm going to hang you." Colt shook his head, smiling at her again. "No, Amy, we're going to tie him up and wait for Marshal Taylor. We'll let the Territory of Wyoming hang his worthless hide if they want to."

Amelia found a piece of rope and brought it to Colt.

"No, you tie him up, and tie him up tight. I'm not going to take the chance he'll try something if I pull this rifle away from his head." Colt grinned at her. "Pretend you're mad at me while you're pulling those knots. That should make sure they're good and tight."

Once Amelia had tied Billy's hands behind his back, Colt pulled the man to his feet, ignoring Billy's groan of pain. He pushed him into a stall and slammed the door, latching it. He lowered the rifle and slipped his finger away from the trigger. The shakes were starting, but not because he'd killed Johnny. This time, he knew it was because Amelia had been hurt and almost killed. Ruthlessly, he quelled his shaking hands. Not yet, he told himself. A few more minutes and then he could start shaking.

Blood had dried at the corner of Amelia's mouth and a bruise in the rough form of Billy's handprint was forming along her cheekbone. "Are you all right?"

She nodded, but he saw her iron will crumbling. He pulled her into his arms. The last of her bravery crumbled and she collapsed against him, sobbing. Colt smoothed her hair, murmuring, "It's okay. You're safe, now."

She pushed away from him and shook her head. "You were right. We're only safe until the next man comes here looking to settle an old score with you."

She spun around and raced to the house.

The fear and agony in the depths of her eyes would haunt him for the rest of his life.

Billy leaned over the stall door. He watched Amy disappear into the house and laughed from his makeshift prison. "Evans, that woman's smarter than she looks. As long as you're here, she ain't ever going to be safe. No matter where you go, someone is going to be looking for you. You're going to spend the rest of your miserable life looking over your shoulder, waiting for the next one who wants to even the score."

Colt raised the rifle. "I could get rid of one right now if you don't shut up."

Billy only laughed louder. "It ain't gonna matter how long you hang onto a plow or a rope, you are always gonna be a shootist, and there is always gonna be someone who wants to prove they're faster than you."

"Shut up."

Colt shut the barn door and sank onto a sawhorse, the rifle held across his hips. Billy asked, "You going to leave Johnny there, staring up at the sky? Least you could do is find a blanket and cover him up."

"If you and Johnny had killed me, would you have done that? Or would you have raped Amelia by my body and then killed her and left the both of us? I should haul him out for the buzzards and the coyotes." Colt spared the body a glance. "Soon as the marshal gets here, we'll get him taken care of. He isn't going anywhere, Billy."

"You're a cold bastard, Evans."

"You knew that when you came out here. You also figured with two of you, you'd get the better of me." Colt tried to ignore the way his insides were shaking like an aspen in a winter gale.

A horse thundered into the yard and Colt rose. He pulled the door open a few inches and peered out. Taylor's horse stood at the rail next to the house and Amelia was pointing to the barn.

"Marshal's here, Billy-boy." He shoved the door open as Taylor turned from the house and walked to the barn.

Colt raised a brow. Taylor was livid, if the expression on his face and his long strides were any indication.

The marshal stormed into the barn. He leveled a glare at Colt, and then shifted his gaze to Billy, leaning over the stall door. "Outside," the marshal hissed at Colt.

Colt followed the man out of the barn. Taylor grabbed him by the shirtfront and slammed him into the barn wall. "I told you if you did anything to put Amy or those kids in harm's way, you'd answer to me. You've got one hour to get saddled up and get the hell out of my county. If you don't, I'll find some excuse to arrest you and another one to keep you locked up for a long time down in Laramie."

Colt shoved the marshal back. "Why don't you just trump up a murder charge and hang me in the town square?"

"Don't try me on that, Evans." Taylor jerked his head in the direction of the house. "The only thing stopping me is Amy. I mean it, one hour."

"I told you before, the only one who can tell me to pull my freight is Amy. Not you or anyone else." Colt straightened, only to have Taylor shove him against the coarse lumber of the barn again. A dull pain flared through him when his shoulder hit the wood.

Taylor leaned closer. "What happens the next time your past comes prowling through my town looking for you? Amy was lucky...this time. You got here in enough time to stop her from getting hurt too much. As long as you're here, Amy, Saul, and Jenny are going to be in harm's way."

Resignation twisted around Colt's heart. "You think I don't know that? Marshal, you really think I would have stayed as long as I did if I thought she could get hurt?" He sagged against the wall. "You think I'd willingly put her in the line of fire?"

"No, I don't," Taylor said. "I think you're a better man than that." The marshal released Colt and stepped away from him. "I told you before that if you have any feelings at all for her, you should leave before it hurts her too much. I'm telling you again, move along, Evans. Care enough to leave her."

Colt looked past Taylor to the small cabin. The pain he felt, a pain that started deep in his soul and lanced outward with knife-edged slashes, should kill a man. "Where are Saul and Jenny?"

"I sent Saul and Jenny to the Lazy L. I had no idea what I'd find here." Taylor glowered at Colt. "Last thing either of them would need to see is their sister injured, or worse, dead."

Colt dropped his gaze to the Winchester in his hand. "That'll make it easier, then. It'll just be Amy here."

"You're leaving, then?"

Colt snapped his gaze up to Taylor's face. There was something in the man's voice that puzzled him. It almost sounded like disappointment. Colt shrugged. "What choice do I have? I don't want to take the chance she'll get hurt again, and I sure as hell don't want to spend my time in a cell in Laramie." He forced a light tone to his voice. "I like this territory of yours, Marshal, but not enough to spend a lot of time locked up in a prison."

"I'll send Bob Young out with his wagon for the dead man." Taylor stepped past Colt. "Can the other one ride?"

"Yeah. I just grazed him but he's squealing like a stuck pig. His horse is tied outside the back of the barn. I saw his horse and his brother's when I snuck in here after Jenny found me."

Colt stared at the cabin. His dreams of a small house nestled in a mountain valley, a couple of kids, a few head of cattle, and a life with Amy faded into the failing light as the sun slipped behind the sugary-white slopes of the Medicine Bow.

Taylor came out of the barn, dragging Billy. He stopped. "Either your shooting was off, Evans, or you really didn't want to kill him."

Colt shrugged again. "No need to kill both of them. Enough died today."

Taylor lifted his brow and tilted his head in a silent query, but Colt didn't explain. Instead he walked to the cabin, aching and battered to his soul.

AMELIA TRIED TO SCRUB the feel of Billy's coarse hands and his vile mouth from her. She felt filthy to her soul. A single lantern dispelled the darkness. Colt had been sitting out on the small porch, silent, looking off into the Medicine Bow since the moment Marshal Taylor had led Billy Matthews away.

"Amy."

Startled, Amelia glanced over her shoulder, instinctively crossing her arms over her breasts. Colt's expression tightened and something pained flared to life in his dark eyes.

"I'm leaving tonight, before Taylor brings Saul and Jenny back."

Her throat clenched around the sudden lump burning there. She pulled on her robe, crossed to the kitchen table, and sank into a chair.

"Everyone except for you and me is right," he continued, his voice flat. "As long as I'm here, you're not going to be safe." He pulled a hand back through his hair, disheveling it. "I kept hoping that everyone, including me, was wrong, that my past wouldn't show up.

But I made a mistake, and it's the kind of mistake that a shootist can't afford. The kind that usually ends up costing people their lives."

It was then she noticed the revolver on his thigh and that his sling was gone.

"If I saddle up and leave now, it'll be several hours before Saul and Jenny get back here, and I'll be long gone from your lives." Colt dropped a small leather pouch onto the table. Amelia cringed. "It's not much, but it should help you and the kids through the winter and repay you for what you've done for me."

"What happens if someone comes along and doesn't believe that you aren't here? What happens then?"

His eyes darkened for just a second, and then that cold mask she had learned to despise fell into place. Ice skimmed the gray of his eyes. "They'll find out in town I've left. They'll all start looking for me in Federal, and the way the gossips in town work, everyone is going to know in a day or two I've left."

He started for the door, paused, and turned to her again. "You are the only decent and good thing to have come into my life in a long time and I guess that's why I stayed as long as I did, but I never should have. I should have left two days ago. I've been accused of a lot of things in my life, most of them the truth. I guess now they can add coward to those accusations because I'm too much of a coward to stay here and risk you or those kids getting hurt because of me."

He turned toward the door again and Amelia knew she had a decision to make. Face life without him, or make peace with his past, knowing that it would forever be a specter haunting them. Her parents had confronted a similar decision, and for eleven of her nineteen years, Phillip McCollister and his wife had lived with that specter as the Reverend and Mrs. McCollister.

Amelia came to her feet. "Colt."

He stopped, shoulders slumping, but didn't turn around. His hand stayed on the latch, but he didn't open the door.

Amelia struggled to form the words her heart wanted to say, to beg him to stay, to tell him that somehow they could make things work, that if they had to they could leave, go far away where no one would know who he was. But she couldn't make any of those words move past the huge lump in her throat. She had thought she could be strong and brave if his past ever arrived to settle any scores with him. She had been so wrong. She hadn't been brave. Or strong. She had just been terrified. After a long moment, Colt opened the door.

If he walked out, Amelia knew he wouldn't be back. She quickly crossed the room, and stepped between him and the open door, struggling to find any words.

His shoulders sagged as a sigh escaped him. "You can't even say it, can you?" His smile was forced, and he caught her chin in his palm, splaying his fingers over her cheek. He traced the line of her jaw with his thumb. "I'm going to do the only truly decent and self-less thing I've ever done in this life, because as sure as Saul wasn't raised by your parents to be a shootist, you sure as hell weren't meant to be a shootist's whore. So I'm going to walk out that door and out of your life."

He lowered his hand, stepped around her and out the open door. Amelia screwed her eyes shut. The dull echo of his boot heels on the porch throbbed into her chest, constricting her heart. Moments later, she heard Angel's hooves beat out a rapid staccato that faded into the darkness. Long after those retreating beats could no longer be heard, Amelia stood with her back to the open doorway, arms wrapped tightly around her waist, hunched into herself trying to as-suage the pain.

Chapter Sixteen

The wind snarled with a bitter fury in the dark, cloud-laden skies, sending ice pellets skittering over the frozen landscape. Colt shivered deep in his coat. The lights of Rock Springs danced in the swirling snow, a welcoming beacon drawing him in from the vicious cold. He tugged Angel's head toward the small town huddled along the banks of the Green River.

Rock Springs was as good a place as any other to hole up for the winter. The mountain passes were snowed in, and he had no intention of trying to cross the Wasatch Range in January.

He left Angel in the livery and made his way down the boardwalk to one of the three hotels in town. After paying for a room, he crossed the frozen mud of the main street to the saloon.

He turned down the collar of his heavy coat and headed for a vacant table in the back corner of the room. As he walked past the bar, a huge man turned.

"Colt Evans, is that you?"

Colt spun, his hand dropping instinctively for the gun strapped to his thigh.

The other man threw his hands up. "Whoa, son. Take it easy. It's only me, Bear."

Colt straightened and grinned. "Bear. I'll be damned. What are you doing here?"

Bear grabbed Colt and hugged him so hard his spine crackled. "I could ask you the same thing, boy."

"Let me go, Bear. My ribs can't take it." Colt stepped back and studied the man's face. Bear wore a thicker beard than Colt remembered, and there was so much gray mixed into it he had a grizzled appearance. His shaggy eyebrows were nearly all steely gray. "What are you doing in Rock Springs?"

"Same as you, I'll bet, Colt. Holing up for the winter." Bear gestured to the bartender. "Gimme a bottle of whiskey and two glasses. And don't bring that trash you cut. Bring a bottle of the good stuff."

A moment later, the bartender handed Bear a bottle and two relatively clean glasses. Bear gestured to the table in the corner of the room. "Your favorite table waits, Mr. Evans. I'll even let you have the back corner seat."

Colt chuckled. "As if I could argue with you if you really wanted it."

Bear sobered, setting the whiskey bottle onto the table. "You worried me half to death when you rode out of Red Deer. Where'd you go?"

Colt eased into the chair in the corner, unbuttoning his coat. He picked up the deck of cards on the table and shuffled them. "Found myself outside of a little town called Federal, over near Cheyenne."

The whiskey gurgled as Bear poured it into the two glasses. He shoved one across the table to Colt. Colt set the cards down and picked up the glass. He swirled the amber liquid, and then set it on the table without drinking.

Bear raised a brow but didn't say anything. Instead, he picked up the cards and began dealing them face up in two separate piles. "Scared the daylights out of me when you left," he repeated, "especially when me and Hank saw the hand you'd been holding just before Mitch Matthews sat down."

Colt glanced at the cards fanning onto the table. Aces and eights...a shiver that had nothing to do with the bitter cold crept up his spine. "Any reason you've cut them out again?"

Startled, Bear looked across the table at him. "Didn't know I was doing it. Sorry, Colt. Guess I'm more superstitious than I thought. I still get a chill when I see that hand."

Colt decided to change the subject. "What have you been up to since I rode out of Red Deer?"

"Turned in my badge. Decided I didn't like being a lawman anymore. Played a few hands over in Deadwood, and then wandered down to Denver for a few weeks. Thought I'd head on out to sunny California and see if I can't finally get these old bones of mine warm." Bear collected the cards and shuffled them. "Too many squatters out on the range now. Times are a-changing, Colt. The wide, open range I grew up with is going to be a thing of the past pretty soon. Maybe I can even find some pretty blue-eyed lady to settle down with out in California."

Colt leaned back in the chair and rested his head against the wall. "Good luck, Bear." He shut his eyes and saw Amelia's face bathed in silver moonlight as she had been that night on the glider swing, heard Saul's laugh, and felt Jenny's slight weight as he carried her from the top of the granite monolith during the thunderstorm.

"Who was she, Colt?"

"What?" He sat up, opening his eyes.

"Who was she?"

"I don't know what you're—"

"Don't bother trying to sell me that snake oil, son. Not as long as I've been looking out for you. You've been dogging my heels, just like a pup, since you was tossed out by your step-daddy so I kinda figure I know you a little better than that." Bear's grin stretched his seamed, weathered face. "Who was she?"

"What makes you think I was thinking about a woman?" Colt picked up the glass of whiskey and swirled the liquid again. "Maybe I was thinking about heading back across the street and hitting the hay for the night."

"And maybe you're handing out a lot of balderdash at the moment too." Bear's grin widened. "She must have been something special if she got under your hide."

Colt lifted the glass to his mouth and swallowed the entire contents. He seized the bottle and poured himself another one. The whiskey burned all the way into his gut. He knew he would regret it, but he quickly swallowed the second glass too.

Bear leaned his elbows onto the table. "Have a couple more, boy. You always got real talkative when you'd had too much to drink."

"Go to hell," Colt said.

"Then again, maybe I'll just catch the train tomorrow and head on into Cheyenne. Can't be that many towns around Cheyenne. I think I can find one named Federal and look her up for myself."

Colt dropped his hand to the revolver on his thigh and pulled the hammer back without sliding the gun from the holster. "You stay the hell away from her, you hear me, Bear?"

Bear's eyes widened and the color leeched from his face at the double click of metal on metal. "You'd pull a gun on me? I ain't wearing a gun and don't intend to ever wear one, and you'd pull a gun on me just because I want to know a little more about the lady?"

Colt eased the hammer down. "Let it go, Bear. She's not in my life and never can be."

"Was she married?"

"I said, let it go." Colt sighed. "Damn it, Bear...I'm sorry and yeah, she's one hell of a special lady. No, she wasn't married. Probably still isn't."

Bear tossed his own drink down and poured another. "Tell me about her."

Colt shook his head. "What's the sense?" He surveyed the saloon, thinking it didn't matter the town, or the name of the establishment, they all were pretty much the same. The sense of loss knifed through him. "What good will that do?"

"Humor me. I'd like to know what kind of a lady got under your hide. I would have bet that it would never happen to you. You got really good at spending the night with a saloon whore and walking away the next morning without so much as a backward glance."

"She isn't anything like that."

"I can imagine she isn't." Bear shuffled the cards again and dropped them onto the table, flipping the queen of hearts up. "Imagine she was a real lady."

Colt stared at the severe countenance of the queen of hearts. "The queen of hearts, she's your best bet...isn't that what you used to tell me?" He shook his head, and pushed back a shock of hair that fell over his brow. "She didn't play by the rules, Bear."

"The lady or the queen of hearts?"

Colt tapped his finger on the card in the middle of the table. "The queen of hearts. The lady nursed me back to health. Every time I close my eyes, I see her face and taste her again. Every damn night, I dream she's still next to me and I can feel her under my fingertips...or at least, until I wake up."

Bear leaned back in his chair and smiled.

"I've got it bad, Bear, I know I do." Colt glared at the card. "Every time she walked into the room, I would feel as if I was something more than a jaded, too-old gunfighter. I really thought I could stay there with her. I thought I could forget who and what I am, and when she looked at me, I knew she never saw me as I am. I almost did forget for a little while what I am."

The amusement left Bear's face. "What are you, Colt?"

Colt tore his gaze from the queen of hearts. "I'm a shootist, Bear, and we both know the only way I'll ever be able to hang this damn gun up is when they plant me six feet under."

"You're sure about that?"

He nodded. "Yeah, damn sure. Two of the Matthews boys tracked me down to her place. I wasn't there at the time."

Bear caught his breath. "Shit."

"I got there before they could really hurt her, and almost got her killed in the crossfire." He poured another whiskey and downed it.

"Did she throw you out then?"

Colt refilled his empty glass. "No. I walked out before she could dredge up the words to beg me to take her and Saul and Jenny with me."

"Who are Saul and Jenny?" Bear picked up the whiskey bottle and poured himself another drink. "She a widow woman?"

"No. She's raising her brother and sister by herself." The alcohol was beginning to affect him. A lethargic numbness crept into his limbs. "Living on the run, always looking over her shoulder, that ain't no way to raise a couple of kids."

"You should know, considering that's how you finished growing up," Bear said. "You know what I think you should do? I think you should get damn good and drunk and go spend the night with one of the girls here. Get her out of your system."

Colt stiffened. To even think of comparing what he had shared with Amy to the cheap and tawdry acts he had once performed with a whore set his skin crawling.

"Maybe, then again...you shouldn't do that." Bear shrugged. "It was just a suggestion. You know, like the hair of the dog."

"Hair of the dog...yeah. I don't think so, Bear." Colt slumped in his chair, tugging his hat down lower over his eyes. "Can't even think about doing that. It's just her I want."

"You do have it bad, son. I never thought I would live long enough to see it. Colt Evans undone by a woman."

Colt could hear the grin in Bear's voice. "Go to hell," he said, no malice in his voice. "Just shut up and go to hell."

A KNOCK ON THE DOOR startled Amelia. She rushed over and flung it open. Disappointment knifed through her. Rachel Taylor stood on the small porch, a heavy cloak wrapped around her. The bitter wind howled over the house and into the doorway, driving tiny pellets of snow in front of it.

"May I come in?" Rachel asked after a long moment.

Amelia stood aside. "I'm sorry. Please, come in, Mrs. Taylor."

Rachel walked into the warm house. As Amelia shut the door, she pressed her hand into the small of her back. With the new distribution of her weight, her back ached more and more. Dr. Archer had assured her that was normal.

"I came out here to check on you and Saul and Jenny," Rachel said. "Are you all right?"

Amelia nodded. "You shouldn't have come out today. Everyone says we're supposed to have another blizzard today or tonight. It's been a winter of blizzards this year."

"I didn't come out to discuss the weather with you."

"To answer your question, we're fine. The money Colt left for us has helped."

Rachel pulled off her black woolen cloak and draped it over a chair back. "That isn't what I meant, Amy, and I think you know it."

Amelia crossed to the stove, ignoring Rachel's unspoken question. "I don't have any coffee to offer you, but I do have some tea left. Would you care for a cup of tea, Mrs. Taylor? I also baked some cookies."

No coffee? How about some whiskey, then? Amelia closed her eyes, trying to silence the whispered memories and banish the recollection of Colt's roguish grin.

"It's Rachel, and hot tea would be nice." Rachel said. "Where are Saul and Jenny?"

"They're at the Running Diamond with the Archers today. Rebecca came out here to get them this morning." Amelia broke a small portion of leaves from the tea block and placed it into a silver tea ball. She pumped water into a kettle and set it on the stove before she turned back to Rachel. "I guess if it starts to really snow, they'll be staying with the Archers for a couple of days."

Rachel nodded and sat at the table. "Amy, are you all right?"

Again that hidden question, buried in such an innocuous query. Amelia braced her arms on the counter and dropped her head. She was never going to be all right again, but she couldn't tell Rachel that. "Dr. Archer says everything is going fine."

"Amy, I could have asked him that myself. That is not what I am asking."

Amelia straightened. "What do you want me to say? Do you want me to tell you I've forgotten all about Colt? Dr. Archer says the way I feel will be healed with time. I've heard from other people in town that I have to move on, that I have to be strong for Saul and Jenny and even for this baby I'm carrying. Dr. Archer said that life goes on and that I'll get through this."

"Yes, you will."

The simple words angered Amelia. "How can I go on when I'm still waiting for him to come back?" Her voice cracked. "Do you know, a few days after he left, I gathered up everything of my father's Colt had worn. They smelled so much like him, and then the truth hit home. He is gone and he won't be back, and I couldn't even tell him one last time that I love him." Amelia dashed her hand against her eyes, wiping away tears she refused to shed and added, "I don't think I will ever stop loving him."

The kettle whistled, rapidly rising to a shriek. She poured the boiling water into a cup, and then set the tea ball in to brew. "So, tell me, Mrs. Taylor, how should I feel? How do I go on?"

"You go on because there isn't any other thing to do. If you love him, how much do you also love his child? Dr. Archer is right and so is everyone else who has said you have to go on. Time will heal this, and for Saul, Jenny, and that baby's sake, you have to be strong."

Amelia sucked her breath in. "Do you know how people look at me now? So many of those women in town actually pull away from me, as if carrying a child is contagious, or as if I'm filthy and beneath their contempt. I've heard them saying my parents would be rolling in their graves if they knew what I've done and what I've become. I'm carrying Colt Evans' child, and worse than that, the baby will be born out of wedlock."

To Amelia's surprise, Rachel grinned, and a laugh bubbled from her. "Amy, pregnancy often has nothing to do with marriage. You weren't old enough when you moved here, and I know you aren't old enough to know all of the gossip this town has ground out its grist mill, but I know exactly what you're facing."

"How could you know?"

"Because I wasn't married when I was carrying Joshua." Rachel crossed the room and took the brewing cup of tea from the counter. She spooned sugar in and stirred the steaming liquid.

"But you married his father."

Rachel smiled and shook her head. "No, I didn't. Harrison is not Joshua's father." She sipped from the cup. "So I know the whispers behind your back that you're hearing when you come into town, and I know the looks that are sent in your direction. And believe me when I tell you that you will survive this. Everyone who has said life will go on is right."

"Everyone was right about Colt too?" Amelia couldn't stop the sarcasm boiling in her voice, but if it had any effect on Rachel, it didn't show in her expression. "They all said he was trouble for me and Saul and Jenny. No matter that Jenny adored him..."

You had chocolate ice cream, didn't you, Miss Jenny?

Memory flickered, and she saw that soft, gentle smile Colt had reserved for Jenny.

You don't talk like that to any lady, but especially not to your own sister.

"...and Saul is trying to be the man he thinks Colt would have wanted him to be..."

Damn the woman. Until Rachel arrived, Amelia had been able to keep most of the memories at bay, except for late at night, when she would sob into her pillow, so that Saul and Jenny wouldn't hear her heartache.

"...and I will always love him. Your husband wasn't right about him. Marshal Taylor was dead wrong about him. Those gossiping old hens in town weren't right about him, but they wanted to believe what those horrid books said about him and not what I know of him. They wanted to believe his past would show up again, and we'd be hurt or killed."

Rachel lifted her brows. "His past did show up, Amy."

"Other than being frightened, I wasn't seriously hurt. Jenny is talking again because Colt was here. Saul is always asking if the things he does would make Colt proud. So tell me again how right everyone was about Colt."

Rachel sipped her tea before she asked, "Are you through with your tirade, Amy?"

"No, I'm not, but I was also raised better than I want to be at the moment. This town is the reason Colt left, not his past. No one in this damnable little, two-horse town, no one, would believe that Colt Evans could be a decent man. Everyone wanted to believe he was a ruthless, cold-blooded killer."

"It was his past, not what anyone believed or didn't believe he was capable of, that made Colt decide to leave."

I can't turn you down because I'm not that noble or that strong. Her eyes slid shut again, but this time she didn't try to banish the memory. She let it wash over her, the moonlight playing over Colt's face, the smell of him, the warmth of him, the feel of him, the amazing contradiction of tenderness and strength in his caresses and embrace.

"He is a decent man, but practically everyone in this town refused to believe that." Amelia rounded on Rachel. "If they had given him a chance, maybe his past wouldn't have mattered so much. But because no one would give him a second chance, his past mattered more than it should."

"Are you through now?" Rachel set her teacup on the table, her steady gaze never leaving Amelia's face.

Anger shot through Amelia. "Do not talk to me as if I am a spoiled child having a tantrum, Mrs. Taylor."

"Rachel," she said. "Harrison said that more than once you've pointed out the day your parents died, you were forced to grow up immediately."

"I did," Amelia said through clenched teeth.

"Then grow up, Amy."

Amelia recoiled. "How dare you?"

"Very easily, as a matter of fact. No one is denying that your burden at this moment is not a light one, and those gossips in town do not make this any easier for you." Rachel lowered her gaze to the table and slowly twisted the cup around by its handle. "No one is denying that you love Colt. I don't think anyone who really thinks about it would deny that Colt cared deeply for you and Saul and Jenny. And if that's true, stop for a moment and consider how he must feel." Rachel lifted her head, her intense gaze pinning Amelia. "If he cared for you, if he still cares for you, he is just as lonely, frightened, and heartsick as you are. He doesn't have what you have, though. He's all alone and you're not."

A choked sob broke from Amelia. She spun away from Rachel's compelling gaze. "He shouldn't have left us," she managed on a choking breath. Angrily, she dashed welling tears away. "We could have managed to do something to hide his past. His past shouldn't have mattered. I should have told him that the night he left. I should have told him...I should have told him anything so he wouldn't leave. I couldn't even tell him that I love him."

"His past mattered to him, Amy." Rachel's voice softened and filled with a gentleness that drew more tears from Amelia's eyes. "It mattered greatly to him because it could hurt you. It did hurt you."

Amelia stared at the low ceiling, rapidly blinking in a fruitless attempt to keep her tears in check. "What if he's dead? What if he's been killed? I'll never know, and I will just keep on waiting for him to come back to me. Those animals didn't change the fact I love him. What if he can never come back to me? I will wait the rest of my life for him, because I know there will never be any other man for me."

Rachel drew Amelia into her arms. The simple gesture of concern and caring broke the dam in Amelia and she sobbed in earnest against Rachel's shoulder. "Even if he never comes back to me, I know the last thing in this life I will listen for will be the sound of his voice."

Chapter Seventeen

Colt Evans learned at an early age never to sit with his back to a door. Any door. He sat at a table in the corner of the room, his back protected, and turned a card up in a losing hand of solitaire. He stared at the queen of hearts, shook his head, and glared at the queen of spades, the only black card facing him.

He'd decided any luck he'd had at cards left when he rode away from Amy. Since that day, he could count on one hand the number of times he had won at any card game. Finances got thin over the winter, and even though he could have sold his saddle and Angel, he couldn't bring himself to part with the horse. Instead, he'd taken on a position as a faro dealer. Very few gamblers were willing to argue how the cards fell when the dealer was also a gunman.

A commotion near the door drew his attention. Colt glanced to the doorway where a burly figure stood silhouetted by the harsh, mid-afternoon sun. The man walked into the saloon and scanned the room. He had a badge pinned to his shirtfront. Colt dropped his gaze to the cards, secure in the knowledge he wasn't the object of the tin star's search.

"Keep your hands on the table, Evans, and stand up real slow."

Colt looked up into the barrel of a Navy Colt, less than a foot from his face. His gaze slid slowly along the barrel, to the badge, and up to the wearer's face. "George Matthews?" A chill traced up Colt's spine. "When did you take to wearing a badge? A better question would be what fool town hired you?"

"Shut up." Matthews grabbed Colt's shirt. "Stand up and keep your hands where I can see them."

"I'm going to miss my shift, George." Colt allowed himself to be pulled to his feet. "Where are we going?"

"I'm taking you to the town jail until I can make arrangements to take you back to Red Deer. They'll just have to hire another dealer." He shoved Colt out the door. "Keep your hands well away from your sides, Evans. If I even think you're dropping your gun hand, I won't hesitate to shoot you."

"In the back?" Colt's boot heels echoed with a dry, hollow thudding on the boardwalk of the curiously empty main street. "Where the hell is everyone?"

"I warned the locals that I was going to be taking a very dangerous man out of the saloon and it would be better for everyone to stay indoors."

"That was thoughtful of you, George," Colt said. "Convenient too, so there won't be any witnesses."

"Just keep walking, Evans, and keep your gun hand away from your side." George shoved him again.

Colt stumbled and forced himself to regain his balance. "Wouldn't it be easier if I just took off my gun belt? That way you don't have to worry about me reaching for my gun."

The sound of George's boot heels seemed to fall farther behind him. Colt's instincts thrummed, and the hair lifted on the back of his neck. Judging by the sound, George had fallen at least five feet behind. Why?

George barked, "Step out into the street, Evans." An icy calm settled over Colt. He stopped, keeping his gun hand several inches away from his revolver. "Why? So you can shoot me in the back, claiming I tried to escape?"

"Step out into the street, Evans."

Without moving his head, Colt scanned the empty street. Sunlight threw a brief, but telltale glint off the barrel of a gun perched on top of the building across the street. A shadow moved behind the plate-glass window in the mercantile.

Two other guns. Hell. The odds weren't getting any better.

A third man rounded the corner of the building, a rifle pointed casually into Colt's belly. "Do as he says, Evans. Step out into the street."

For a second, Colt closed his eyes. A deep regret filled him. *I'm sorry, Amy.* He could probably take George and the rifle out, but the other two across the street would finish him.

Well, if they were going to kill him, he was not going to hell's gates alone. He was taking some company with him. Two out of four, hopefully, before they got him.

He stepped off the boardwalk. George and the other gun closed ranks and they had just bettered his odds.

Another step and he'd be in the middle of the street. Colt knew with his next step, the gunfire would start. He didn't dare lift his gaze to the gun on the roof. If he looked up, the gunman on the roof would know he'd been spotted.

The first shot rang out, grazing his thigh. The lead burned more than caused any damage, though the shock forced Colt to one knee in the dusty street. He whipped his revolver out, and fired two rapid shots, one at the roof, the other into the mercantile. Shooting at a shadow in the mercantile had been an act of desperation, but one Colt knew he had to take. The gunman on the roof dropped to the street and didn't move. The mercantile window shattered and another bullet grazed Colt's arm.

A chill settled over him. They weren't trying to kill him instantly. Neither shot had been fatal, nor apparently was intended to be. They were going to take him apart with gunfire. But why hadn't George or the other gun fired?

He was pinned down in the street, forced to his knees, and shot twice. What the hell were they waiting for? Sunlight glinted on the barrel of the rifle emerging from the storefront's shattered glass. Colt gritted his teeth, turned to his side, and fired.

Another gunman fell, sagging out the storefront window.

Colt faced George and the other gun. A badge glinted in the sunlight on the chest of George's other gun. The third gunman brought his rifle up. Colt fired, but not soon enough. Another bullet grazed his thigh. Colt spared one second to aim and dropped the rifleman. "You need to hire better guns, George. They're shooting from point -blank range and so far, I've only been grazed. You're down three hired killers."

From behind the protection of a large barrel, George shouted, "And you've only got one shot left, Evans. Think you can get me before I get you? I've still got all six shots left."

"Tell me something I don't know," Colt muttered. He shook his head to clear the sweat from his eyes. He didn't dare lower his revolver. "Step out from behind that barrel and give me a clean shot. I only need one."

With a laugh, George fired. The bullet tore into Colt's shoulder and spun him partially around. He crumbled to the ground with a groan. Small rocks dug into his skin. Pain rolled over him in nauseating waves. He had it figured out now. The hired guns were only meant to wound him so that George could finish him off without being killed himself.

"I want you to beg me, Evans, like my brother begged you. Beg me, so I can kill you like you killed him."

The silence was deafening. He was not going to die like a dog in the street and he sure as hell wasn't going to beg. He was going to die shooting, at least. Colt forced himself to rise to his knees. George slowly rose from behind the barrel.

One chance. Colt whipped the revolver up, dropping his left hand to the ground to steady his last shot, ignoring the agony of his injured arm and shoulder. He knew he was fading fast. He squeezed the trigger and completely missed George.

With another groan, Colt collapsed face first to the ground, his gun hand pinned under him. George's boot heels thudded hollowly on the dry ground. Colt slipped his hand into his shirt, fingers curling around the single-shot Deringer hidden in the waistband of his trousers.

George stood over Colt. "I should shoot you in the back, Evans. Gun you down like a dog, just like you killed Mitch."

Keeping his face in the dirt, Colt growled, "I didn't shoot him in the street. He drew on me first, in the saloon. I at least had the guts to look him in the eye when I shot him."

George shoved the toe of his boot into Colt's ribs and flipped him over. More out of instinct than accuracy, Colt rolled with George's boot and allowed the Deringer to come up with the motion. George's eyes widened in startled surprise. Even as Colt squeezed the trigger, another bullet tore into him, high on his ribcage. His own bullet hit with deadly accuracy.

George fell face forward into the street and sprawled, motionless and not breathing next to Colt.

Colt shut his eyes. The heat of the sun bathed him and took away some of the numbing chill creeping through him. Bear had been right. Dying wasn't much of a living. And this time, he had stepped over the line.

AMELIA PAUSED ON THE porch, shaded her eyes, and glanced up at the sun. Only noon, and already her dress was clinging to her. The blistering, withering heat was too hot for late September, especially considering the killing frost of a week ago. Saul's angry voice carried to her.

"You blasted mule! Pull in a straight line!"

Amelia sighed. She could only guess how much Saul was struggling with the mule. Drake Adams had warned Saul the beast was stubborn, but Saul had insisted on renting it to plow the garden under for the winter.

"Whoa!" Saul yelled. A moment later, he shouted again, his voice breaking, "Amy, come here, quick!"

Amelia ran around the corner of the house. Jenny followed with Michael in her arms.

A white horse walked slowly toward the house. The rider slumped lifelessly over the horse's neck as it trampled the frost-killed herbs. Blood had dried on the gelding's shoulder in a garish pattern. Baby ran toward the strange horse, barking and growling a challenge.

"Colt!" Amy rushed to Angel's side and grabbed his reins. She dragged the horse through the barren garden patch in the straightest path to the door. "Saul, help me get him into the house."

Saul's new height and build made the task easier than the last time they had carried Colt Evans into the house. Amelia's heart wrenched. He was so pale and barely breathing. Carefully, they lowered him into her bed.

"I'm going for Dr. Archer." Saul's voice broke.

"Tell him to hurry, Saul." Amelia set about pulling the blood-caked shirt from Colt. Jenny set Michael down and joined Amelia in the bedroom. Together, they pulled his boots from him.

Jenny grimaced as she set down his left boot. "It's full of blood."

"Go get me some hot water and washrags. Hurry, Jenny. We've got to get this bleeding stopped. And start ripping a sheet into bandages."

Jenny ran from the room. Amelia tugged off Colt's trousers. He had a bullet wound in his shoulder, another below his arm and high on his ribcage, one had deeply grazed his upper arm, and two more had scored his thigh. How had he managed to survive?

Her eyes filled with scalding tears. He couldn't die...not when he had just come back to her. "Please, God," she breathed, "don't take him. Please don't take him. Not now."

Jenny returned with a pot of heated water and several clean towels. Tears streamed down her face. "Amy, he's gray."

"I know, Jenny. Go on and take care of things while I tend to Colt." Amelia forced a thin smile to her face. "It's going to be okay."

As gently as she could, Amelia washed the dried and caked blood from Colt's ravaged body. At least this time there was no raging infection. The water in the wash basin rapidly grew bright red.

"Amy."

His voice was little more than a breath. She dropped to her knees at his side, and brushed her hand over his face. "I'm right here, Colt. You're safe, now."

"Had to come back...see you one more time." He twisted his head on the pillow. Pain scored deep lines into his face and darkened those gray eyes to nearly black. "One more..."

"Don't you dare die, Colt Evans!"

A watery smile lifted his mouth. "...love you always..." His eyes slid slowly shut.

"Colt!"

His chest barely rose and fell, and he was icy cold. Frantic, she pulled the blanket over him. Cleaning his wounds suddenly wasn't as important as keeping him warm.

"...will always love..."

She collapsed next to him, her arm draped over his chest, and sobbed silently.

Dr. Archer pulled Amy to her feet. "Go. I'll take care of him."

Startled, Amelia stared at the doctor. She had never heard him ride up. Archer gently pushed her to the door. "Go on. I'll take care of him."

Blinded by searing tears, Amelia staggered from the room. She fell into Saul's arms.

"It's going to be okay, Amy." Saul wrapped his arms around her. "He came back. Everything is going to be okay now."

She had no idea how long it was before Archer emerged from her bedroom. Amelia ceased her frantic pacing. Jenny slipped her hand into hers and Saul froze near the doorway.

Exhaustion etched Dr. Archer's face and shaded his eyes. "Don't know how that man made it this far." He sank into a chair at the table. "He was damn lucky again. The bullet in his chest missed vital organs."

Afraid to hope, Amelia stared at Archer. "He's still alive?" Her hands crept to her throat and her body quivered.

"For the moment. He's lost quite a lot of blood, and when I tried to dig the bullet in his shoulder out, he lost even more. I had to leave it because I couldn't get it out. Amy, if he makes it through the night, it will be a miracle. If he does make it, he's going to walk with a limp for the rest of his life. There was a lot of damage done by one of the bullets he took in his leg." Archer sighed. "Have you got any coffee?"

Amelia shook her head. "I haven't had any in a year. Colt was the only one who drank it."

"How about a whiskey?"

"There's a bottle in the cabinet. I'll get it for you." Her hands shook while she poured out a glass for Archer.

Unable to stand the waiting, Amelia handed Dr. Archer his whiskey and let herself into her bedroom. Colt was as pale as the white pillow under his head. Silver liberally shot through his black hair and the hard lines to his face had deepened in the last year. He had aged ten years in one.

What had his life been like, never being able to let down his guard, always wondering when and where the bullets would come at him?

She sank to her knees next to him. Gently, she smoothed the silvered hair from his brow. "Oh, Colt..."

Even unconscious, he responded to her touch. Ever so slightly, he turned his head into her caress. Tears burned her eyes. "Don't leave me again," she whispered. "Not when you've just come back to me."

She dropped her head onto the bed next to his and slipped her arm over his chest. "Don't leave me again." A loud knock on the door of the cabin jolted her to her feet. She left the room, to find Dr. Archer ushering Marshal Taylor into the house.

Taylor's face was set in granite, his expression inscrutable. "Where is Colt, Amy?"

Amelia tilted her head over her shoulder in the direction of her room. "He's in there."

"I have to take him into Federal. I have to arrest him for shooting and killing two law enforcement officials over near Rawlins Springs."

"No." She backed against the bedroom door. "You'll take him from here over my dead body."

"You're not moving that man anywhere, Harrison," Archer said at the same time. He moved to stand with her to guard the doorway.

"Doc, move. I've got a job to do."

"Harrison, I think my oath to do no harm trumps your oath to uphold the laws of this territory. You're not moving that man."

"If he can't ride, he can go to Federal in the back of a wagon." Taylor pushed the doctor out of the way.

Amelia braced her arms in the doorjamb. "You're not taking him."

"Amy, any other time, I wouldn't be here. Not after I stopped at the Archers and Becky told me Colt had been all shot to hell. I would figure it could wait. But not this time. Those deputies said they shot him up while he was riding out of town after killing Marshal Matthews."

Archer bristled, reminding Amelia of an angry terrier. "They're lying, Harrison. He wasn't shot while riding out of town."

Marshal Taylor raised his brow. "How the hell can you know that? Were you there?"

"I didn't need to be. I can tell you beyond a shadow of a doubt they're lying about when and where they shot him."

Taylor looked from Amelia to the doctor. "Want to tell me that again?"

"I said they're lying. When did you get hard of hearing? Unless they shot at him while they were riding into town at the same time he was riding out, they're lying. Not a single one of those bullet wounds was caused by a shot from behind." Archer advanced a step on the marshal. "I just spent the better part of four hours in there, taking lead out of that man and sewing him back together. You are not going to kill him by moving him."

"You're certain he wasn't shot from behind?" Taylor's expression lost some of its granite quality.

"As sure as I'm standing here." The doctor once more positioned himself between the marshal and the closed door. "He wasn't shot from behind. If I had to guess, I'd say he was led into an ambush."

"Then why would those deputies say he shot and killed some marshal and a deputy?"

Amelia studied Taylor's face. "You said his name was Matthews. Didn't Billy Matthews have one other brother?"

Taylor's brows snapped together. "You think there's a connection? Matthews is a fairly common name."

Amelia couldn't stop her sigh of relief as Taylor stepped away from the doorway, his brow knitting.

"If he woke up now, could he make a run for it, Doc?" Taylor asked.

Dr. Archer laughed bitterly. "He couldn't crawl away, right now."

"I'll give him a couple of days, but I'll be back." Taylor dipped his head to Amelia. "I'll give him the benefit of the doubt until then. When I come back, even if I don't take him into Federal, I'm going to have some questions for him and he's going to have to tell me what happened."

"Provided he survives," Amelia murmured, and then bit her lower lip to stifle a sob.

Taylor studied Amelia, his expression softening. He cocked his head at Archer. "He's that bad, Doc?"

Archer nodded. "I've got a couple of questions of my own. If Colt shot and killed that marshal and a deputy, how did they manage to shoot him five times? And why were there different entry angles with those bullets? One of those bullets came from high up, like from a roof."

"Let me see him."

Amelia looked to the doctor. Archer nodded, then stepped aside, gesturing for her to do the same. Taylor shoved the door open. She followed Taylor into the room, Archer behind her. Colt hadn't moved and she had to strain to see his chest rising and falling.

The marshal's swift intake of breath whistled through his teeth. "My God, I've seen dead men who looked better. And you're certain that every shot was from the front?"

"Yes," Archer said. "What are you getting at?"

"I'm not sure." Taylor shook his head and shrugged. "Maybe nothing. But I'm going to take a hard, fast ride down to Laramie and depending on what I find out there, catch the train into Rawlins Springs." He paused next to Amelia. "I want your word, Amy, if he wakes up before I get back to talk to him, you won't let him leave. I don't want to have to spend a couple of months tracking him all over the damn territory."

"I can't promise you that." Amelia lifted her hands. "I couldn't stop him from leaving a year ago. If he thinks he's wanted for killing—"

"Then don't tell him. Besides," Taylor said with a smile, "he's got a lot more reason to stay for a while, this time, hasn't he? I'll be back in a couple of days. Keep him alive, Amy."

"So you can hang him?" Amelia hated the aging marshal at that moment more than she ever thought she could hate anyone.

An enigmatic smile crossed Taylor's mouth. "Just keep him alive."

COLT JERKED AWAKE, gasping. He'd shot and killed two lawmen in Rawlins Springs, as well as two other men that George had probably deputized.

Where was he? He scanned the room. The familiar sights of Amy's bedroom, the low ceiling, the short chest of drawers, and even the battered nightstand slowed the terrified pounding of his heart. He licked parched lips and let a moment of relief cascade over him.

Amy dozed in the rocking chair in the corner of the room. His heart wrenched. Even in sleep, she appeared exhausted. Dark circles smudged the smooth skin under her eyes, and lines had etched themselves into her face. "Amy." His voice was little more than a croak.

She sat upright, her eyes lightening when she settled her gaze on him. A tremulous smile broke over her mouth and she leaped from the chair. She sank to her knees and ran a trembling hand over his brow. She stared at him, awe and relief coloring her expression.

He caught her hand and pressed it to his lips. Still gripping her hand, he lowered it to his chest. "How long have I been here?"

"Ten days." Her voice broke. "Dr. Archer and I didn't think you were going to make it."

"I can't stay, Amy." He tightened his hold on her hand when she tried to pull away. "I shot and killed a couple of lawmen in Rawlins Springs. If Taylor hasn't been here, he soon will be."

Anger filled her eyes. "So you're going to run again?"

He shook his head. "I'm tired of running and tired of looking over my shoulder. I can't stay because as soon as I can stand, I'm going to turn myself in. Maybe that will rate me a new rope in his tally book."

"I see," she said, in a voice so soft Colt strained to hear it. She pulled her hand free of his hold and stood. "I'll be right back."

Amelia left the room. She stopped at the table, braced herself on her hands, and gave in to the tears she had wanted to cry for the past ten days.

In his bassinet, Michael waved his chubby arms at her. Amelia scooped him up and hugged him fiercely. Instinct shouted to carry him in to meet his father, but she didn't. If she had to keep Michael hidden for a few more days from Colt, she would. She wanted to know he was going to stay because it was what he wanted, not because of an obligation he might feel to their child.

She went to the door and called for Saul.

The thirteen-year-old boy ran from the barn. Amelia couldn't stop the smile breaking over her face. "He's awake. Go into town and tell Marshal Taylor."

AMELIA OPENED THE DOOR and stood just inside, allowing Taylor into the bedroom.

Before Taylor could say a word, Colt said, "I'm not going to run, Marshal. At this point, I couldn't. I give you my word, as soon as I can, I will come into town and turn myself in."

"I don't think so, Evans."

Colt's gaze dropped to the coiled rope in Taylor's hand. It was old and frayed. Weary resignation filled him. Even offering to turn himself in hadn't earned him a new rope. He tried to push himself up. "Let's make this quick then, Marshal, and as painless as possible for Amy and the kids."

Taylor barked, "Don't get up."

Colt frowned. He looked from Amelia to Taylor. "What's going on?"

"I've been to Laramie to talk to Billy Matthews. He had an older brother named George. Last Billy heard of George, three months ago, George worked a roulette wheel in Deadwood. I then made a real fast trip to Rawlins Springs. Seems no one had ever heard of George Matthews when he rode into town with three other men. I sent a wire to a judge I know in the Dakota Territories, asking him if George Matthews had been sworn in as a marshal. He never was."

Taylor leaned a shoulder into the doorjamb, and slapped the rope in a slow, steady rhythm against his leg.

That coiled rope held Colt's gaze.

"But he was wanted for the killing of a federal marshal over at Council Bluffs about five years ago. George took the man's badge as a trophy, it seems, because when I was in Rawlins Springs, I got that badge. Several folks there were amazed that you survived that ambush. They said it was over in less than ten seconds, and most of them had never seen shooting like that." Taylor spared the rope a glance. "I also had a long talk with the two deputies in town who claimed they shot you while you were leaving. They admitted they hadn't, and they also admitted they stayed out of sight while George and his three hired guns bushwhacked you. They're not wearing badges anymore."

Amelia edged closer to the bed. Colt finally pulled his gaze from the rope and glanced at her, trying to read her unusually expressionless features. He tried to push himself up again.

Taylor barked, "Damn it, Evans, I said don't get up. I sure as hell don't want to hear about it from Doc Archer and Amy if you start bleeding again. Doc said he'd shoot me himself if that happened."

Amelia sank to the edge of the bed and took his hand into both of hers.

Colt demanded, "What's going on?"

"I'm going to ask you a question, Evans, and I want a totally honest answer from you," Taylor said. "If you had an ironclad guarantee no one was ever going to come looking for you, and you knew Amy and the kids would never be put into harm's way because of your past, would you stay here with her?"

Colt shot his gaze to Amelia's face. The fathomless lines of her expression were crumbling. He shook his head. "It's not possible, Marshal. If it was, I would have married her a year ago and stayed. But we both know it isn't possible."

"It is if we buried Colt Evans two days ago," Taylor said.

"What?" Colt's gaze skipped from Amelia's sudden smile to the marshal's poker face and back to Amelia. "What the hell is this?"

Amelia's smile grew. "The whole town turned out for Colt Evans's funeral according to Saul. Of course, Jenny and I weren't there, because I was too distraught, and Jenny stayed here to take care of me."

"I'm asking you again, Evans, if you had an ironclad—"

"Who the hell did you bury?" He glared at Taylor.

"Colt Evans was in that pine box." Taylor tossed the rope onto the battered trunk at the foot of the bed.

Ignoring Amelia's attempts to hold him flat on his back, Colt pushed himself up. "Who did you bury?"

"More like what. We buried a sizable chuck of Medicine Bow granite two days ago." A smug grin altered the severe lines of Taylor's face. "I need a full-time deputy. You think you're up to that job?"

"Deputy?"

"Deputy Evans. It sounds right. Even if someone talks that the shootist Colt Evans isn't dead, I'm figuring most of the folks who might still be looking for you are going to hesitate drawing on a lawman."

Colt fell back into the pillows. His head spun with the possibilities opening up. Being able to spend the rest of his life with Amy, never having to look over his shoulder again, never worrying about another bullet with his name on it in another man's gun. He squeezed Amelia's hand.

"It's the closest anyone is going to come to an ironclad guarantee for you, Colt. Are you going to stay?" Amelia asked in a small voice.

"If you had a preacher-man here, I'd marry you now." He paused, searching her face. "That is, if you want me."

Her eyes flooded with tears. "Yes, I want you. I want you to stay. If I'd been honest that last night you were here, I would have told you I never wanted you to leave in the first place, but I was just too scared to find the words."

Taylor cleared his throat. "Want me to send in Reverend White, Colt?"

Amelia sat still as a marble statue, breathless. Slowly, Colt nodded. "Yeah, if she doesn't mind being wed to a man flat on his back. I know this isn't how most ladies see their wedding day, but I told you the day I left here I was doing the only decent thing I'd ever done in my life. I was wrong. I'm finally getting around to that decent thing."

AMELIA STOOD IN THE doorway, Michael in her arms. Colt lifted his head. His brow furrowed, his eyes narrowing, and then his expression went blank. He pushed himself up against the thick pillows.

Amelia waited for him to say anything. His gaze skipped from her face to Michael's chubby countenance and his eyes widened as he gulped a ragged breath. A body would have to be blind, Dr. Archer had said, not to know the boy was Colt Evans all over again. Even with her eye color, Michael was just a younger, gentler version of Colt. At long last he breathed, "Did you know when I left?"

She shook her head. "Not for two months after." She didn't move closer.

"Why didn't you tell me before Marshal Taylor got here?" A flicker of anger glittered in the depths of his gray eyes.

"I had to know you wanted to stay with me because it was what you wanted, not because it was out of a sense of obligation."

"Obligation? What makes you think I'd feel any obligation?"

"Don't you? Isn't that why you left in the first place, because you felt if you stayed here, we'd all be in danger?" She shifted Michael in her arms. The infant chewed on his fist, drooling onto her dress.

Colt's features softened. "How old is he?"

"Four months. His name is Michael. I gave him your middle name, if that Bible you carried had your name right."

"It's right." He looked again from her face to Michael's. At long last a smile broke over Colt's face. "This is a hell of a way to meet your old man for the first time. Tell your momma to bring you here, Michael."

At his name, Michael twisted toward Colt. Colt held his one good arm up to the boy, and carefully, she lowered Michael onto his lap.

Colt cradled his son, looking down into the baby's face. "An ironclad guarantee...a chunk of rock gave me an ironclad guarantee."

Michael gurgled happily, chewing on his fist.

Her heart was swelling so full it should be breaking open. "Marshal Taylor and Dr. Archer both told me I should tell you right away about Michael, but I had to know that you were staying this time because you wanted to, because when they buried that granite, they buried your past with it."

Colt smiled down into the infant's face. Michael latched onto Colt's finger and pulled it into his mouth to gnaw on it. "They buried my past and gave life to a future, Amy."

To her amazement, he was trembling. He lifted his head and the gray of his eyes was soft as the dawn. "They gave life to a future with you."

A word from the author...

I hope you enjoyed this revised version of *A Long Way from Yesterday* (formerly published as *The Devil's Own Desperado*). Please consider leaving a review. If you want to follow me, I'm on Facebook at https://www.facebook.com/lyndajcox. My webpage is www.lyndajcox.com.